ARKHAM

The Weird of Hali

ARKHAM

The Weird of Hali

Book Seven

John Michael Greer

Published in 2023 by
Sphinx Books
London

British Library Cataloguing in Publication Data

A C.I.P. for this book is available from the British Library

ISBN-13: 978-1-91257-397-4

Typeset by Medlar Publishing Solutions Pvt Ltd, India

www.aeonbooks.co.uk/sphinx

That is not dead which can eternal lie
Beneath cold stone or far, forgotten sea,
And with strange eons even death may die.

Those Great Old Ones who dwelt beyond the sky
Shall bear their age-long slumber patiently:
That is not dead which can eternal lie.

The fate of mortal things has passed them by.
Until time has an end, they yet shall be,
And with strange eons even death may die.

They need not fear the ages as they fly,
Nor count them up in hours of reverie:
That is not dead which can eternal lie.

Those who cast down their fanes with dreadful cry,
And willed that they were dead, failed utterly,
And with strange eons even death may die.

Until those cold bright hieroglyphs on high
Come right at last and set the Old Ones free,
That is not dead which can eternal lie,
And with strange eons even death may die.
        —"A Villanelle for Alhazred" by Justin Geoffrey

CONTENTS

CHAPTER 1

THE BOOK OF INNSMOUTH

Owen came down the cracked stairs, leaving the solemn brick mass that had once been Arkham's East High School and was now, two previous buildings having been outgrown, the local parochial school of the Starry Wisdom church. A right turn on High Street started him up the uneven sidewalk toward home. Cold light of an autumn afternoon spilled carelessly across Arkham's gambrel roofs; further off, gray hills topped with standing stones clung to shreds of mist. Creak of wooden wheels and rhythm of hooves on much-patched pavement told of a wagon going by a street or two away, coming up from the newly rebuilt quay along the Miskatonic River. Trucks had done such things for more than a century, but two years had passed since the last working truck in Arkham threw a piston rod and got hauled to Ken Whateley's smithy west of town to be cut up and hammered into more useful things.

Owen was close to fifty, and gray showed in his sandy hair—the beard he'd worn for most of twenty years was gone, sacrificed ruthlessly once it started to go white in random patches—but he set a brisk pace up the street. Houses slipped past: Victorian, most of them, with bits of ornament softening the harsh lines of New England's native architecture. Old habits of protective camouflage remained firmly in place, and the houses looked tumbledown and foreboding. Even so, every house he passed had signs of occupancy for those who knew how to look. That was less noticeable than the absence of trucks, maybe, but offered testimony all the same to two decades of tumultuous change.

He turned after a few blocks, went to 638 South Powder Mill Street, a clapboard-covered house three stories tall, with bay windows on the first two floors. He let himself in, shed tweed jacket and woolen necktie, allowed a sigh of relief: home.

"Owen, dear?"

He turned and went into the parlor, smiling. "Laura."

The parlor, old and comfortable, had full bookshelves, faded lithographs on the walls, a pert little fire crackling in the Franklin stove. Laura sat in her wheelchair next to the sofa as usual, papers piled on her lap. Looking up at him, she met his smile with one of her own.

He sat on the sofa next to her, reached for her, kissed her. She was as beautiful as she'd been when they'd first met, he decided, though her brown curling hair had silver in it, and wrinkles showed, thin as threads, at the corners of her eyes and mouth. The salt scent all the folk of lost Innsmouth had about them called back twenty years of memories. So did the two slender shapes that slid out from beneath her skirt to coil around his ankles in an additional caress: the tentacles she had in place of legs, sign of her less than half-human parentage.

The kiss finished, he sat back, let out a long ragged breath. "Long day?" Laura asked.

"Just the usual," he said. "The kids kept me hopping. I hope your day was pleasant."

A luminous smile answered him. "Very much so. I went over to see Annabelle—Belinda will be bringing her over this evening. The new class of priestess candidates is turning out just as good as I'd hoped, and I'm going to ask Jenny to teach them a little sorcery if she can spare the time." Then: "And I spent a good hour paging through the book, of course."

The book in question didn't need any further label. On the side of the sofa away from the Franklin stove, a wooden crate two feet on a side sat on the floor. It had the word **ARKHAM** painted on one side in block letters, and the lid had been pried off to reveal, under waterproof wrappings, a double row of identical hardback volumes bound in green cloth.

"Of course," Owen repeated. "It's been a little while since your last publication." Laura blushed, and turned her attention pointedly back to the papers she was correcting. Owen laughed, got up, and fetched himself a beer from the kitchen—they'd gone back to an icebox most of a year before the electricity went out for good, and got deliveries of ice every few days, the way families in Arkham had done two centuries before.

Back in the parlor, he settled on the sofa again, picked up his copy of the book from the coffee table in front of him, sipped beer and considered the gold lettering on the cover:

Tales and Traditions of Old Innsmouth
Laura Merrill

Ten years, he thought. It had been that long ago, the summer they'd moved to Arkham from the little mountain village of Dunwich, that she'd started gathering up everything left of Innsmouth's folklore and folkways. Hours at the kitchen table tapping away at the old manual typewriter he'd brought back from Providence, more hours with pencil and paper in hand as white-haired Innsmouth folk recounted everything they remembered about the abandoned town: she'd somehow managed that while doing her share of raising their two children and taking on an ever-larger role in the local lodge of the Esoteric Order of Dagon. Now it was done, and he turned to the bookmark he'd left between two pages and started reading.

* * *

He'd spent maybe a quarter hour at that pleasant task when the clicking of clawed feet came dimly up from below. The door to the cellar creaked open to reveal a figure no taller than a child, dressed in a hooded black robe that concealed almost all his form. Owen glanced up from Laura's book, said, "Hi, Pierre." Pierre made a little bobbing motion, perhaps a bow, perhaps something else, and made his way into the kitchen. Moments later he returned, a glass of salted water clutched in what was all too clearly a squamous, rugose tentacle, and settled in an armchair close to the Franklin stove. Owen turned back to Laura's book; Laura reached for another stack of papers—incantations written neatly in the Aklo language, Owen noted, part of the work the Esoteric Order of Dagon assigned to its priestesses-in-training.

A comfortable silence returned. Pierre put the empty glass aside, brought three oddly shaped stones from inside his robe, set them on what he had instead of a lap, and contemplated them. Laura finished correcting the last of the papers. "Time to get things started," she said.

"Need any help?"

"Not yet." She gave him a sly smile. "Rest while you can." She unfastened the brakes on the wheelchair, coiled her tentacles around the footplates, and headed for the kitchen.

Only a few minutes passed after that before the front door rattled and opened. A glance at the entry showed something like a fifteen-year-old version of Owen, thinner than he'd been at that age, tense and awkward in a way he'd never been at any age. The newcomer had half a dozen thick hardback books in his arms and a distracted look on his face. Owen knew the look, smiled, and said nothing as his son Barnabas headed for the stair and clumped up it. He'd be back down at six o'clock exactly—you could set your watch by it—to help with dinner.

A few minutes later voices sounded low outside the front door. Owen glanced up again, grinned, and returned to the old Innsmouth tale he was reading. Minutes passed before the voices stopped, and after another minute or so the door opened again to let in his daughter Asenath. She had a creature perched on her shoulder the size and shape of a large rat, with an odd humanlike face and paws that looked like little pink hands: a kyrrmi, the witch's familiar of old legends.

Everything about her recalled to Owen the way her mother looked twenty years back, the same cascade of brown curly hair, the same coltish build beginning to fill out into womanhood, though her eyes were violet in place of Laura's brown. Her nineteenth birthday wasn't all that many months away, Owen reminded himself, and shook his head. Sometimes it seemed only a little while since she'd been a little girl running barefoot through the woods around Dunwich.

He set aside the book, presented a cheek for a filial kiss, said something pleasant in response to the kyrrmi's friendly chirr, asked about Asenath's day, and when she'd finished telling him more than he needed to know, said mildly, "How's Robin?"

She turned as pink as her light brown complexion allowed, stumbled through something innocuous. Owen, who knew perfectly well what the real answer was, smiled. When she'd finished, he said, "I hear Annabelle's coming over with the Martenses."

"They'll be here in a bit," said Asenath. "I figured Mom would need some help."

"I offered," said Owen.

Asenath's expression told him what she thought of that. "Oh, for Mother Hydra's sake, Dad. You don't offer, you just do it." Shaking her head, she went into the kitchen. Owen glanced at Pierre, who gave Owen an unreadable look in response— four eyes the color of onyx, and a conical face that split open into four fanged jaws, made that easy.

All at once Owen started to laugh. Twenty years back, he remembered vividly, he'd been an ordinary student pursuing an ordinary master's degree at a small Ivy League school called

Miskatonic University, working on a thesis about a horror writer named H.P. Lovecraft, and it had never occurred to him to wonder if there might be anything to the obscure myths and occult lore Lovecraft wove into his stories. Now? Owen's wife was just eleven thirty-seconds human, had tentacles for legs, and was into her third year as Grand Priestess of the Arkham lodge of the Esoteric Order of Dagon; his daughter was training to be a witch, and his son spent his spare hours studying the kind of science that gave Victor Frankenstein a reputation for eccentricity; one of his two closest friends was a sorceress who wielded a magic ring older than the human race, the other was covered from head to toe in barley-colored fur; and when he taught composition, literature, and history five days a week, few of his students were entirely human and the school where he taught was run by the Starry Wisdom church.

He hauled himself up off the couch. "Sennie's probably right, you know," he said to Pierre. "Time to get to work."

Pierre tucked the stones back inside his robe, slid to the edge of the chair and plopped to the floor. The two of them had just started for the kitchen when a knock sounded at the door. "I'll get it," Owen said. Pierre nodded and went on as Owen doubled back toward the entry.

* * *

"What a cutie," Owen said.

Little Annabelle, just a few days old, had a wizened face, violet eyes, and a cluster of two-inch-long pink tentacles around her mouth. When Owen reached a finger toward her face, the tentacles closed on it and squeezed. He laughed, and Belinda Martense laughed too.

She was Laura's younger sister, and she had the same curly brown hair, the same brown-touched-with-green complexion and brown eyes. The muumuu and knitted shawl she wore, though, did little to conceal the half-human shape of her body and the dozen tentacles she'd been born with in place of human limbs. The muumuu had panels to allow for nursing, and two of her arm-tentacles curled protectively around Annabelle, who was bundled up neatly in a blanket embroidered with seaweed and octopi. Strictly speaking, the baby wasn't hers—infertility ran in many of the Innsmouth families—but the Black Goat of the Woods was prodigal in her blessings, and Belinda had used spells and potions to waken her breasts to their duty.

As he motioned her to the couch, the rest of the first wave of guests came back from the kitchen, where they'd left big platters of sandwiches on homebaked bread. Justin Martense, Belinda's husband, looked like a barley-colored sasquatch; a rare form of porphyria ran in the Martense family, and he had a fine case of it. He hurried over and helped Belinda settle onto the couch. Behind him came Justin's son Robin, seventeen now and as tall as his father, and his five-year-old sister Josephine. Two dark-haired girls came next, Emily and Sylvia d'Ursuras, who were staying with the Martenses; Emily was starting her first year at Miskatonic University and Sylvia, a witch in training with a kyrrmi peeking out of her purse, was in Owen's classes. Behind them came Asenath and Laura, and Barnabas last of all—he was meticulous about helping out before and after parties, so that he could make himself scarce during them.

"If anybody starves to death tonight it won't be our fault," Justin said with his lopsided grin, once he'd made sure Belinda and Annabelle were comfortable.

"I'll have you know," said Asenath, "that I spent all day helping Mom bake rolls and make a big pot of fish chowder, so nobody was going to starve anyway."

"All day?" Belinda asked. "I don't think that was what you were doing an hour ago."

Asenath blushed furiously and mumbled something inaudible, and Robin looked away. Owen suppressed a laugh; the budding romance between his daughter and Justin's son had been a subject of amused discussion in both families for the past two years.

A convenient knock sounded on the door just then, and Asenath went to answer it. As voices sounded in the entry, Owen turned to Justin and Belinda and asked, "Jenny?"

"She'll be here," Belinda said. "She went to the university to discuss something with Miriam, and you know how Miriam is."

"I should hope he does," said a familiar voice. Dr. Miriam Akeley came through the doorway: white-haired and lean as a heron, dressed in her signature black dress and white sweater. Another kyrrmi sat on her shoulder, chirred a greeting to the other kyrrmis present.

He gave her a hug and then turned to the one who followed. "Hi, Jenny."

Thin and plain, with a mop of unruly mouse-colored hair well mixed with gray, Jenny Chaudronnier was also the greatest sorceress of that age of the world. A heavy ring of unusually red gold with a violet stone glinted on her right index finger, but not everyone there could see it. She smiled, and they exchanged pleasantries and wandered apart for the moment.

Not long thereafter another knock sounded, and Asenath let in a couple Owen knew well, John and Sybil Romero. He had straight black hair and a face like an Aztec statue, she had curling brown hair and the familiar Innsmouth brown-tending-to-green coloring. Sybil had been Laura's chief assistant in the research that had produced her book. Owen waved them in and went to the kitchen for another beer.

He was on his way back when Miriam raised her voice. "If I can interrupt everyone for a moment," she said, and paused while the talk died down. "Laura has a few things to say before we get down to serious eating and drinking."

Laura opened her mouth, closed it again, drew in a deep breath and tried again. Owen kept a smile off his face by raw effort. He'd watched her conjure titanic powers out of the depths of the ocean and quell bitter feuds among members of the local lodge of the Esoteric Order of Dagon with a raised eyebrow, but it didn't surprise him at all that talking about the book on which she'd lavished ten years of hard work left her tongue-tied.

"Thank you, all of you, for coming tonight," she said at last. "Every one of you helped me make this book happen in one way or another, and I'm more grateful for your help than I can possibly say. Owen, dear, if you could—"

He'd already set his beer aside and started for the crate. "Of course."

Asenath, who'd discussed strategies with her parents before the Martenses arrived, gathered up the children and teens and led them into the kitchen, from which bursts of laughter sounded promptly. Only little Annabelle stayed behind, and she was sound asleep in Belinda's lap. In the relative hush that followed, Owen began pulling copies of *Tales and Traditions of Old Innsmouth* from the crate and handing them out.

The hush deepened as the guests began leafing through the book. Jenny was the first to say anything. "Laura, this is really impressive. I'm having to fight an urge to run down to the nearest seashore and try some of the spells."

"They're mostly little sorceries," Laura protested. "That's what we had in Innsmouth."

"Simple but useful," said Jenny. "Some of these could really come in handy."

"I'm more interested in the stories and the history," Miriam said. "There are some real treasures here." She closed her copy. "I'm going to want to give this a very thorough reading, but a party's probably not the right place to do that." Then, smiling: "Laura, I wouldn't at all be surprised if this ends up being considered an important tome."

Laura blushed. "Compare it to the *Necronomicon*," Miriam went on. "In both cases you've got histories, legends, narratives, lore about the Great Old Ones, incantations—"

Laura found her voice. "The *Necronomicon* doesn't have recipes for clam chowder!"

"No, but think of some of the things it does have," said Jenny. "It's not that different."

As Laura began to protest, Sybil Romero grinned, tapped her fingertips against the arm of her chair in an odd rhythm, and whistled a bit of melody. Laura blushed again, and Owen stifled another smile. Sybil was one of a dozen or so people in Arkham who'd learned the way the Innsmouth folk used clapping and chanting for music, back when they were too poor to afford musical instruments, and the tune she'd sketched out was called "Smile and Take the Praise."

A moment's silence, and then Belinda spoke from the couch. "*The Book of Innsmouth*. I bet that's what they call it. Thank you for writing all this down, Lolo."

At her childhood nickname, Laura blushed even harder. "*The Book of Innsmouth*," said Owen. "That does have a nice sound, doesn't it?"

* * *

Fortunately for Laura's self-possession, the conversation veered elsewhere, and food and drink made their appearance. The temporary division of the guests, children and teens in the kitchen, adults in the parlor, gradually unraveled. Asenath and Emily ended up sitting together on the floor over by the bay window, and their voices tumbled over each other's as they talked about Miskatonic and their classes; Robin made off with his father's copy of the book, found a quiet corner, and started leafing through it; Josephine nibbled on party food, listened wide-eyed to the talk, and after a while curled up and fell asleep.

Pierre headed back to the cellar shortly after the guests arrived, and Owen expected to see Barnabas slip quietly upstairs, but each time he went into the kitchen, there his son was, talking earnestly with Sylvia d'Ursuras. He pretended not to notice, and said to himself: well, why not? Sylvia had a reputation as the bookish one in her family, and if she and Barnabas became friends, that would give the boy a chance to work on his social skills. He loaded up his plate with squid fried Innsmouth style and headed back toward the parlor.

He was most of the way to his place when, unexpectedly, another knock sounded on the front door. Owen glanced at Laura, who met the glance with a fractional shrug. Meanwhile Asenath scrambled to her feet, went to the door, opened it and let out a squeal of delight. Turning back toward the parlor: "Mom, Dad, it's Mr. and Mrs. Mazzini and Molly."

A black-haired girl with thick glasses came in. Owen, who had known Molly Mazzini since she was eight, greeted her and went to the entry, while Molly said hi to everyone, followed Asenath to the bay window and plopped down next to Emily.

"Owen!" Sam Mazzini, scruffily dressed as always, flung his arms around Owen. He was nearly bald now and had glasses thicker than his daughter's. "Damn, it's good to see you." Then, glancing around with a startled look: "I hope we're not interrupting anything private."

"Not at all," said Laura. "I'd have invited you if I'd known you'd be in town."

"It's her book release party," said Owen.

Sam grinned. "Everyone in Providence either has a copy of that book or wants one. I hear there's already going to be a second printing." He veered over to greet the other guests. His wife Charlene, who was thin and voluble and had her hair tied back in a graying ponytail, greeted Owen with equal delight but more decorum, and he asked about their other children down in Providence before going in search of more chairs.

"Yeah, we made good time," Sam said once he was settled, with a beer in one hand and a plate of party food in his lap. "Not what I would have called good time back when the trains and buses were still running, but who's complaining?"

To Justin and Belinda: "I hope it won't be any kind of problem that we got here two days sooner than we expected."

"Not a bit," said Belinda. "These days, we're used to it."

Evening deepened outside. Owen went into the kitchen to get one more round of food, and Sam happened to be on the same errand. Barnabas and Sylvia were still talking, though they had well-stocked plates in front of them. She was explaining something in animated tones while her kyrrmi, whose name was Wilbur, perched on the table between them and nibbled on a piece of fried squid.

"Do you know a Mr. Ambrose?" Sam asked him unexpectedly. When Owen shook his head: "He dropped off a letter for you at Sancipriani's a week ago. Julie gave it to me to bring up here. She didn't know him either."

While Owen was still processing this, Sam pulled an envelope out of the inside pocket of his jacket and held it out. Owen took it, glanced at it. The paper was yellowed with age, but the address was written in a script that was already old when paper envelopes were invented:

Owen Merrill
Arkham Marrachurettr

There was no return address and no stamp. Owen opened it. Inside was a sheet of paper equally yellowed, with a paragraph written in the same archaic script at the top and a tracing of a dozen lines in a very different script further down. The writing at the top of the page was in the half-barbarous Latin of the Roman Empire's chaotic final years, but Owen had learned medieval Latin years back to study eldritch texts, and had no trouble deciphering it. It read:

> *Master Merrill, a friend we have in common tells me that you*
> *are a learned man, therefore I trust my manner of writing will*

not trouble you. You will know of a book that was taken from its rightful keepers fourteen years ago, a few lines of which are copied below. That book is presently in a place known to me. Should you wish to see it returned to those who should have it, it would be well for you to journey to the town called Partridgeville (this word was in English) *in the region called New Jersey* (this was also in English), *where I will await you. Do not fail to heed this message, for the fate of more than one world depends on it.*

Owen looked up from the letter. "This is—really odd."

"I couldn't make a bit of sense of it," Sam confessed. "It's Latin, isn't it? Way over my head." Then: "Do you have any idea what the stuff is down below?"

Owen pondered the writing that filled the lower half or so of the page. It wasn't a script he recognized, that was certain. Ornate glyphs that looked a little like words in Arabic and a little like Chinese characters spilled across the page, carefully traced out in ink. He pondered them, frowned. It wasn't until he'd begun to fold the letter again that the realization struck him.

Fourteen years ago: that was the key. That year they'd driven down to Kingsport for the summer as usual, Asenath in the front seat beside him, Laura in back where she could take care of little Barnabas. He'd followed the old highway along the Miskatonic River to Arkham, drove up Peabody Avenue until it turned into Old Kingsport Road, rose out of the Miskatonic valley and descended again to the blue Atlantic and the slate roofs huddled beneath the soaring gray crags of Kingsport Head. The driveway of the big Georgian mansion on Green Street waited, and they'd spilled out of the old station wagon to a warm welcome from the Chaudronniers.

Only later, as night wrapped Kingsport and fog rolled in from the sea, had Jenny told him the appalling news—the men with guns lying in wait a few days before, the sorceries that had narrowly saved her from sudden death, the guardians in

Spain and Ghana who weren't so lucky. Of the three treasures of drowned Poseidonis, she'd saved one, and another came back a week later in a way that still made him wince to recall. Then there was the third—

The *Ghorl Nigral*, the Book of Night.

Maybe, he thought. Maybe. He thanked Sam, and the two of them went back into the parlor to join the others.

CHAPTER 2

THE MISTRESS OF THE CATS

It had been the town green once, Owen recalled: a broad rect-
angle of grass south of Church Street with a big elm at one
end, back when Arkham was a village huddled between a
bend in the Miskatonic River and the forests of a distant age.
When the smoke of the Revolution was still drifting on the
wind and every town in New England dreamed of having a
college, the town meeting sold the green for one Continental
dollar to what was then Miskatonic Liberal Academy. The first
wooden buildings rose soon thereafter, replaced by some of
New England's ugliest Victorian architecture in the 1850s and
then by dignified brick buildings in the 1920s.

Once the gleaming new postwar campus rose north of the
river, the old campus had been handed over to malign neglect
and a few tag-ends of college bureaucracy. The wheel had turned
again, though: now the new campus stood neglected and crumbling while the old buildings murmured with life. As Owen
walked up to the doors of Hutchinson Hall that sultry morning, he could hear voices from the quad beyond, past the elegant
brickwork of Upham Library, and the notes of a violin further
off. One of Erich Zann's compositions? He thought so, but a door
closed and shut out the trilling notes before he could be sure.

Inside was a space that doubled as entry and stairwell, with
steps going down to the basement and up to the higher floors.

A bulletin board with handwritten flyers announced classes, lectures, performances by local garage bands with names like Squidface and Hatheg-Kla. Beyond another door, dark wooden wainscoting and yellowed plaster met his eyes. Here and there, old paintings and photos in the ornate frames of an earlier era gazed down on him. Quiet sounds filled the air: footfalls on the floor above, low voices through open doors. Owen turned left, passed six doors, tapped on the seventh.

"Please come in," Miriam's voice called out.

The office inside had the same blend of plaster and wood, and bookshelves lined all the walls but one, where tall windows looked out on the Miskatonic quad. The desk was as cluttered with books and papers as ever, but the computer he remembered from Wilmarth Hall was gone.

Miriam waved him to a chair. From a small pillow on a bookshelf, her kyrrmi glanced up sleepily, let out an amiable chirr, and curled up again. "Jenny and Abelard should be here any minute," said Miriam. "I admit I'm eager to have another look at that letter."

"Easily done." Owen handed it over. She thanked him and cleared a space on her desk, sending a book sliding. Owen caught it. *The Secret Watcher*," he said. "Halpin Chalmers?"

That got him another smile. "Yes, Jenny and I have been following up some clues he left. It's ironic that the letter mentions Partridgeville—that was his home town, you know."

Since none of the other books on the desk looked likely to dive, Owen sat back and considered her. Miriam had been his adviser twenty years back when he'd been a grad student at Miskatonic. Now she was the president of what remained of the university, which had about as many students as it had when those first white buildings rose on the former town green, almost all of them from among the worshipers of the Great Old Ones.

Another knock sounded on the door. "Please come in," Miriam called again.

"Hi, Miriam," said Jenny as she came into the office. "Hi, Owen." She sat and turned toward Owen. "I want to see that letter again."

"As soon as Miriam's done with it," Owen replied cheerfully. He'd taken Jenny and then Miriam aside at the party, shown them the letter, and arranged to meet with them the next morning. Later still, when the guests had gone and Asenath and Barnabas had gone upstairs, he and Laura had discussed the letter at length. He'd already made arrangements to seek another source of guidance on the subject, but that wouldn't be available until evening.

"Fascinating," said Miriam after a few more moments. "But I'm not at all sure what to make of it, and I know I've never seen the script at the bottom." She handed it to Jenny.

"Could I have the envelope too?" Jenny asked. Miriam handed her the envelope. Jenny pulled a magnifying lens out of her purse and examined the envelope with utter concentration.

Just then a quiet tap sounded on the door. "Please come in," said Miriam a third time. The door opened to admit an old man with a wrinkled face and flyaway white hair: Abelard Whipple, the librarian in charge of Miskatonic's restricted collection of occult tomes. "Miriam, Jenny, Owen," he said, beaming at them with a vaguely distracted look. "Good morning."

"Good morning, Abelard," said Miriam, and motioned him to a chair.

The others made small talk while Jenny subjected the letter and the envelope alike to a meticulous examination. Finally she handed both to Abelard, slipped the magnifying lens back in her purse, and put on a bland expression that told Owen at once that she'd found something. Abelard considered the envelope, read the Latin text of the letter with slowly narrowing eyes, then glanced down at the strange script below, and stopped. A moment passed; then he looked up and said, "I wonder if any of you have the least idea of what this second text is."

"I think," said Owen, "that it might be a passage from the *Ghorl Nigral*."

In the sharp-edged silence that followed, Abelard regarded him. No slightest trace of distraction showed in the old man's bright blue eyes. "Why do you think that?"

"The letter says fourteen years ago, and that's when the *Ghorl Nigral* was lost," said Owen. "And von Junzt says the keepers of the *Ghorl Nigral* had to translate it for him because he didn't know the script. You know better than I do how thoroughly he knew ancient languages, so it must have been something really exotic." He motioned at the letter. "Like this."

Abelard regarded him a moment longer. Then: "You may well be right. There are three samples of text from the *Ghorl Nigral* in the books we have, and this appears to be the same."

"I wonder if this is a trap," Miriam said then. "We know who has the *Ghorl Nigral*."

Jenny stirred. "If it is, it's a very odd trap, because there are some really strange things about this letter. Look at the paper— it's at least seventy years old, and probably more than that."

"The yellowing?" Owen asked.

"Yes, but also the watermark. Both the sheet and the envelope have one, and it's the same on both. Envelopes with watermarks went out of style in the middle of the twentieth century."

Owen raised the envelope so that light from the window passed through it, and saw the mark: the words WARD BOND in an ornate script, with a crest above them. "Okay."

"It's been kept in a sheltered place the whole time," Jenny went on. "The condition of the paper's too good for anything else. Now look at the writing—it wasn't done with any kind of pen I'm familiar with, though the ink's ordinary enough."

Abelard gave her a startled look, then turned to Owen and extended a hand: may I? Owen gave him the letter and envelope, and he examined them both. "You have good eyes," the librarian said to Jenny. "This was written with a pen made from a bird's wing feather. The knife that cut it wasn't perfectly sharp. You see this sort of thing often in medieval manuscripts."

"Of the same age as the script and vocabulary of the Latin text?" Owen asked.

"Or a thousand years in either direction." Abelard handed the letter and envelope back.

"Do you think it's worth taking the risk of going to Partridgeville?" Owen asked.

For a moment no one spoke. Abelard sat back in his chair, his thoughts veiled behind a vague smile. "I don't know," Miriam said. "I really don't."

"I have one suggestion," said Jenny. "You should get Justin to read the cards for you."

Owen grinned. "Already on the schedule. I'll be visiting this evening."

Just then, Miriam glanced up at the clock on the wall and sighed. "No rest for the wicked. I've got to meet the faculty senate in fifteen minutes." Her expression brightened. "You haven't seen the latest additions to the quad, Owen. If you can spare a moment, I think you'll appreciate them." Jenny stifled a laugh; Owen gave them both a wry look, and nodded.

* * *

A heavy wooden door swung open, letting in sunlight. Beyond it, three steps led down to a flagstoned walkway that ran between banks of close-cropped grass and a double row of cherry trees that raised bare branches to the wind. Owen went down the stairs, followed the walkway to the middle of the quadrangle, looked to both sides, and started laughing.

At each end of the quad stood a bronze statue. The one to the west inspired no laughter: the image of Great Cthulhu that had kept watch for years in front of the long-defunct Lovecraft Museum on Derby Street. The tentacle-faced, dragon-winged Great Old One loomed up as though rising from the sea, one mighty fist raised to grasp nothing in particular. Back in the day, Owen remembered well, student wags vied with each other to find silly things to put into the Great Old One's grip and absurd hats to perch on his bulbous and many-eyed head.

Times had changed. A block of stone stood in front of the statue now, holding offerings: silver coins, shells, red cords knotted with Tcho-Tcho incantations, plaited chaplets of dried seaweed: the gifts the people of the Great Old Ones offered up to seek dreams from the Dreaming Lord, or hasten the hour when the stars would come right at last.

Owen turned next toward the cause of his amusement. There stood the statue of H.P. Lovecraft that once graced Love-craft Park, with three bronze tentacles writhing about his feet and an eye on a stalk peering up from under the edge of the pedestal. Lovecraft's long mournful face was turned toward Cthulhu's, and he seemed to be regarding the Dreaming Lord with a dazed look. Half a dozen cats sunned themselves on the grass at the pedestal's foot: a pleasant homage to the man, Owen thought, for Lovecraft had been a passionate cat-lover in his day.

He turned to go, then glanced back, for no reason he could name. Someone was sitting on the grass next to Lovecraft's statue, where no one had been an instant before: a woman dressed in rumpled nondescript clothing, her taffy-colored hair uncombed, looking at him.

He stood very still for a moment, then walked over toward her. He'd seen her before, though a decade had passed since the two of them had traveled together. Her presence in the Mis-katonic University quad set his nerves instantly on edge.

"Owen Merrill," she said then. Her voice had a curious silken quality.

"Great Lady," he replied, bowing.

"You laughed," said the woman. "It amuses you to see me sitting at Lovecraft's feet?"

That got an unwilling smile from him. "I admit it's quite an irony."

Her laugh rang like muffled bells; her tawny eyes, vertically slitted like a cat's, regarded him. She gestured at the grass near her, and without any volition on his part, Owen found himself sitting there, facing her. The cats took brief notice of him and returned to sunning themselves.

"I met Lovecraft, you know," she said then. The nearest of the cats, a lean black and white tom, padded over to her and rubbed its face against her fingers. "One winter day he gave me one of his aunts' cast-off coats. He said he couldn't stand seeing me shiver. I wasn't shivering, but—" The cat twined itself around her hand. "I've received stranger offerings."

"A bowl of cream comes to mind," said Owen, thinking of an afternoon in Arkham.

She laughed again. "Oh, that was once highly traditional." Then, in a reflective tone: "Many millions of years from now, when these children of mine rule this little Earth, they will long for a taste they cannot remember except in their deepest dreams. They will wish for cream made from cow's milk, when cows will long since have perished from the world."

The black and white cat rubbed its face against her, gave her an uncertain look, and then tucked its paws under it and settled down to drowse in the sun.

"A little while ago," she said then, "on the road to Providence, I spoke of the ancient quarrel among the Great Old Ones, and of what would come of that if it ran unhindered."

"I remember," said Owen.

"Good. The time of decision is almost here."

Owen gave her a troubled look.

"Good," she said again. "You know what's involved."

"Some of what's involved," said Owen. "I know this Earth may not survive."

"Exactly. Listen well. You will leave Arkham soon, and meet someone you know. He'll bring you a certain thing."

He nodded, and she smiled. "Then there'll be more for you to do—much more. The Weird of Hali approaches its fulfillment. Are you ready for your part in that?"

Owen stared at her. "I have no idea," he admitted.

Her smile broadened. "Good." Then, with sudden terrible intensity: "Far more is at stake than you can imagine. From the pavements of Carcosa to the halls of R'lyeh—" A gesture scythed through air. "Everything. If you do as I instruct you, things may still turn out as I desire."

"For you," said Owen, "and your children."

"And for you and yours," she replied.

He could find no words to answer her. All at once she and the cats were gone. Owen blinked and rubbed his eyes. Had another voice spoken?

"Owen?" It was Jenny's voice, from behind him. "Are you okay?"

"Yeah." He got to his feet. "Yeah, I think so." Then: "What is it?"

She was staring past him, eyes wide. "One of the Great Old Ones was here," she said.

"I know," said Owen. "Phauz."

That got him a long steady look. "You saw her."

"She talked to me." Most of what she'd told him wasn't to be mentioned to anyone else, not yet: he could feel the warning she'd set in the deep places of his mind. But one thing— "She said that the Weird of Hali is awake."

The words hung in the unquiet air for a time. Finally Jenny began to nod. "I thought the time might be close," she said. "But if it's here—" She left the sentence unfinished.

* * *

"The Lightning, the Coffin, and the Mice," said Justin Martense, turning over the three cards he'd just dealt. In the warm light of an oil lamp, the faded colors of the cards seemed to glow faintly from within. "That's the past." He paused, pondering them. "Sudden violence, death, and the theft of something important. That's clear enough."

They sat in a pleasant room on the second floor of the Martense place, a sprawling Federal-era farmhouse on Benevolent Street. The window next to Owen showed evening light fading slowly over the hills west of town. Low murmurs hinted at voices in the parlor below. A blue gingham tablecloth on the table between them set off the reds and golds of the card designs.

Justin dealt out three more cards and turned them over. "The Moon, the Letter, and the Ship. That's the present. A secret revealed by a letter, and a voyage to follow." He glanced up at Owen. "Nothing you didn't know already."

Owen nodded, said nothing. He knew the cards nearly as well as he knew Justin, having met both for the first time within days of each other. The Great Old One Shub-Ne'hurrath in one of her temporary human forms had dealt and read those same cards for the two of them on a day neither would forget, and given the cards to Justin a few nights later. Over the eighteen years since then, Owen had watched Justin slowly master their intricacies.

"The Rider, the Key, and the Bear." The cards gleamed in the lamplight. "That's the future. Someone will come to meet you there, bringing information you don't have, something that will show you the way forward. There are other people involved, too. They might be friends or enemies, but they've got their own agenda in all this."

The cards whispered against one another as Justin dealt three more, turned them over. "The Swords, the Clouds, and the Park. That's the road. There's danger ahead, and the only way out of it leads straight into the unknown. On the other side of it there's a place you haven't been before, or maybe more than one place. That's where you'll find the way you need to go."

Three final cards joined the others on the table. "The Book, the Scythe, and the Roads," Justin said. "There's a secret at the heart of this, and you might be able to find it out. You only have so much time until something happens; I can't tell what it is, but the Scythe in the middle position's a really bad sign. There's a way past that, and you might find it or you might not." He motioned at the last card, which showed a crossroads with one road leading toward the rising sun and the others veering away into shadows. "That's as far as I can see."

"One question," said Owen. "Any sign a trap's been laid for me?"

Justin studied the cards for a long moment. "No," he said at last. "There are things you don't know, things that are hidden, but not to deceive you. It's deeper than that."

Owen glanced from his face to the cards, nodded slowly, and said, "Thank you, Justin."

Voices greeted them as they came down the stairs: Belinda's, Robin's, Emily's, Sylvia's, Molly's. The Martense home wasn't quite a rooming house, but it felt like that sometimes, and half the children in town made a beeline there during the hours when their parents were busy and school was out. Aunt Bee and Uncle Beast, the children called Belinda and Justin, and adored them. The third permanent member of the household got respectful silences, wide eyes, and whispered stories told about her once she'd left the room.

It was the third member of the household who came into the living room from the kitchen as soon as Owen got to the bottom of the stair. "Hi, Owen. Can you spare a moment?"

"Sure." Owen followed Jenny into the kitchen, sat at the table. "What's up?"

"You're going to Partridgeville, aren't you?"

"Two days from now. John Romero will be taking my classes until I get back."

"You know that Miriam and I have been following up on some of Halpin Chalmers' work, right?" When Owen nodded:

"Partridgeville was his home town, and the university library there used to have all his papers. I wonder if you could see what they've still got."

"Anything in particular I should look for?"

"Two things." She reached for a book on the table, opened it, handed to him and tapped one of the open pages. "Take a close look at the last paragraph here." Owen read:

```
What if, parallel to the life we know,
there is another life that does not die,
which lacks the elements that destroy our
life? Perhaps in another dimension there is
a different force from that which generates
our life. Perhaps this force emits energy,
or something similar to energy, which
passes from the unknown dimension where it
is and creates a new form of cell life in
our dimension. No one knows that such new
cell life does exist in our dimension. Ah,
but I have seen its manifestations. I have
talked with them. In my room at night I
have talked with the doels. And in dreams I
have seen their maker. I have stood on the
dim shore beyond time and matter and seen
it. It moves through strange curves and
outrageous angles. Some day I shall travel
in time and meet it face to face.
```

He glanced up at Jenny, and then reread the paragraph. "That's really odd," he said then. "Everything we've got says that there haven't been doels on Earth for millions of years."

"I won't argue," said Jenny. "The Mother of Doels gets some discussion in the *Pnakotic Manuscript* and the *Eltdown Shards*, but you know how old those are, and the more recent tomes don't mention her at all." Owen conceded the point, and Jenny went on. "I thought at first that Chalmers encountered Noth-Yidik in the Dreamlands, but Miriam spent every night for the past year searching for any trace of her there and found nothing."

She turned to another page, where an ink drawing showed spirals and whorls traced in delicate lines. Below it were words in English: THE TREASURE HOUSES OF THEM THAT DWELL BELOW. "This is the other thing," Jenny said. "Do you recognize the writing?"

"It looks familiar," Owen admitted, "but I can't place it."

"I'm pretty sure it's in the same script as the tablet Dr. Muñoz gave me seven years ago. I just noticed this drawing a few months ago, and I know I've seen something like it somewhere else, but—" She shrugged. "If you can find anything, that would be good."

"I'll give it a try," Owen said. "This is helpful, you know. All I know from the letter is that I'm supposed to go to Partridgeville and wait for somebody to contact me. People won't be anything like so suspicious if I have something else to do."

"True enough." After a moment her smile faded. "It's a long shot, I know. If the *Eltdown Shards* are right and Noth-Yidik is supposed to play a role in Cthulhu's awakening, anything we can find out about her might lead us somewhere. I figure it's worth trying"

Owen nodded. "It's all we've got left at this point."

That was true, and they both knew it. More than eighteen years back, one evening in Dunwich, he, Jenny, and Laura had settled on an audacious plan to find the lost incantations that could waken Cthulhu from his sleep. They'd known that it wouldn't be easy, if it could be done at all, for the same thing had been tried many times before. Despite their hopes and hard work, the trails they'd followed led to one blind alley after another.

So much had been lost down through the centuries, so many books burnt, so many loremasters murdered before they could pass on what they knew! Capable though Jenny was, the scraps of lore that remained gave her no way to reach realms of power through which sorcerers and sorceresses in ancient times had roamed at will, and initiates such as Owen and Laura had to make do with even less. So far, none of it had opened the way to the secret they sought.

We're not out of options yet, Owen told himself, but the words rang hollow.

* * *

Two days later, Owen said goodbye to Laura and the children, shouldered a well-worn duffel, and set out into the sultry morning. It was a familiar routine. Over the years, the journeys he'd made in search of forgotten lore, or in response to some cryptic request from the Great Old Ones, had mounted up to the point that he had to strain to keep them in order. Chorazin, New Orleans, Providence, Brooklyn in the United States; Caermaen in Wales, Anchester in England, Vyones in France, a summer in Greenland, another summer crossing Laos and then climbing up onto the forbidden plateau of Leng: memories from all these and more jostled each other, recalled dangers he'd escaped, people he'd known, and always at the end of it—

Arkham. For ten years, it had been as close to a home as he'd ever had.

All around him, a hushed autumnal life huddled beneath the town's gambrel roofs. Habits reinforced by bitter experience kept that life hidden, taught the people of the Great Old Ones to veil their presence behind a facade of decadence and destitution, so that it took a keen and knowledgeable eye to notice the burgeoning gardens, the houses tenanted for the first time in decades, the shops where local products stayed out of sight of the windows.

Some of the changes couldn't be seen at all by those who walked above ground. Down in the stone-lined tunnels beneath

Arkham, where bootleggers had hidden rum in the 1920s and escaped slaves had waited for the next ship to Canada most of a century before, a colony of shoggoths had found comfortable homes. They belonged to the smallest subspecies of their polymorphous kind, frail and delicate by shoggoth standards, but Owen had seen more than one of them shrug off the worst an assault rifle could do and rip the gunman limb from limb in a matter of seconds. It comforted him to know that they were there, and on excellent terms with Arkham's human and half-human residents: a bulwark against a certain very ancient, secret, and powerful organization that every worshiper of the Great Old Ones knew and feared.

The Radiance. Someday, Owen knew, they'll whip up mobs against us, or send their own heavily armed negation teams to do the job. Someday it'll be Arkham's turn to see dreams shattered and memories flung to the winds. That's the way things are—

Until the stars are right.

The ancient phrase, bent under its burden of half-forgotten hope, offered him no solace.

French Hill Street took him to Church Street, and that brought him to East Street. He walked past the East Street playground, heard the sounds of girls jumping rope and the chanted words of the ancient rhyme they used to set the rhythm:

"The King is in Carcosa, the Goat is on the hills,
And there and back the One in Black goes wand'ring as he wills,
But down below the ocean, the Dreaming Lord's asleep,
Until the night the stars are right and call him from the deep:
He waits for ..."

The words dissolved in laughter; clearly someone had missed the step before they'd even started counting years. Asenath had chanted that same rhyme with friends in Dunwich and

Kingsport when she'd been of age for such games. When the stars are right, he thought. Was that what Phauz was hinting at? He knew better than to think he could tell.

He shook his head, came down the last long slope to the new quay along the Miskatonic River, where a sturdy two-masted schooner was tied up, taking on cargo. Barrels and crates stood heaped alongside the quay waiting for burly young men to haul them belowdecks. As Owen reached the quay, he saw ornate letters on the schooner's stern:

Abigail Prinn
Salem

"Mr. Merrill!" The shout came from aboard the schooner, and Owen looked up to see a man in his twenties standing on deck. He waved a casual greeting, and an instant later recognized the face: Joe Eliot, one of the Innsmouth Eliots, a student he'd taught a few years back.

He went to the gangplank, let Joe help him aboard, shook his hand. "Good to see you, Joe," he said, and watched the younger man grin in delight at being recognized. "Last time I talked to your dad he said you were with the fishing fleet."

"I signed on to the *Abigail Prinn* this spring," said Joe. "Purser—yeah, quite a step up. All that math Mr Waite drummed into my head paid off." He took the duffel. "Let's get you settled. The other passengers are already aboard, so we'll cast off in under half an hour."

Like most of the ships that worked the coastal routes now that the highways were all but abandoned, the *Abigail Prinn* had cabins for passengers. Owen's wasn't much larger than a closet, but it was pleasant enough, with a berth against the aft bulkhead and a single porthole letting in daylight. He thanked Joe, latched the door when the younger man headed back up on deck, spent a little while getting his clothes and gear stowed below the berth, and then sat atop the berth as footfalls beat on the deck overhead.

He opened Laura's book, found a pencil, set to work copying a spell into a little volume of useful lore he'd collected over the years. Though he was no sorcerer, as an initiate of the Starry Wisdom he knew how to bind and loose the currents of voor—the life force that flowed through all things—and how to drive off those beings for whom humans were no more than prey. To the things he'd been taught in the Starry Wisdom he'd added incantations from obscure texts and others learned from initiates, witches, and sorcerers he'd known. Those had saved his life and the lives of others more than once, and he rarely began a journey without reviewing them.

A sudden lurch to port told him that the *Abigail Prinn* had left the quay. He glanced out the porthole, watched the half-wrecked buildings across the river begin to slide past. An attempt to force his attention back to the spell he was copying didn't accomplish much, and after a while he put the books away, watched as the last buildings slipped past and greenery took their place.

Not that many minutes later he was on deck. The Mazzinis stood looking back toward Arkham; they welcomed Owen when he came on deck, but he could tell that they didn't really want company, not with their oldest staying behind at college. He leaned on the starboard rail, watched the shores slip past. On both sides of the river, young trees rose above the ruins of suburban tract housing, and hills rose higher still. Highest of all, the soaring crags of Kingsport Head stood against the paler gray of the sky to starboard. In the distance, framed by the river's green banks, the Atlantic showed a deeper gray as it rolled in restless sleep.

It was a familiar sight, one he'd seen a dozen times since the roads had gotten so bad that sailing was the better option. As he stood on deck and Arkham slid out of sight, though, a strangeness seemed to gather around him. It felt somehow as though the world had passed from the control of known gods or forces to that of gods or forces which were unknown.

CHAPTER 3

THE SECRET WATCHER

The wind blew steadily, and by noon two days later the *Abigail Prinn* had left the low dark line of Martha's Vineyard behind and was bound for the mouth of Narragansett Bay. The great bridge across the bay's mouth still stood, though Owen glanced up at the cracked concrete and steel, and wondered how long that would last. He could see all at once the way it would crumple in the face of a howling nor'easter, but when? The gift of seeing outside his own time he'd received twenty years before didn't give him any way to tell.

The middle of the afternoon saw the bay narrow and the empty skyscrapers of downtown Providence come into sight, and the sun was still above the hills to westward when the *Abigail Prinn* tied up at the new quay at Fox Point, not far from where clipper ships had tied up two hundred years before. As the longshoremen came aboard, the Mazzinis said their farewells. Sam tried to talk Owen into staying in Providence for a few days and slapped his shoulder when the effort failed. Charlene asked him to make sure Molly was fine once he got home. Then the two of them headed down the gangplank, waved, and flagged down one of the horsedrawn carriages that had replaced taxis once the price of gasoline soared past that of oats and hay.

He went below as soon as they were gone, tried to distract himself copying a spell into his notebook of lore: an incantation from Laura's book, used to strengthen a hand's grip on rope or spar. Meanwhile thumps, muffled shouts and footsteps on the deck spoke of an exchange of cargoes. The sun still hadn't set when the *Abigail Prinn* left the quay and scudded down Narragansett Bay again with a brisk wind off her starboard beam, and the west still glowed crimson when she headed out into the Atlantic.

Day followed day: five days in all, as the *Abigail Prinn* worked her way down a coast where few lights shone and tumbled ruins outnumbered buildings that anyone lived in. Owen knew what to expect from recent journeys, but it still left him feeling as though he'd entered a different world. The days when jetliners drew white stripes across the sky and cars thronged the freeways were still vivid in his memory. Though he could recall just as easily the changes since then—cascading economic crises, political gridlock, roads and bridges and power lines falling apart as the funds to maintain them ran out, and more recently a spreading silence in place of news from outside Essex County—the gap between the world he'd once known and the one he saw from the *Abigail Prinn*'s railing seemed too vast to fit within the span of a single life.

The abandoned Mulligan Point lighthouse came into sight early on the afternoon of the fifth day. Not long thereafter the *Abigail Prinn* slipped through the narrow opening that linked Partridge Bay with the Atlantic. A soaring white steeple caught Owen's eye first, and then the rest of the town spread before him: the old downtown close to the waterfront, a hill to the left with the church atop it and roofs clustered all around, stark gray shapes of the university buildings further off, and beyond them a larger hill, blocking the way to the pine barrens.

He went below while the schooner crossed Partridge Bay. When Joe came to let him know it was time to disembark, he shouldered his duffel, slipped a revolver into one of his jacket pockets in case of trouble, thanked his former pupil for an assortment of small but welcome favors, and went down the gangplank. He could see easily enough how the rising seas had drowned the old waterfront and forced a new pier to be built a block further inland.

That too would be temporary, he knew, and guessed that the people of Partridgeville knew it as well, for the only buildings that showed any sign of habitation were well up the slopes of the hill. Once he'd passed the longshoremen and the cargoes waiting to be hauled on board, and voices behind him faded out into silence, the cracked streets of Partridgeville reached away between empty buildings. The old downtown seemed uncannily silent, a habitation of ghosts.

Smoke rising from chimneys to his left led him toward the steeple, and once he reached the foot of the hill, signs of life made their appearance: gardens first, burgeoning with autumn produce, then houses that hadn't been abandoned to the weather, and then people. A child stared at him from a porch, and scuttled inside; a block further, an old man with a white beard and dark brown skin greeted him politely and asked if he was looking for something. Owen thanked him and asked, "Is there a place in town for travelers to stay?"

That got him a measured smile. "Why, yes," said the old man. "Go up to the church." His gesture indicated the steeple. "The parsonage is just past it. You go there and tell Reverend Ross who you are and what your business is, and she'll show you the meaning of Christian charity."

Owen thanked him again, said the expected things, and went on. He could feel eyes on him the whole way to the parsonage. It felt oddly familiar—he'd have fielded the same blend of caution and courtesy, he knew, if he'd come as a stranger to Innsmouth, Dunwich, Chorazin, or Arkham in its latter days. That raised questions he couldn't begin to answer: was it just the ordinary wariness of a small town far from anything? Or was something else involved?

The First Baptist Church was a splendid eighteenth-century Neoclassical structure, the house next to it a big Victorian home of red brick with mansard roofs and a vast comfortable porch. A stout African-American woman in a sober black dress sat on a rocking chair on the porch. She gave him a casual glance as he came along the sidewalk, then a second look, far from casual. Something about her face seemed familiar, but he couldn't place it. Still, a sign out front identified the Victorian house as the parsonage, so he turned up the walk to the front door. She got up to greet him as he climbed the stair to the porch.

"Good afternoon," he said. "My name's Owen Merrill—"

"I thought so," the woman responded with a broad smile. "But I wasn't sure I could believe my eyes." Then, seeing his surprise: "You don't recognize me at all, do you?"

Something in her voice, maybe, set off the memory her face hadn't quite awakened: a memory from twenty years before, when he'd been a grad student at Miskatonic, living in a rental house on Halsey Street, and one of his housemates was—

"My God," he said, blinking in amazement. "*Tish?*"

"The very same." She took his hands in hers. "Owen, it's so good to see you again! You're looking for a place to stay, aren't you? You come right on in."

* * *

"Yes, I heard that you were okay," said the Reverend Dr. Letitia Martin Ross, sitting back in the big rose-colored armchair. Around her, the parlor of the parsonage sprawled in comfortable disorder, stocked with mismatched furniture. A clatter of plates and a burst of laughter from the next room told of a late lunch in preparation. Outside, the afternoon drew on.

"I stayed in touch with Jenny for a while," she went on. "This was when Will and I had just moved here, and she wrote to tell me that you'd turned up again. She said you'd been involved in some business you couldn't talk about and had to hide for a while—oh, thank you, Aramelia." A girl of fourteen or so, her hair a torrent of long slender braids, had come from the kitchen with tea and sandwiches. Owen thanked her as well, got a luminous smile in return.

"You're okay now, I hope," Tish said then.

"Pretty much," Owen allowed. "I think the people involved have a lot of other things to keep them busy these days." He sipped at his cup, recognized the blend of local herbs.

"That's good to hear. So what have you been doing with yourself? Tell me everything."

That, Owen thought, was exactly what he couldn't do. Fortunately he'd had years of practice at saying only what he knew his listeners could handle hearing, and there was plenty to tell without straying into things better off left unsaid. It was easy enough to talk about Laura without mentioning that she was a Grand Priestess in the Esoteric Order of Dagon and had tentacles instead of legs, to mention his children without breathing a word about witchcraft or kyrrmis, to summarize twenty years of teaching without letting on that the parochial schools where he'd taught belonged to a church that worshiped the Great Old Ones.

Tish was beaming by the time he'd finished. "That's marvelous," she said. "I don't suppose you've got pictures of your wife and children."

He grinned in response. The last brief flickers of cell phone service had shut down all over the east coast four years back, but the people of the Great Old Ones had learned many years before to avoid electronics that could be used to track them, and Arkham had its share of old-fashioned film cameras and basement darkrooms. Owen pulled out his wallet, extracted the photos, handed them to Tish, who made appropriate noises and handed them back one at a time.

They talked a little more about Owen's life, and then Tish sipped more tea. "Me, I've had a lot of changes, too," she said. "The Lord knows I didn't expect to become a minister, for one."

"You were in med school at Miskatonic, weren't you?"

"Yes indeed. Graduated, did my residency, passed my boards, got a job at a community health center here. Will and I were married by then, Emalinda was on the way, and he'd gotten a good IT job with the city government, so everything looked like it was supposed to." She gave him a bleak look. "But the economy had other ideas. Even before the dollar collapsed, things were bad, and before long we were struggling. I honestly don't know what I would have done if it wasn't for the church."

"I remember," said Owen. "You used to go to church every Sunday no matter what."

A reminiscent smile told him she remembered as well. "I started attending the First Baptist Church here as soon as we moved. Will went a few times, but he didn't like it, so Sunday became his sleep-in day, and after I started Bible study on Wednesday nights, that became his night to go out with his friends. I thought everything would work out fine."

She refilled their cups, went on. "But it didn't. Church turned into a sore spot between us. He started trying to talk Emalinda and Aramelia into not going, even though they had friends at Sunday school, and he even tried to keep me from taking Josiah once he came along. But I'd started the advanced classes and was learning about the real meaning of scripture, the secrets hidden from the foundation of the world. Then Meryl, who was the minister then, offered to take me on as an assistant. This was right after the state defaulted on its debts and all the community health centers shut their doors, and I was thrilled, partly because it meant doing the Lord's work, and partly because it meant food on the table. But that very same night Will told me that either I was going to give up my faith or he was going to walk out the door. So I told him I loved him but I loved the Lord more, and away he went. He got a new job somewhere out west, or so I heard."

"I'm really sorry to hear that," said Owen.

The words felt hopelessly inadequate, but she smiled. "Thank you. I cried and cried, of course, but it was probably for the best."

"Did he know how you spent your Sundays before the two of you got married?"

"Good heavens, yes. That wasn't the problem." She sipped her tea. "The problem was that he couldn't handle finding out that when the Lord comes back, He's not going to come down from heaven. He's going to rise up out of the sea."

Owen's gaze flicked up from his teacup, but he kept his reaction off his face.

"I suppose that doesn't matter much to you," she said, with a hint of an apologetic tone in her voice. "As I recall, you weren't a churchgoing man when you were at Miskatonic."

"No," said Owen. "But I've become more openminded about that than I used to be."

That got him a bright smile. "I'm glad to hear that. The Lord chooses whom He wills, and if He hasn't called you yet, why, that's no business of mine to judge." She finished her tea, refilled their cups. "Now why don't you tell me what brings you here to Partridgeville?"

* * *

Dinner was a communal affair, nearly twenty people sitting around a big sturdy table and passing platters and bowls up and down. Before they sat down, Owen got introduced to all of them. He ended up sitting next to Ezra Cowley, the assistant pastor, a sturdily built black man in his forties, who treated him with a hint of wariness. Watching the way the man glanced at Tish from time to time, Owen guessed what the issue was, and made a point of saying something about Tish that was complimentary but made it clear that he wasn't interested. That broke the ice promptly, and before long they were chatting pleasantly.

Later, in the comfortable upstairs room Tish had given him, Owen stared out the window for a time before going to bed. Partridgeville had no more electricity than Arkham, and fewer lamps. Only the pale glow of the stars over the great sprawling hill in the middle distance—Hob's Hill, Tish had called it—broke the tremendous darkness of the night.

He shook his head, thinking of the conversation earlier with Tish. He'd known for years there were worshipers of the Great Old Ones all over the world, some in secretive groups like the Esoteric Order of Dagon, some passing on family traditions, some who'd found bits of lore all on their own—but Baptists? Maybe they'd used the Baptist identity as a cover, he reminded himself, or maybe Tish's teacher had stumbled across the old lore by herself. Maybe.

He pulled the curtains shut, doused the little oil lamp, and went to bed.

It took a while for him to chase off straying thoughts, but once he managed that he plunged deep and slept hard. Toward dawn, vague unremembered dreams gave way all at once to vivid glimpses of huge squared masses of dark stone, covered with hieroglyphs and fronds of wet seaweed, dripping with water, tenanted here and there with little scuttling crabs and sea worms. He seemed to be walking up a broad avenue or processional way, or perhaps down it instead, for the route wasn't level but Owen couldn't tell which way it slanted. Off in the distance ahead, a colossal monolith rose up toward a prismatic sky—

All at once Owen blinked awake to find the first pallid light of dawn creeping in through the window. Low noises from below told him that the household had begun to stir, so he put fifteen minutes into his Starry Wisdom meditations and twenty into his morning workout, then got dressed enough to be decent and went in search of hot water. Half an hour later, washed, shaved, and ready for the day, he sat at the kitchen table with Ezra Cowley and half a dozen other early risers, bowed his head while Cowley said grace in words that could pass for a Christian prayer if you didn't happen to know which Lord was being addressed, and then filled up on pancakes, bacon, applesauce, and ersatz coffee made of chicory root. Half an hour after that, he loaded a backpack with flashlights and notebooks and pocketed his revolver, and he and Cowley started down the hill toward the gray silent buildings of Partridgeville State University.

"It finally shut down six years ago," Cowley said as they walked down an empty street. "I don't think there's a university still open in New Jersey any more. Thaddeus Waldzell, he's our church librarian, says you still got one in business up in Massachusetts—is that right?"

"More or less." They reached the foot of Angell Hill. "It's smaller than the high school I went to—thirty professors and about a thousand students—but yeah, it's still going."

"That's good to hear," said Cowley. "I wish we had something like that, but that's about how many people there are in Partridgeville these days."

They turned toward the university buildings. A rusted street sign announced the intersection of Church Street and Meeker Street, but it had been knocked so far askew that Owen couldn't tell which was which. "What happened?"

Cowley shrugged. "We had some bad flu seasons and something else came through and took a lot of folks, some kind of fever. Mostly, though, it was jobs. Once the university shut down, a lot of people headed out west. There was still supposed to be plenty of jobs there."

A few blocks more brought them to a gray concrete building with weathered plywood over the windows. "Hancock Library," said Cowley. "When the university shut down they handed the keys to the city manager, and we got 'em from her when she joined our church."

"I'm surprised the government didn't say something about that," said Owen.

"The government? I'm not sure we've even got one any more." Cowley met Owen's startled look. "We take a truck of fish and produce over the barrens to the market at Bordentown when we can spare the biodiesel, and that's not far from Trenton, where the state capitol is. The thing is, Trenton's next thing to empty. Folks go in there to get glass and metal from the buildings, and that's about it. As for Washington, well, I bet you heard what happened there."

Owen nodded; the news had taken its time getting to Arkham, but once it arrived there'd been no shortage of little huddled groups discussing it in shocked tones.

"So there you are." Cowley pulled a ring full of keys from one pocket and handed it to him. "Here you go. Just lock up when you're done, and if you find anything you need, take it." Owen thanked him, and Cowley shook his hand and headed back up the hill.

It took Owen a few tries to find the key for the front door, but that was the only obstacle. Inside darkness and dust shrouded a typical university library, apparently untouched since the day the librarians locked the doors. The beam of his flashlight played over tables, some with books sprawled on them; a checkout counter decked with disused scanning machines; a cobweb-draped escalator rising into shadow. A few minutes of searching turned up a directory on one wall, and a few minutes more and two of the keys got him into the closed stacks in the basement below the special collections reading room. Chalmers' papers were in sixteen archival boxes, and someone had taken the time to sort them out roughly by subject, so he only had two boxes to haul up the stairs to the reading room above, where skylights let him spare his limited supply of flashlight batteries and the dust wasn't quite so choking as elsewhere.

Luck was with him as he searched the papers, too. Maybe a quarter hour after he started, he found a notebook full of curious geometrical diagrams, and in the middle of it, half a dozen pages of whorls and spirals paired with words and phrases.

The words across the top of one page—*The Treasure Houses of Them that Dwell Below*—settled the matter. The pages that followed were dotted with references to the serpent folk of old Valusia, and Owen pondered those, his chin in his hand. Was that simply a matter of ancient history, or had Chalmers made contact with members of that ancient race who dwelt among humans, disguised by their strange hypnotic powers? The notebook did not say.

Further on in the same notebook Owen found much about doels, along with references to the deepest and most perilous strata of the old lore: Zemargad, Dzannin, Psollantha, Vermazbor, the Dho-Hna formula, the Yr and the Nhhngr, the Aklo Sabaoth, and the Black Flame of Yuzh. On one page Chalmers had written out a strange word in capitals: N O D I A S A H T. Owen nodded slowly: there were powers of the outer voids so terrible their names could not safely be repeated even in thought, and the letters concealed the name of one of them.

Over the next two hours, the stack of notebooks and papers destined for shipment to Arkham grew rapidly, and in the process Owen traced the last three years of Halpin Chalmers' life. First the dreams had come: vivid and troubling, breaking in on his sleep beginning late in February 1925, reminding him of obscure passages in certain primal myth-cycles. The dreams stopped abruptly on April 2 of that year, but by then Chalmers had visited Harvard's Widener Library to consult the *Necronomicon*, and begun collecting other archaic tomes—Owen spotted quotes from von Junzt, the Greek *Pnakotica*, and *The Seven Cryptical Books of Hsan*.

In those tomes, Chalmers found incantations that allowed him to travel to far realms in his dreams; when those proved insufficient, he turned to strange drugs; and one of those, the last and strongest he'd tried, had taken him to realms humans could not enter with impunity. They'd found him not long afterward, his head torn off and his naked body smeared with a stinking blue ichor. Owen nodded again, recognizing the mark of the Hounds of Tindalos, the beings that guard the boundary between curved and angular time at the uttermost edge of existence.

Chalmers' encounters with the doels came in the months before that, while he labored on *The Secret Watcher*, his last book. His notes described plunging or soaring through midnight-hued abysses, at times clawing through obstacles that dimly resembled clouds of thick vapor, at other times encountering sensations for which no human language had a name. *I have stood on the dim shore between time and matter*, Chalmers wrote in one notebook, the script a feverish scrawl. *I have seen her—I have seen the Mother of Doels.*

After that, things he would not describe began to follow him back through the abysses. Notes written in trembling script described his frantic search for spells that would keep the things at bay, the troubles he'd had getting ingredients for amulets to ensure his safety, his dread of the night sky and in particular of a certain point between the stars Polaris and Algol. Finally, though, he learned to communicate with the things, and identified them as the doels of archaic legend.

De Marigny was quite wrong, Chalmers wrote hurriedly, *and the book by "Swami Chandraputra"—I think I know who hides behind that pseudonym, and why—is utter nonsense. The doels do not feast on the hearts of planets. Their origin and destiny is far stranger. They said to me*—What followed, though, was written in a script Owen recognized at once, made of whorls and spirals. Evidently Chalmers had not been willing to risk putting the secret of the doels into plain English even in his private notebooks.

* * *

As the skylights yellowed with afternoon sun, Owen read the last notebook. Half its pages were blank. The last page with writing on it said only this: *I shall have to take the risk. The secret*

is in the earth—that much I know, but the rest remains hidden from
me. The drug is prepared, and tomorrow I shall call Frank and ask
him to help me. Perhaps that will be enough.

The remaining documents in the box were pure anticlimax,
a mass of letters Chalmers had exchanged with a Cincinnati
book collector named Oliver Woadley. Owen flipped through
them, made sure they contained nothing more interesting than
long discussions about fine editions of Jane Austen and the
myriad faults of rare-book dealers, and set them aside. The
papers he meant to take back to Arkham were enough to fill
one of the document boxes, so with a silent apology to the vanished librarians, he packed the papers he didn't need in the
other box and hauled it back to its place in the lightless stacks
below.

He'd just set the box down on the steel shelf where he'd
originally found it when a voice spoke out of the darkness
around him: "Owen Merrill."

It was a man's voice, elderly and hoarse, with an accent
Owen couldn't place. He turned toward it, fast, but the beam
of his flashlight revealed only bookshelves reaching away into
empty space. A dry laugh sounded from somewhere else in the
room, and from yet another place, in the same voice: "*Gratias
ago tibi ut veniveris.*" It took Owen only a instant to translate the
words out of Latin: I thank you, that you have come.

"*Qui es?*" Owen responded: who are you?

The laugh whispered off concrete walls. "That matters not,"
the voice said, still in Latin. "You received my letter. Ask whatever you will, that you may know it came from me."

"You wrote of a mutual friend," said Owen. "Who is that?"

"It is Charles Dexter Ward, whom you know well."

"Where did you get the paper for the letter?"

"From his laboratory beneath the earth, by the river called
Pawtuxet."

Owen nodded, remembering the place. "Where is Charles
now?"

"Good. He dwells with Lydia his wife in a city between the mountains to the east and the sea to the west, with an emerald sky above."

"*Bene*," Owen said after a moment; it was the nearest he could come to "Okay." He drew in an unsteady breath, then said, "Your letter mentioned a book."

"The *Ghorl Nigral*," said the voice. "Yes."

"Do you have it?"

"With your help and that of another person, I will secure it."

"Why did you send for me?"

"You know one who can pass through the hidden paths of space and take the book to safety." The dry laughter sounded again. "Convenient, that it is your own daughter."

Owen stared at the darkness, horrified that an unknown person knew so carefully guarded a secret. Before he could speak, the voice went on. "Will you assist me in this?"

It could be a trap, Owen knew, and the message of Justin's cards were a slender thread on which to risk his own survival and Asenath's as well. Still, he didn't hesitate. "To regain the *Ghorl Nigral*? Of course." Then: "I know one who should see it once it is regained."

"I know her as well," said the voice, "though she does not yet know me. We are children of the same father, she and I."

Owen tried to think of something to say, and failed.

"Tomorrow morning," said the voice then, "pass this building by, and go west upon the street called Meeker. Follow it until it becomes the road of Mulligan and passes into the wood of Mulligan. Come alone, be ready to travel, and bring a lamp."

"*Bene*," Owen said again.

"Do not fail to come," said the voice. "Much depends on it."

An instant later something shifted in the unlit basement room, and Owen knew he was alone. He stood there for a while, shaken, and then headed back up the stair to the reading room.

A few minutes were enough to pack the documents he wanted in the box, and he hefted it under one arm and made his way out of the abandoned library into the warm damp air of a sultry afternoon. He locked the door behind him, glanced up at the cracked and boarded-up face of the library, and thought of the books and archives inside. He was enough of a scholar to want to save them, enough of a realist to know that Miskatonic University and the Arkham branches of the Starry Wisdom church and the Esoteric Order of Dagon had their hands full with their own libraries, and the First Baptist Church had probably already taken on as much as it could handle. After a moment he turned and headed off into the silent downtown district.

On the way back up Angell Hill, he thought of the glimpses he'd had of the First Baptist Church of Partridgeville: close to a thousand people living in the neighborhood that surrounded the church, growing food in gardens where squash leaves and potato greens made miniature jungles through which lean half-feral cats stalked their prey, and meeting most of their other needs out of the salvage of a departing age. Tish was the hub around which it all revolved, Owen had seen that quickly enough, with Ezra Cowley and a dozen others circling close around her and others finding orbits further out. He wondered how many other communities like it had taken root in the little towns of the eastern seaboard—and how many of those had found their way back to the worship of the Great Old Ones, the half-forgotten gods of Earth.

* * *

"I hear you found what you were looking for," Tish said.

The parlor of the parsonage glowed with lamplight and the red gleam of flame from the fireplace at one end. Tish's three children sat close to the fire, busy with homework—the First Baptist Church had put together its own school, Owen gathered, once the public schools ran out of money and shut their doors. Dim noises from elsewhere in the big Victorian house spoke of other members of the household busy with their own lives, but for the moment Owen and Tish had one end of the room to themselves.

He glanced at her, startled. "Yeah. I'm curious how you knew."

That got him a long considering look. "You said earlier that you've got an open mind these days when it comes to religion. Mind if I put that to the test?" Owen motioned, inviting her to go on, and she said, "I heard it in prayer today from the messenger of the Lord."

"He's well-informed," said Owen.

Tish laughed. "He always is." Then, abruptly serious: "But he said something I'm to pass on to you. He said you've got a journey ahead of you. He said it's further than—" Her brow furrowed. "I didn't hear the name of the place clearly—Koyasan, maybe, or Corazon—"

"Chorazin," Owen said, concealing his surprise.

"That sounds right. But he said it's even more important."

Owen began to nod. "Okay," he said. "He's right. I'll be leaving tomorrow morning."

"On the schooner that just came in?"

"No, I'll be heading west up Mulligan Road."

She gave him a dismayed look. "Are you sure that's wise? That way you get to the pine barrens, and the Jersey Devil's been seen up there more often than I like to think about."

Owen wondered what that meant. "That's the way I need to go, though." A guess occurred to him. "The Lord's messenger—have you seen him?"

"Oh, yes. Do you know who he is?" Before Owen could reply: "He's the prophet Elijah, who walks up and down the world to prepare the way for the Lord's coming."

Owen took that in. "Really tall?" he ventured. "Wears a long black coat and a black hat? Lean brown face, big beak of a nose, eyes the color of outer space?"

To each question Tish replied with an enthusiastic nod. "You've met him."

"He's the reason I've got an open mind about religion."

"Owen," she asked then, "there are things you didn't tell me, aren't there?"

He weighed that, nodded.

"That's okay." Beaming. "You tell the servants of the Lord up in Arkham that if any of them ever want to come down to Partridgeville we'd love to meet them."

"I'll do that," said Owen. "And we'll see what happens."

Words neither of them spoke hovered in the still air of the parlor, questions he couldn't be sure it was safe to answer and she apparently knew better than to ask. Owen thought then of the Esoteric Order of Dagon, the Starry Wisdom Church, the Tcho-Tchos in exile from distant Leng, the old families of Kingsport in exile from long-drowned Poseidonis—all the scattered fellowships who prayed to the Great Old Ones and waited for the stars to be right at last.

He thought about that again later that night, after he'd arranged to have the box of Halpin Chalmers' papers sent to Arkham and written a note to Jenny telling her about Tish, then said his goodbyes and promised Tish to visit again and invited her to come stay with him and Laura sometime. Clouds came in that evening, blotting out the stars, and darkness stood outside his window like a wall. He reread his little notebook of useful incantations, then pulled an old favorite from his duffel, Justin Geoffrey's *The People of the Monolith*. He flipped it open, read:

```
A VILLANELLE FOR ALHAZRED
That is not dead which can eternal lie
Beneath cold stone or far, forgotten sea,
And with strange eons even death may die.


Those Great Old Ones who dwelt beyond the sky
Shall bear their age-long slumber patiently:
That is not dead which can eternal lie.
```

```
The fate of mortal things has passed them by.
Until time has an end, they yet shall be,
And with strange eons even death may die.

They need not fear the ages as they fly,
Nor count them up in hours of reverie:
That is not dead which can eternal lie.

Those who cast down their fanes with dreadful
cry,
And willed that they were dead, failed
utterly,
And with strange eons even death may die.

Until those cold bright hieroglyphs on high
Come right at last and set the Old Ones free,
That is not dead which can eternal lie,
And with strange eons even death may die.
```

Someday, he thought, but the word twisted and clawed at him.
The poet who'd written those lines had been locked up in an
asylum in 1926 and murdered there. Maybe death would die
eventually, but for the moment it served the Radiance all too
faithfully. He closed the book, put out the lamp and made himself try to sleep.

CHAPTER 4

THE STAIR IN THE TOMB

He was up before dawn after another round of strange salt-scented dreams, breakfasted with Ezra Cowley and the other early risers, shouldered his duffel, pocketed his pistol, and headed down Angell Hill. Fog turned the buildings of the university into gray spectral shapes and hid Hob's Hill in an impenetrable vagueness. He passed the university, plunged through what had been a small-town business district. Signs on empty buildings marked what had been a laundromat, a funeral home, a grocery of the venerable First National chain, before the unraveling of the economy turned them into empty shells.

More blocks passed before the buildings thinned out. He went by one last burst of empty fast-food places and a rental truck lot with no trucks in it, and then Meeker Street turned into Mulligan Road and plunged into a darkness beneath writhing pines. Hob's Hill rose to Owen's right, a dim presence more felt than seen. Dead pine needles blanketed the road. The main highway out of town crossed Mulligan Road on an overpass, swinging northward around the hill, while Mulligan Road itself turned more gently southward, crested a long slow rise, and descended again. The immense sweep of New Jersey's pine barrens was almost invisible in the fog, an unquiet gray expanse in which dim shadows spoke of nearby trees.

Owen stopped on the crest, considered the landscape ahead. He was not utterly surprised when a hoarse voice he recognized sounded off to his right, under the trees: "Owen Merrill."

He turned to face the voice. If the shadows under the pines had been untenanted, he would not have been surprised, either, but there before him stood the most extraordinary man he had ever seen. Not five feet tall, with a wispy white beard and long white hair tied back loosely behind his neck, he had eyes the color of polished steel set in a lean expressive face. He wore a hooded raincoat that would have gone just past the hips on a taller man, and on him, fell to the knees; the sleeves had been hacked short to reach to his wrists; under it another garment showed the marks of equally rough surgery; a piece of cord wrapped three times around his waist made a belt, and supported a hefty knife in a makeshift sheath on one hip and a cloth bag neatly tied shut on the other. Sweat pants showed below the jacket, covering his feet as well as his legs, with a pair of sandals strapped on over the cloth. The oddest detail of the entire costume was that the old man stood and moved as though his bizarre clothing was perfectly normal.

That was not what made him extraordinary, though. Owen's years of training had developed the subtle vision of the pineal gland to the point that he could see the way voor gathered around sorcerers and initiates. He knew well the sea-colored glow that was Laura, the brilliant violet sunrise that was Jenny, the distinctive voor that surrounded other masters and mistresses of sorcery. Never before, though, had he seen the blowtorch intensity that approached him that morning, so dazzling that he nearly had to blink and look away.

"*Veni*," Owen managed to say in Latin: I have come.

"So I see." The old man came out from under the pines, glanced up at Owen. "Alone, as I asked, and at the time called for. I thank you for that. Are you ready to travel far?"

"I didn't bring food or water for a journey."

"That does not matter. We will not go on foot." A wry smile answered Owen's startled look. "Our mounts will arrive soon."

"Who are you?" Owen asked.

"You have not guessed?" The old man seemed amused. "You may call me Ambrose."

"All I know," said Owen, "is that you've met Charles Dexter Ward, you know something about my daughter that's been secret for years, and Nyarlathotep knows what you're doing."

"Nyarlathotep," said Ambrose. "Yes, that is one of his names, is it not? He knows a great deal about me, and I know a little about him."

"Is this his idea?"

"No." The same dry laughter Owen recalled from the stacks of the deserted library sounded again. "He does not disapprove of it, but the plan is mine." Before Owen could ask him what that plan might be, he held up a hand for silence, then motioned down the slope and led the way a short distance, to where the pines fell back from the road and weeds grew thick. Owen followed, wondering what the old man had in mind.

He heard the sound first: slow heavy wingbeats, half muffled by the fog, coming out of the pine barrens to the southwest. Uncertain, he glanced at Ambrose, who said nothing. The wingbeats grew louder, and then two huge dark shapes shot across the sky above Owen, slowed, and landed in a flurry of wingbeats that set dust and debris swirling up in the air.

Owen stared. The creatures stood as tall as elephants and their heads resembled those of horses, but they were of reptilian form, kin to the pterodactyls, with scaled bodies and leathery wings. They turned to face Ambrose and bared long sharp teeth, but he raised his right hand and traced a symbol in the air, and the creatures hissed at him and bowed their heads.

"Do you know them?" Ambrose asked. "They are called Jersey devils." It took Owen a moment to parse *diaboli Jerseyi*. "In the waste lands nearby, there is a portal to the place where these dwell, and that is fortunate. We must travel fast and far, and they will bear us."

Owen finally found his voice. "Those are shantaks."

"Good," said Ambrose. "You are well instructed. Let us mount; we must hurry."

Another gesture of the old man's hand made the shantaks crouch. Owen approached one of the creatures, set his hand on the massive scaled neck. When the shantak seemed amenable to the touch, he got his duffel settled, crouched, and sprang. It took some scrambling to get atop the creature, as its scales were as slippery as wet glass, but after a minute or so he was perched astride the thing's neck just in front of the great bunched muscles at the root of the wings.

He glanced at the other creature in time to see Ambrose spring lightly astride it, as though mounting a scaled hippocephalic horror was an everyday occurrence for him. "You are ready?" the old man asked Owen. When he nodded: "Then we ride the winds."

The old man gestured again. Owen could feel the creature he rode tensing beneath him, the powerful muscles crouching. Then the great wings swept down, and the pine barrens fell away beneath him as the shantaks took to the air.

* * *

It was not a brief flight. Fog wrapped the land below them in a shroud of featureless gray, so that only now and then could Owen catch a glimpse that helped him guess where he was. The blurred bright place that marked the sun's position told him that they were flying southwest. After a time Owen guessed was measured in hours, open water seen through thin places in the fog marked Delaware Bay, and patches of green countryside some time thereafter marked Maryland's eastern shore. Later, the upper end of the Washington Monument rising out of the fog told him that half-flooded and more than half-ruined

Washington D.C. was off to his right. Those were the only land-marks he could see. All else was hidden from him.

The shantak flew tirelessly on, and Owen clung to its neck and wondered where it was taking him. A little ahead and to one side, the strange old man rode the second shantak with what looked like perfect ease. The sun reached its highest point and began to sink; wind whipped past, damp with cloud, and the great heavy wingbeats of the shantaks kept a steady rhythm.

Finally the old man traced a symbol in the air with one hand, and the shantaks began to descend. The fog swallowed them utterly, so that for a time Owen could scarcely see the great beast he rode. Then all at once black shapes of trees appeared below, looming out of featureless gray; the great wings flapped hard, and the shantaks slowed and settled to the ground in the midst of a clearing surrounded by tall cypresses.

The air seemed preternaturally still as the old man slid effortlessly from his mount, motioned for Owen to follow. As soon as they were both on the ground, Ambrose waved Owen away from the creatures, and then gestured again. The shan-taks crouched down, and all at once dense fog swept in, hiding them completely.

The old man turned to Owen. "Attend," he said. "You have a short distance to go, and then you will meet someone you know. Do you carry a weapon?" Owen nodded, and the old man went on: "Do not be quick to use it. You will not be betrayed, though you may think otherwise."

Owen nodded again, warily.

"You will follow the path." The old man's gesture indi-cated a faint track that vanished into the shadows beneath the cypresses. "Go on until you come to a graveyard where you will find a stair that leads into the earth. Do not stray far from it. One will come to meet you there. If all goes well, bring him here, and I shall call another shantak. If matters go amiss, the stair leads to refuge. Descend without fear and do not turn back. Do you understand?"

"You aren't coming with me," Owen said. "Why not?"

"You know Charles Dexter Ward and his work," said Ambrose. "I am one whose life he restored. Shall I speak of certain vulnerabilities that go with that condition, or of certain foes of yours and mine who know how to make use of those?"

"Foes." The word—*hostes* in Latin—hissed in the still air. "Are they waiting for me?"

"No, but they may follow the one who comes to meet you." The old man gestured again at the trail. "You must hurry. There is little time."

"*Bene*," Owen said. "I will be back soon if I can."

"Do not stray far from the stair!" Ambrose said, and waved him on.

The trail wound through dense forest broken here and there by clearings full of rank grass, moss, and curious creeping weeds. Owen made sure his revolver was ready in his pocket, set a steady pace through the wood. Fog coiled and flowed among the black foliage, and birds he didn't recognize called to one another in the dimness. The ground grew damp as he went on; pools of standing water showed in some of the clearings, fringed by cattails and the sprawling leaves of skunk cabbage. Finally a pallid shape dotted with moss rose from the forest floor, canted at a random angle: a tombstone, its inscription all but erased by time and weather.

A little further on he spotted another, and then another. The trail sank into a damp hollow, and there the tombstones clustered, leaning at crazy angles or fallen flat. A statue loomed up suddenly from behind a cypress: an angel, its robe streaked with moss, its face weathered away to eyelessness. He walked on, following the trail. After another two minutes, maybe, he saw a low mound of fresh earth sprawled across the floor of the hollow. That looked promising, and he went toward it. The stair was just beyond the heaped earth, edged with flagstones; the slab that had once sealed it lay sprawled to one side, as though it had been flung there by some force from underneath. The stair itself descended into unbroken blackness.

Not far past the stair, the hollow ended in a low slope thick with cypresses, and the tombstones thinned out. Owen looked around, and then stood by the stair, waiting. Fog swirled around him, and the strange birdsongs sounded, muffled by distance.

He heard movement before he saw anything: footfalls, quick and furtive, running through the woods toward him. He turned to face the sounds, glimpsed someone moving in the middle distance. A few moments passed, and then the same figure appeared briefly between the trunks of two cypresses: human, Owen was sure of it, moving low and fast, dressed in what looked like ordinary nondescript clothing, wearing a cheap nylon backpack that moved as though it had something heavy in it. Owen reached into his pocket and slipped his hand around the grip of his pistol; then, mindful of the old man's words, released it.

Then the running figure came out from behind a tree, saw Owen, and stopped cold.

It took Owen less than a heartbeat to recognize the face—harsh and angular, with cold blue eyes—and in that moment he almost reached for his gun. He'd seen the same face lit by strange lightnings at a little town in western New York named Chorazin, seen it again three times in and around Providence when he'd gone seeking the lost rituals that might raise Cthulhu from his tomb. A servant of the Radiance, the commander of one of its armed negation teams—

"Michael Dyson," he said aloud.

* * *

Dyson stared at him a moment longer, then sagged in visible relief. "Good," he said. "The old man said you'd be waiting here but I wasn't sure I could believe him. There were two teams on my trail. I think I slipped them but we need to get out of here right now."

If the man had suddenly sprouted feathers, Owen would have been less flabbergasted. "Okay," he managed to say, then: "Come on—"

At that same instant Dyson turned sharply, looking up into the shadows beneath the cypresses. As Owen looked the same way, something small and black darted out of the shadows high above. Owen drew his gun at once, but Dyson was quicker; an automatic pistol barked in his hand, and the shape lurched and tumbled out of the air.

"A drone?" said Owen.

"Yeah." Dyson looked haggard. "I'm not sure we can get away in time."

"Then it's down the stairs." He motioned past the heap of earth. Off in the distance, muted by the fog, the sound of helicopters in flight came filtering down from above.

"You're serious?" Dyson said, the blood draining from his face. "Don't you know what's down there?"

"I've got no idea," Owen snapped back, "but that's the way the old man said to go, and I know what's going to be up here in a couple of minutes." He hurried over to the top of the stair, got out a flashlight, and Dyson swallowed visibly and followed him.

The stair plunged straight down into blackness, the steps damp with moisture, the walls encrusted with gray-white niter. Something drew a ragged line down one side of the stair, the cracked and corroded fragments of something too stiff to be cordage. The beam of the flashlight caught from time to time on spots of green verdigris on the fragments, and that gave Owen the clue he needed. "How close are we to Gainsville, Virginia?"

"Too goddamn close." The man's voice echoed in the silence. "About five miles east of town, just south of the old Gainsville Pike." Then: "Yeah, I saw the phone line too."

Obscure noises came down the stair after them. The negation teams? Owen glanced over his shoulder, kept moving. Suddenly the stair seemed to turn a corner, though Owen couldn't have said which way it bent. The moment they rounded it, the noises from above fell silent.

"Okay," said Owen then. "That ought to slow them down a good bit."

"Don't be so sure of that," Dyson said. "We got all Harley Warren's papers after he died down here. Everything he knew, we—" He caught himself, managed a bitter laugh. "I keep on having to remind myself that it's not 'we' any more. Everything he knew, the General Directorate of the Order of the Radiance knows, and they'll move heaven and earth to get back what I've got with me. I'm betting you already know what it is."

"The *Ghorl Nigral*," said Owen.

"Yeah." They hurried down the stair. "I killed seventeen people to get it," Dyson said then. "Two of them were guys I'd known for years."

"Why?" Owen asked him.

Silence broken only by their footfalls answered him at first. Then, in a precise and bitter voice, Dyson went on. "Because everything I ever believed in turned out to be a lie."

Owen glanced back over his shoulder at Dyson, realized to his surprise that he could see the man's face. He turned forward again, to find a gray phosphorescent glow filtering up out of the deeps ahead. That was when he realized where the stair was taking them.

They kept going. The dim gray glow slowly strengthened. Then, all at once, the stair ended at another doorway of roughly carved stone. Beyond it, the gray light filtered down onto jagged slopes, glinted on impossibly high pinnacles. Though they could not have descended more than a few hundred feet, the mountains rose thousands of feet into a glimmering gray sky, and the desolate landscape visible beyond the nearest peaks had nothing in common with Virginia or anything within two thousand miles of it. Ahead of them, a pathway wound its way down a narrow ravine, passing the mouths of dozens of caves before it vanished from sight.

Just past the doorway, an odd cluster of shapes on the ground, dark and light, caught Owen's attention. He glanced down at it, saw the corroded remains of old electrical gear framed by rotted wood, and next to them, a scattering of bones.

"This is where Harley Warren died," said Dyson. His rigid face told Owen at a glance that he expected to die there too.

"I know," Owen replied. "Give me a moment." He stepped forward, raised his left hand, traced a geometrical figure in the air with the first two fingers and thumb pressed together, and intoned three long words made entirely of vowels. Nothing happened, but then that was the point of the spell: the caves ahead remained silent and still, their hideous inhabitants unseen.

He turned to Dyson. "Do they know that one? Harley Warren didn't."

"I don't know. I really don't."

Owen started down the trail into the ravine, motioned with his head for Dyson to follow. Dyson braced himself visibly and came after. "Where are we?" he asked.

"The Peaks of Throk," said Owen, trying to recall what he'd learned about otherworldly geography from the *Necronomicon.* "Off that way—" He pointed to the right. "The Vale of Pnath. We don't want to go there. Off that way—" He pointed to the left. "The Sunless Lands of N'kai. We don't want to go there either. Straight ahead there's a stair that reaches the upper Dreamlands by way of the ruins of Sarkomand. I'm pretty sure that's where we want to go."

"The Dreamlands," Dyson said, his voice flat with suppressed horror.

Owen glanced at him with a raised eyebrow. "My daughter," he said, "has been coming here every night since she was eight."

Dyson shot him an unfriendly look, but Owen met it squarely, and after a moment Dyson looked away. "Your daughter," he said, "is only half human."

"Just over two-thirds," Owen said. "A lot of people who come here are as human as you are—and you probably came here when you were a kid, before the crap that gets pushed at children slammed the door of dreams in your face."

Dyson drew in a breath to respond. Before he could say anything, a sound like distant thunder came echoing down the ravine behind them.

"Your former friends?" Owen asked.

"Bet on it." An assessing glance flicked over Owen. "You're no younger than I am. What kind of speed can you keep up?"

"Let's find out," Owen said.

* * *

Time passed—two hours, Owen would have guessed if he'd been in the waking world. Time ran differently in the Dreamlands, all the old tomes said that, but what that meant in practice he had no idea. The path he and Dyson followed ran alongside a streambed that looked as though it filled with water maybe once in a million years. Bare slopes soared to either side, pitted here and there with caverns, and the gray phosphorescence filtered down from above.

The two of them moved fast, stopped briefly at long intervals to catch their breath. Old hands in the Army had taught Owen that on a long march, men would cover more distance in fifty-five minutes of walking and five of rest than they could in sixty minutes of uninterrupted effort. He didn't have to explain that to Dyson. Though they'd met only briefly before, and in those days they'd been on opposite sides of a war more than two millennia old, they fell quickly into soldiers' habits Owen knew well: communicating with gestures, sharing out the work of eye and ear that might give them a few moments' warning of pursuit.

Maybe a quarter hour after they'd left Harley Warren's bones, sounds rang out behind them: a clattering that hinted at gunfire, dim sounds that might have been human voices. After that, silence closed in again. The first time they stopped to rest afterwards, Owen said in a low voice, "I couldn't tell if the negation team survived that or not."

"Neither could I," Dyson replied in a matching undertone. "But there'll be somebody with them who knows sorcery. We've had people studying that for a while now."

"I know," said Owen.

Dyson gave him a look of bleak amusement. "I bet. Your side couldn't have missed figuring that out once the project at Binger State University went pear-shaped." He fell silent again, listening. Owen gave him a puzzled glance, wondering what had happened at Binger State University, but knew better than to speak. After another minute, they stood and hurried on.

That was far from the only question that circled in Owen's mind as they hurried down the trail. Above all else, why had Dyson turned his back on everything he'd valued, and stolen the one thing the Radiance most needed to keep out of the hands of the servants of the Great Old Ones? The silence of the barren slopes around them weighed on his nerves, but Owen knew better than to do anything that might distract either of them. He cleared his mind, kept going.

The trail wound onward, and the peaks around them finally slanted down into foothills and then to a bleak plain dotted with vast low mounds. From the crest of each mound, a standing stone rose up stark into the dim gray light. "Okay," Owen said in a low voice. "This is the Plain of Dead Gods. If Alhazred's right, and nothing's changed, we're about halfway to the stair." Dyson nodded, and the two of them headed out across the desolation.

More time passed. The vast gray plain stretched on and on. One after another, the great mounds and the standing stones atop them loomed up, towered over Owen and Dyson, fell slowly behind. Maybe an hour into the journey across the plain, they stopped to catch their breath at the foot of one of the mounds, and after a moment Owen went around to the side of the mound furthest from the Peaks of Throk, clambered up to the standing stone atop it, crouched, and peered. At first he could see nothing but the bare plain, the mounds and stones, and the Peaks of Throk rising in the distance to unguessed heights. After a few moments, though, he caught a hint of movement far off, then spotted tiny dots where the plain blurred into gray distance.

He scrambled back down to where Dyson waited. "Company," he said. "A long way back, better than five miles, but there's a lot of them—at least twenty."

Dyson hauled himself to his feet. "No surprises there. A second team'll be following in case the first one runs into trouble." He motioned with his head, Owen nodded, and the two of them set out at the fastest pace they could maintain.

Therafter they took only the briefest of rests, and angled their course to keep at least one of the mounds between them and their pursuers. Hours went by. Once, as they caught their breath at the foot of a mound, Dyson scrambled to the top, came down almost at once. "Two miles back, maybe," he said. "No more than three. I hope those stairs aren't too much farther."

As they hurried on, dim uncertain shapes rose up in the distance ahead of them. Clouds, Owen thought at first, but as they kept walking, the shapes became clearer: two titanic masses of stone in the shape of winged lions. Their crannied faces gazed down with derisive snarls. Between them lay a vast arch of stone, and beyond that, shadow.

"There," he said to Dyson. "That's the stair to Sarkomand." Dyson glanced at him and nodded, then glanced back the way they'd come and let out a muffled profanity. Owen glanced the same way, and saw the thing he feared most just then: tiny shapes of men in the distance, spreading out and moving toward them.

They hurried on. The stone lions rose up above them, tall as mountains. The shadow between them remained impenetrable. Another glance backward showed the negation team closing nearly to within rifle range. Owen motioned to Dyson, who nodded, and the two of them broke into a trot. It was a futile gesture, Owen knew as he made it; even if they reached the stair, their chances of climbing up the hundred thousand steps to the ruins of Sarkomand with a negation team at their heels weren't worth worrying about. Still, he flung himself forward, saw the archway between the winged lions loom closer. Another hundred yards—

All at once black winged shapes burst from the darkness within the great arch. Bats, Owen thought at first, from the way they swooped and darted, but his sense of scale reasserted itself after a moment, showed him that the winged things were taller than he was. By dozens, then by hundreds, and finally by thousands, they streamed out of the abyss, plunging through the air above Owen and Dyson toward the negation team: winged, horned, cadaverously thin. Their great leathery wings, as they lashed the air, made no sound at all.

Assault rifles spat three-round bursts behind Owen. A hurried glance backward showed the negation team crouched in a defensive formation, guns blazing. He broke into a run, crossed the last twenty yards or so to the foot of the stair. Once in the shadow of the arch he stopped, his heart thudding in his chest, and looked back. The negation team was besieged by a swarm of winged nightmares that had to be ten thousand strong.

Dyson reached the stair a moment later and panted, "Night-gaunts?"

"Yeah," Owen managed to say.

As if to settle the point, half a dozen of the winged creatures fluttered to the ground near the stair and crouched there. It wasn't accurate to say that they faced Owen and Dyson, for the heads that turned toward the two men had no faces, just smooth black skin that gleamed in the uncertain light. Long barbed tails lashed back and forth behind them.

Owen was trying to figure out how to respond to their arrival when an improbable voice sounded from the shadows of the great stair above him: Asenath's. "Hi, Dad."

He turned, laughed in sheer relief. "Hi, Sennie. Are the night-gaunts friends of yours?"

"No, the most remarkable old man taught me how to summon them." She came hurrying down out of the darkness, dressed in billowing robes of many-colored silk—dream-garments, Owen guessed, for she had nothing of the sort in her closet in Arkham. Rachel the kyrrmi, perched on her shoulder, chirred at Owen. "The old man said you need to come to the ruins of Sarkomand with me right away. He says it's really important. Do you mind being carried by night-gaunts? I promise they won't tickle you, and it's a lot faster than climbing the stair."

Owen glanced at Dyson, who gave him a weary look and nodded. "Sure."

"Okay, good. Hold your arms out like this." She spread her arms, glibbered at the crouching night-gaunts. All at once two of them sprang up, seized her by the arms, and carried her up into the blackness. Owen gave Dyson another glance, saw him clench his eyes shut and spread his arms, and made the same gesture. An instant later both of them had been seized by the night-gaunts and soared up into the shadows of the stair.

Up they went. For an interval Owen couldn't even begin to measure, the night-gaunts flew on, their silent wings beating hard. At last a faint trickle of light began to seep down from somewhere high above; it brightened until Owen could see the night-gaunts carrying Asenath further up, and caught some sense of the immensity of the stair up which they flew. Finally the light turned into the pallid glow of a gibbous moon, and the night-gaunts carried Owen out between the two winged lions carved of diorite that stood guard over the Gate of the Abyss in fallen Sarkomand. Their faces made the same derisive snarls as their counterparts far below.

Around him the ruined city spread its shattered grandeur. Owen could see black broken pillars and crumbling walls, fallen remnants of sphinx-crowned gates, the sweep of great round plazas where the paving stones were framed by straggling grass and wrenched asunder by frequent shrubs and roots. Then, as the night-gaunts soared over the city, he spotted a point of red light close to the dead city's long-abandoned wharves. The night-gaunts sensed it in some fashion of their own, and flew straight toward it.

In a silent flurry of wingbeats, the creatures that carried Owen brought him safely down to a pavement of black stone not far from the glimmering sweep of the Cerenerian Sea. They released him, flapped a short distance away, and crouched. The two that had carried Asenath were already there, and a little afterward Dyson landed on the pavement and the last two night-gaunts joined the others. Asenath glibbered at them, and at once they sprang up and flew off in total silence. Moments later Owen, Asenath, and Dyson stood alone on the pavement beneath the unfamiliar constellations and the vast golden moon of the Dreamlands, facing the little fire that leaped and glowed nearby.

Dyson gave Owen a shaken look and said, "I think I'm the first negation team officer who ever got a ride from night-gaunts and didn't end up in something's jaws." Then he turned toward Asenath and said with evident discomfort, "Thank you."

"You're welcome." Rachel made a low, wary chirr, and Asenath glanced at her and then asked Dyson, "Do you really think I'm a monster?"

Taken aback, Dyson opened his mouth, closed it again. "I suppose you can't help what you were taught," Asenath said then, "but it's rude to think it so loudly, you know." She turned and started toward the fire. "Come on. The old man said we don't have a lot of time."

* * *

What would be waiting by the little fire, Owen had no idea, but it didn't come as a great surprise when he saw the old man he'd met west of Partridgeville. The odd clothing he'd worn then had been replaced by dream-garments, a plain robe of unbleached wool and a cloak colored brownish-gray. The eyes that rose to meet them glinted like polished steel, though, and the voor that flowed through the old man was just as dazzling as before, brilliant as a thunderbolt.

"Welcome," said Ambrose, in accented English. "I thank you all for doing as I asked. We are safe here until the sun rises." To Dyson: "I need not ask if you have the book. If you will—" He extended a hand, and Dyson extracted a flat shape wrapped in cloth from his backpack.

"Even so." The old man took it in one hand, gestured with the other. "Sit. When dawn comes, each of you must go a different way, but you must learn certain things first." He turned to face Dyson again. "The others must hear your story. Begin with our first meeting."

"Okay," said Dyson. "Two years ago I led a negation team into the Providence area. That's a high-risk zone, and our people who go there—" He caught himself. "There I go again. Radiance personnel who go there usually don't come back. It was bad enough before your side crashed the economy, and it's gotten worse since then."

"We didn't crash the economy," Owen said. "I figured your side did."

Dyson gave him a baffled look, then shook his head. "It wasn't us. The economic crisis messed us over good and proper." Then: "But our briefing said that an extremely dangerous alchemical revenant had been detected there. Our job was to go in, shoot it on sight, dissolve the body in acid. Any other alchemical revenants we found were to be treated the same way." He shrugged. "The short form is that we didn't find any of them, and I lost almost three-quarters of the team. I don't know what got them. All we ever found were bloody bones.

"We finally got orders to head back to base. That night—" He motioned with his head toward Ambrose. "He showed up in the place we were staying. He used sorcery so I couldn't move or call out. He sat on the foot of my bed and I was sure I was about to die, and he said—"

He stared at the fire, his face haggard. "He said, 'You did not find me, but I have found you. No, I do not mean to kill you. When you are back where you began, ask Olson how it goes with Project 638.' Then he was gone, just like that, and I could move again—but I didn't."

He was silent for a time, and then Owen said, "Project 638. What's that?"

"Something nobody on your side is supposed to know about," said Dyson. "Something most Radiance personnel never hear about. The negation teams find out a lot of stuff they're not supposed to, and word gets around, but you don't talk about it to anybody outside your squad—and you never, *ever* mention Project 638. That's our—that's the Radiance's ace in the hole: a network of shelters deep underground, where essential personnel can retreat if things spin out of control topside. The first shelters went in under the Alps and the Blue Ridge mountains more than a hundred years ago, and at this point there's quite a few of them."

Owen nodded, remembering a conversation with Nyarlathotep twenty years before.

"Carla Olson was a negation team coordinator," Dyson went on. "A friend of mine, one of the very few who got out of Oklahoma when Binger went south and we lost half the state."

"What the hell happened there?" Owen asked.

"That was our—the Radiance's base for research on sorcery. What I heard was somebody got cocky and called up something they couldn't put down." He shrugged. "There was no official announcement, just a lot of killed-in-action reports and Binger was off our maps. Carla got clear in time, though, and so did someone else you know, Clark Noyes."

Owen gave him a wry look. "I wasn't sure he was still around."

"You could say that," said Dyson. "He's the Director—the head of the entire Radiance. He was there in Binger when things went wrong, but he walked out. Don't ask me how."

"Go on," Ambrose said then. "The woman Olson."

"Yeah. She'd been assigned to the Denver dirigency for a couple of years, running security for Project 638, but when I got back she'd just been reassigned to the Philadelphia dirigency. So we spent some time catching up, had some drinks—well, I'll spare you the details. The short version is that we got to talking, and she told me—" He drew in an unsteady breath, went on. "Something that put a stake through the heart of everything I thought I could trust.

"She said that the Denver dirigency had been stripped of authority over the deep shelters in the Rockies. That the shelters were reassigned to the Liaison Office. That all the maintenance staff had been sent elsewhere and all the supplies for long term survival hauled away. That the shelters were being handed over to—something else."

The expression on Dyson's face when he said those final words reminded Owen suddenly of the way the man had looked at Asenath. A guess rose abruptly, kindled by memories from six years back: darkness pierced with flashlight beams, stagnant air reeking of stagnant water, shoggoths and sorcery and a Radiant negation team, and in the midst of it—

"Oh my God," he said aloud. "The fungi from Yuggoth."

CHAPTER 5

THE TWILIGHT YEARS

Dyson stared at him, his face gone bloodless. In a strangled voice: "How did you know?"

"I saw one commanding a negation team in New York City six years ago."

A hard-edged silence came and went. "What I heard," said Dyson then, "was that there were no survivors of that operation on either side."

"We didn't lose anyone," Owen said. "If your side did, it wasn't our doing—one of our sorceresses used the Fourth Sign of Terror to chase them out of there in a hurry."

Dyson stared at him a moment longer, then nodded slowly and let his gaze drop. "Okay," he said. "That just figures, doesn't it?" Then: "Yeah, the shelters were handed over to the Mi-Go, and stocked with their food and supplies instead of ours. That's what Carla told me. I didn't believe her. The next morning, we made arrangements to meet that evening—and sometime during the day she got picked up by the Directorate of Security and her name was off the active list by nightfall. The official story was she was killed in action."

"I'm sorry," Owen said.

Dyson went on as though he hadn't heard. "The same thing—the exact same thing—happened to everyone in the team she'd led. They all got reassigned, and within a week turned up dead. And the same thing happened to other teams who handled security when other shelters got handed over to the Mi-Go. Every shelter in North America's theirs now. Every single one."

Another silence passed. The vast golden moon of the Dreamlands slipped westward. Off the other way, a first hint of pale light touched the horizon's edge.

"I spent the two years from then until now figuring out what was behind it all. I had some help." He nodded at Ambrose again. "He showed up from time to time. He never gave me any of the data himself. He just told me to talk to this person, read this file or that book—but that's all he had to do. I got the pieces of the puzzle one by one and put them together. And—"

He hunched forward, his face ashen. "I said to you when we were going down the stair in the graveyard that everything I ever believed in was a lie. That's what I found out. I thought I was fighting for the human race, trying to keep us free of the alien overlords your side calls the Great Old Ones—and the whole time, I was just a puppet of a different set of alien overlords. We were told that the Mi-Go are our allies—the allies of the Radiance, I mean. They aren't allies. They're masters. The Mi-Go use the Radiance the way your Great Old Ones use you."

Owen tried to think of something to say in response, but Asenath forestalled him. "It's not like that," she said. "Shub-Ne'hurrath is my grandmother. Phauz is my goddess and my teacher and my friend. You've been told so many lies about so many other things. Why can't you see that you've been told lies about them, too?"

Dyson's gaze flicked over toward her, harsh as a whip. "I hope you aren't trying to convince me that they care about the human race."

Owen found his voice. "Depends on what you mean. The crap about humanity as the pinnacle of evolution, the conqueror of nature, the measure of all things—they have no time for any of that. To them we're just another species. But—" Once again, memories surged: Nyarlathotep's dark intent face by lamplight in an abandoned farmhouse in the Massachusetts hills; Shub-Ne'hurrath, the Black Goat of the Woods, sheltering him beside the white stone of Arkham, counseling him in a little dark cabin beneath Elk Hill near Chorazin; Yhoundeh speaking to him in dreams, sending the animals that served her to save Laura and Asenath and the people of Dunwich from a negation team; Phauz, the goddess he prayed to, bending to kiss his forehead in the silence of a Providence night. "They aren't our enemies. They are what they are, we are what we are, we pray to them—and sometimes they answer."

Before Dyson could reply, Ambrose said, "Enough. We have little time." Owen gave him a rueful nod, fell silent.

"So that's what I found out," Dyson said then. "That, and one other thing. It's the other thing that got me to cut the tracking chip out of my shoulder with a knife, leave Philadelphia in a stolen car, zigzag at ninety miles an hour through the mountains to a research station in Virginia and leave a whole lot of corpses there. The thing—" He swallowed visibly. "Do you, either of you, know what the Nhhngr is?"

Owen glanced at his daughter, and she beamed and said, "Of course. One of the two forms of matter furthest from the one we're made of. It's balanced by the other one, the Yr." With a little toss of her head: "We learn that in Sunday school."

"Now tell me what happens when it's not balanced by the Yr," said Dyson.

Asenath's smile vanished. "Then it's really dangerous."

"Yeah. And what if somebody was to get a really large quantity of it, enough to spread all over the surface of the Earth, and did that with it?"

The blood drained out of her face. "Then everything would die, if it stays long enough."

Dyson's face tautened. "Oh, it'll stay a good long time— something between a few decades and a hundred years is what

I heard, unless Cthulhu wakes up and gets rid of it sooner. That's why the Mi-Go took over the shelters. They ran a test a while back—they dropped a piece of it on a corner of Massachusetts, where there's a reservoir now."

Owen forced words out through a mouth gone suddenly dry. "'The Colour out of Space,'" he said. "The Lovecraft story."

"Yeah," said Dyson. "The Radiance was supposed to keep humans or the elder races from using sorcery to open the way for the Great Old Ones once the old psychonoetic barriers break down." His face twisted in a ghastly smile that had no trace of humor in it. "That was what was behind all that crap about reason and science and the destiny of humanity: a bunch of extraterrestrial bugs trying to keep their mining claims out of the hands of the original owners." The smile trickled away. "But we—but the Radiance failed, so the Mi-Go are going to make sure there's nobody and nothing left alive to cast those spells."

* * *

Owen was still trying to process this when Ambrose spoke. "Now you know the peril we face. There is still time before the baleful thing descends, and this book—" He motioned with the wrapped volume. "—it holds the key."

"You're a sorcerer," Owen said. "Can you work the spells?"

"I? No." With a little shrug: "My present condition forbids that." Then: "But there is one known to you who can work them. This book must go to her."

"I can take it to her," Asenath said at once.

"And you shall, once the sun rises—if that is possible." He leaned forward, handed her the book. "Attend. There are forces at work of which you know nothing. The working that failed in the place called Binger opened a gate that should never have been opened and summoned a being whose tread this Earth was never intended to bear. That being may stop you from reaching the one you must seek. I have called one to assist you if that happens. You know her name. Go with her wherever she may take you." Asenath looked uncertain, but nodded.

The old man turned to face Owen. "Once the sun rises, you will pass through a portal I have opened to the waking world, and there you will meet one you know. You will tell him about the recovery of this book. Some of the Great Old Ones wish it to be recovered, others wish the opposite, and if the latter learn about this before the former, all our hope is at an end. But the one you will meet is the soul as well as the mighty messenger of the Great Old Ones, and what he knows, they all know." Owen nodded, accepting the task.

"And me?" Dyson asked.

"Once the sun rises, you will come with me. We have a different portal to seek."

The old man got to his feet, then, and gestured for the others to rise. He gestured again, and the little campfire went out as though someone had dumped water over it. In the firelight's absence, the vast ruins of Sarkomand rose black against a sky already tinted by the unseen sun.

"Once the sun rises," said Ambrose, "foes will come here. Yes, they have already entered the Dreamlands in force—did I not say that there were powers at work you do not know? All those who come here will die, for that which lurks beneath the waters hungers for their blood. Even so, we must not be here when they arrive." He turned to Asenath. "Go. Do not let anyone see the manner of your leaving." To Owen: "Go west upon that street." He pointed. "You will find at its end an opening in the cliff half blocked with rubble. Do not enter that. Go instead to the north, where you will see a doorway marked with the head of a cat. Enter it, and seek the nearest road." To Dyson: "We will wait until they are gone."

Asenath went to her father, gave him a hug and a kiss on the cheek, forced a smile, and said, "I'll see you back home soon." Rachel chirred at him. A moment later she hurried away.

Owen watched her go and then turned to Dyson and said, "Thank you." Dyson nodded uncomfortably, and Owen turned away and started up the street Ambrose had indicated.

He reached the cliff as the first light of sunrise kindled the eastern horizon to flame. The opening half blocked with rubble was easy enough to find, but it took him a few minutes to spot the doorway with the cat's head over it, and it looked far from promising, a shallow niche carved into the face of the cliff. Still, he walked straight toward it, and an instant before his face hit stone, darkness opened up before him and sent him tumbling through an unexpected abyss.

Then the darkness gave way to daylight, and he was stepping onto ground scattered with fallen pine needles. He blinked and looked around. Low haggard pines surrounded him, sending clutching roots into the sandy soil. A few scraps of mist coiled here and there, and he looked around, wondering if he'd see Hob Hill somewhere close by, but as far as he could tell, the land around him stretched away flat to the edge of sight. Ahead of him, though, something interrupted the pines, and after a moment he was sure it was a road.

It took him some minutes to get there, weaving through the pines, but eventually he stepped out onto the verge of a two-lane road. From where the sun stood, Owen guessed that the road ran north and south; it reached straight in both directions toward unguessable distance; other than the road itself, the only sign of human presence was an old wooden billboard that had long since been bleached to illegibility. Lacking any better ideas, he turned north and started walking.

After a mile or so, he heard the sound.

The sound came whispering through the unquiet air from somewhere to the south. Owen recognized it at once. He turned to look back along the road, and presently saw something low and black moving with uncanny speed toward him. A slow smile spread across his broad square face as he recognized the car's fluid shape, knew what—and who—it had to be.

The car slowed as it approached him. He knew better than to look at the license plate, or even to try to tell whether the car had two doors or four.

It stopped and the passenger side window slid down. Owen glanced inside, saw the figure he expected: tall and lean, clad all in black, with a hooked nose like a hawk's beak and black eyes that opened onto unfathomable abysses.

"Good afternoon, Old One," Owen said.

"Good afternoon, Owen," said Nyarlathotep, the soul and mighty messenger of the Great Old Ones. "I suspect you'd welcome a ride."

"Please and thank you." Then: "Where are you going?"

"Providence," Nyarlathotep said.

"Works for me." Owen opened the door, climbed in, tossed his duffel into the back seat.

* * *

The long black car accelerated, whipping around the curve at a speed no human driver could have attempted and lived. The car radio played a fine version of the Delta standard "Cross Road Blues." Listening to it, Owen felt a sudden flash of recognition: he'd heard the same performance in a converted warehouse on Fish Street in Arkham twenty years back.

"Yes, that's Isaac Jax and His Cottonmouths," said Nyarlathotep.

Owen glanced at him. "That radio will play any music you've ever heard, won't it?"

"Of course. I think you'll appreciate the playlist between here and Providence."

"I remember the one you played on the way to Dhu-Shai."

The Crawling Chaos gave him a cryptic glance, slowed just enough to take a curve without spinning out of control, floored the pedal as the road went straight again. Around the car, the New Jersey countryside blurred past. Houses and businesses that had fallen in on themselves outnumbered those that still showed signs of occupancy by more than ten to one.

"I'm supposed to tell you something," Owen said, as Isaac Jax and His Cottonmouths moved on to another piece of classic blues. "About a book."

"The *Ghorl Nigral*."

"Yeah. Did you know it's been recovered from the Radiance?"

The car veered around a pothole large enough to swallow a child. "I knew the attempt would be made," said Nyarlathotep. "That it succeeded is welcome news. The Radiance didn't have the lore or the skill to make much use of it, but it's better out of their hands."

Owen considered the Crawling Chaos for a long moment, and Nyarlathotep gave him a look of cool amusement. "Yes, my masters know what you intend to do with it."

"What do they think of that?"

"They are not of one will in that matter, as you know." The road stretched away into blue distance ahead. "Some favor your intention. One opposes it. Since their will is divided—" The Crawling Chaos glanced at him again. "I can neither assist your purpose nor hinder it."

"Giving me a ride doesn't count?"

The fathomless black eyes glanced at him again. "We'll agree that it doesn't."

Owen pondered that as the car whipped past an abandoned strip mall. Beyond it, more empty buildings stretched off to the edge of sight.

"Is it okay to ask why you're going to Providence?" Owen asked after a while.

"Of course. The humans there need to know about a certain imminent danger."

"I think I know what the danger is," said Owen. "The Nhhngr?"

Nyarlathotep nodded. Owen glanced at him, could think of nothing to say.

Well before the roads began to flow together toward New York City, Nyarlathotep veered inland. After a time the uneven crests of the Watchung Mountains rose up against the northern sky, and the last traces of the twenty-first century melted away into resurgent forests and scattered farms where draft horses had long since replaced tractors.

"It seems like a dream sometimes," Owen said, as the car shot past a cluster of old farm buildings up against a hill, set glowing by slanting evening sunbeams. Only after the words were out did he realize that he'd spoken them aloud.

Nyarlathotep glanced at him. "The world you grew up in?" He nodded, and the Crawling Chaos went on: "It always was a dream—the dream of the Radiance." Hands glittering with rings turned the steering wheel, and the car hurtled around a curve. "And it strayed from their intentions the way dreams generally do. Now comes the awakening."

Owen gave him an uneasy look.

"There are friends of the Great Old Ones in these valleys," Nyarlathotep said then. "I'll stop just before we reach the Ramapo Mountains to get you some food, then drive through the night. We'll be in Providence around dawn tomorrow. The following evening I'll pass on my message, and the next day I'll be elsewhere."

"And after that?" Owen asked. The Crawling Chaos glanced at him, said nothing.

The promised stop came later that afternoon, as the sun sank toward ragged mountain crests on the western skyline, and it was brief—the black car pulled into the driveway of a little house surrounded by woods on three sides and the road on the fourth, and a thin middle-aged woman darted out the door with a basket in her hands. She passed the basket through the open window to Nyarlathotep, who gave it to Owen and then placed a hand atop her head and blessed her in words that were ancient before the land around the house first rose from primal seas.

Owen watched her as the car backed out of the driveway, with her hands clasped to her chest and her face awash with awe and delight. He wondered what tangled geometries of persecution and survival had played out in those hills while the communities he knew—Arkham, Innsmouth, Kingsport, Dunwich, Chorazin—had struggled with their own parallel destinies. As the woman and the little house went out of sight behind dark autumnal trees, his thoughts strayed to all the other worshippers of the Great Old Ones scattered around the planet, clinging to an archaic knowledge that all the glaring lights of the Radiance could not obscure, waiting for the hour when the stars would come round right and set Earth's ancient gods free at last.

Several miles slid past before he remembered the basket. He pulled open the cloth wrapping inside it. Inside were two robust chicken salad sandwiches on homebaked bread, an apple tart, and a brown bottle with screw-on lid that turned out to contain a pleasant homebrewed ale. Once he'd finished the meal, he said aloud, "Please thank her for me."

"I already have," said Nyarlathotep.

Later, as the sun set, the black car shot across the Hudson River on a bridge north of Peekskill so rusty and rickety that Owen wouldn't have risked it on foot. Beyond the river, only scattered farms showed any signs of life. Awakening from a dream, Nyarlathotep had called it, but a different metaphor circled in Owen's mind as they drove. These are the twilight years, he thought drowsily. The harsh sun of the Radiance is setting, and night's peace comes at last.

A less metaphorical night closed in as the black car hurtled onward. The last thing Owen remembered before sleep took him was Nyarlathotep's lean dark face, caught in a stray splash of lamplight from a farm near the road. The black eyes were unreadable as always, but something in the set of the Old One's expression seemed to deny even the possibility of hope.

* * *

"Providence," said the Crawling Chaos.

Owen blinked awake in response. Light of a gray dawn came filtering in through the passenger side window, spread across high thin clouds. Through the driver's side window, off past Nyarlathotep's black silhouette, a gibbous moon showed through a gap in the clouds.

"What now?" Owen asked.

"I have certain preparations to make before tomorrow night. I trust you won't be inconvenienced if I drop you off on Federal Hill."

"Not at all."

Nyarlathotep's glance, half visible in the dim light, communicated nothing.

Owen watched empty buildings slip past, noted rusting hulks of abandoned cars beside the curbs. A stray dog trotted along the sidewalk. Weeds rose through cracks in the pavement, and here and there saplings had begun to shoulder their way up through concrete. Ahead, the tall silent buildings that marked Providence's downtown rose up against a featureless sky. After a short distance, without any obvious act on Nyarlathotep's part, the radio came on, playing the opening measures of a piece of avant-garde jazz.

"Sun Ra?" Owen asked, recognizing the sound instantly.

"Yes." The Crawling Chaos slowed to evade more potholes. "He really was from Saturn, you know." Owen gave him a questioning look, but Nyarlathotep said nothing more.

As Sun Ra and His Intergalactic Arkestra played on the radio, Nyarlathotep drove through a maze of surface streets veering at random angles and finally reached a neighborhood Owen knew. The car slowed as it reached a windswept open square, pulled up at a sidewalk next to a stone wall topped with a rusted chainlink fence.

"Will this do?" Nyarlathotep asked.

"Of course. Where should I be tomorrow night?"

"You'll see the signs."

A few moments later, Owen stood on the sidewalk, his duffel slung from his shoulder, as the long black car drove away. He looked around, sorted through memories scattered over a decade of visits, and then set out for the one place he guessed would be open so early. Off the broad avenues as quickly as he could, down a narrow brown alley to an unmarked door: it was nearly as familiar as the streets of Arkham. He tried the door, found it unlocked, went through.

Inside, wooden tables glowed in the light of oil lamps, and stained glass spelled out the name of the restaurant—Sancipriani's—over the room's far end. A familiar rush of scents rose to greet him. A plump gray-haired woman behind the counter glanced up, did a double-take, and in a delighted tone said, "Owen! You didn't tell us you were coming!"

"Hi, Julie," he said, returning her hug. "I didn't know until yesterday." In response to her startled look: "I got a ride from someone who drives a big black car."

The smile dropped off Julie Olmert's face. "He's supposed to be here tomorrow night."

"He's here now. He just dropped me off by the Mother Church."

She put the smile back on with an effort. "Well, anyway, it's so good to see you again! You'll want breakfast, of course—and do you have a place to stay yet? No?" She glanced up at the clock. "I give it thirty minutes before people are fighting to offer you a room."

It didn't come to that, but that was mostly because Sam Mazzini, red-faced and puffing, flung open the door a few minutes later, having gotten some message Julie sent. He gave Owen a bear hug that might have cracked ribs on someone less robustly built, plopped himself into the seat facing Owen's, and said, "Charlene will wring my neck if you don't come stay with us. You're okay with that? Oh, good." Julie came over, beaming, with a cup of chicory coffee, and he ordered a breakfast as hearty as the one in front of Owen.

They were halfway through their respective meals, and Sam's disjointed account of the latest doings in Providence, when the door opened again and another familiar figure came through, a woman with white hair and round glasses, dressed in the sort of clothing Owen was used to seeing on construction workers. "Owen," said Ellen Chernak. "I just heard you were here. You've got a place to stay? Good. It's so good to see you again." Another hug later, she accepted coffee from Julie and settled into a chair.

"So things have been going well," she said later, after filling in some of the gaps in Sam's account. "For us, at least. Providence is doing better than a lot of places these days, but that's not saying much. It's got maybe a third of the population it had when you first came here."

Owen choked on his imitation coffee. "What the hell happened?"

"A bunch of things. We've had some really bad flu epidemics over the last couple of years, and a fever—our people got through it fine, but we've got witches to turn to and most other people in town wouldn't go to them, not at first. Mostly, though, it's jobs. There aren't many here, not any more, and there's supposed to be plenty of work out west."

"Or something," said Sam.

Owen considered that. "I heard a little about that in New Jersey."

"I bet," said Ellen. "You know I used to do a lot of carpentry for outsiders, right? I heard from people I worked for that there were ads all over TV and the internet—go to such and such website, apply for a job and pack your bags, that sort of thing."

"Yeah," said Sam. "And you know what? I talked to people who had friends and family who answered those ads and moved out west, and after they went, they never wrote back or called or anything. You answer those ads, nobody ever hears from you again."

* * *

It took a good two hours before Owen and Sam managed to pry themselves loose from the crowd of friends at Sancipriani's, but Owen didn't mind. After the days just past, it was good to see familiar faces, hear about who'd gotten married or had a child or been initiated into a higher degree since he'd last been there. As he and Sam wove their way through narrow brown alleys atop Federal Hill, the pressure of the terrible news he carried faded for the moment.

"Here's something you ought to see," Sam said a few blocks from Sancipriani's, as they came to one of the broad avenues that crossed Federal Hill. He pointed to a sheet of yellow paper stapled to a telephone pole. It had an image on it that stirred decades-old memories: a crossroads under a crescent moon, with a tall figure in a broad-brimmed hat and a long coat backlit by the moonlight. The poster in his memories had the name of a blues band across the top, though, and this one replaced that with a familiar but improbable name: Nyarlathotep. Down below was an address in Providence, a date that worked out to the next day, the time 7 PM, and nothing else.

Owen turned to Sam. "I knew he was giving some kind of talk," he said. "I had no idea he was doing it under his real name."

"Everybody's been talking about that since the signs went up. I was hoping he might have mentioned something about it to you."

"I wish." Then, as they started walking again: "Who put up the signs?"

Sam shrugged. "No clue. They showed up first thing Wednesday. Every dog in town was howling around three that morning, so I'm guessing whatever stapled them up wasn't human."

Sam's house was a pleasant clapboard-sided place with a view west, over outspread roofs and the gray belt of an abandoned freeway, toward the mostly empty suburb of Olneyville and the purple slopes beyond. A sprawling garden spread south of it, where another house had been ten years earlier;

an altar to the Black Goat of the Woods stood in the traditional place between seedbed and compost bin. The back door swung wide. Owen wiped his boots solicitously on the coarse fiber of the doormat, clumped up the short stair inside after his host, and had just reached the kitchen when Charlene came hurrying over to throw her arms around him.

After that came more coffee and more conversations. Toward noon he got his things settled in Sam and Charlene's spare bedroom upstairs, and made time for a few hours of sleep. After that, though, Sam and Charlene's two younger children got home from school, and by the time Owen had finished fielding their questions, a knock on the door announced another of Owen's Providence friends. By dinnertime the Mazzini house was full of guests, potluck dishes made their appearance from neighboring kitchens, and wine had begun to flow. "Oh, it's local," said Sam, as he popped the cork on another bottle. "We've got vineyards here these days, the weather's gotten that warm." He poured Owen a glass. "Give it a try."

It was close to midnight before things wound down and Owen made his unsteady way up the stairs. Sleep came quickly enough, but toward dawn unremembered wanderings gave way to the same vivid images that burst into his dreams in Partridgeville: stone ruins dripping with sea water and strewn with wet seaweed, a soaring monolith against a prismatic sky, a road that rose or fell toward it. He woke as the first gray light showed through the eastern window of the room, lay there for a while trying to decide whether the dreams were wishful thinking or maybe, just maybe, offered a hint that a time long awaited was approaching at last.

"Got any plans today?" Sam asked him over breakfast, as a chicory brew that smelled tolerably like coffee splashed into cups. "Before Nyarlathotep's talk, at least."

"Yeah." Owen took the cup gratefully. "Off to visit George Gammell Angell."

Charlene's face lit up. "Please tell Dr. Angell we'd love to see him any time."

"I'll do that," said Owen.

* * *

"Owen," the old man said, beaming. "Please come in. Tea? Excellent."

The house at 17 Wayland Lane seemed to have slipped out of time, and the same was true of its occupant: thin and stooped, bald except for a thin halo of white hair, wearing clothing of a style that went out of fashion before the Second World War. He unchained the door, let Owen in and then shook his hand. The skin felt abnormally cold and dry, with a curious coarse texture.

Owen waited while the old man locked the door. "It's good to see you again."

"The pleasure is entirely mine," said Professor Angell. "I trust all is well with Laura and the children? Very good. And Miriam? Also very good."

Owen let himself be guided into the library, settled into a chair at the table there while his host made clattering sounds in the kitchen. Scents of leather and old paper tinged the air. Elegant white curtains shut out the half-abandoned neighborhood outside, made it possible to believe for a moment that the calm of a less troubled age still lingered.

The two of them caught up on the doings of mutual friends while the teakettle heated, finished that end of the conversation with the first few sips of tea. "Now," said Angell. "I'm quite sure you didn't come all this way just to sip tea and gossip. What can I do for you?"

"I wasn't actually planning to come to Providence at all," Owen admitted. "I went to Partridgeville, New Jersey to do some research in the papers of a man named Halpin Chalmers."

Angell's eyebrows went up. "Chalmers," he said after a moment. "Now there's a name I haven't heard in a very long time."

"Did you know him?"

"Oh, yes. He worked for the Manhattan Museum of Fine Arts, you know. They always had forgers trying to palm off fraudulent antiquities on them, and he'd come up on the overnight boat from New York to ask about anything in my field of study. I won't say we were close, but cordial, yes." He glanced up at Owen. "Yes, I know about his other interests as well. I have an autographed copy of *The Secret Watcher*, a gift from him. It came in the mail just days before I heard that he'd died."

"Do you recall the passage where he mentions talking to doels?"

That fielded Owen a startled look. "No." He went to the shelves, brought back a familiar volume. "But it's been quite some time since I last read it. Do you recall where the passage is?"

It took Owen a little searching to find the page Jenny had shown him in Arkham, but finally he handed the book to Angell, who put on a pair of gold-rimmed glasses.

"That is very remarkable," said Angell finally. "What do you make of it?"

"If von Junzt's right, there haven't been doels on this world for millions of years."

"Yes, von Junzt does say that, doesn't he? Only the *Pnakotic Manuscript* and the *Eltdown Shards* speak of doels in the present tense; the more recent tomes say they've been gone for ages. The thing that puzzles me most, though, is the reference to the maker of the doels."

"Noth-Yidik," said Owen.

"Precisely. Do you recall the discussion of her in the *Liber Rerum Celandum*?"

"The *Book of Hidden Things*? That's a rare one."

"It is indeed." The old man smiled. "There was a copy at the John Hay Library. I'm not sure what became of it, but fortunately I obtained a photostat in 1937." Angell got up again, went to a file cabinet over against one wall, came back with a manila folder full of sheets of stiff paper. "Here it is," he said, sitting down again. "Let us see." Pages fluttered. "Ah. Here we are. *Liber Quinque, capitulum duodecim, De origine doelum et matre fonteque eorundem.*"

He pushed the sheet across the table to Owen, who translated the chapter title at a glance—"On the origin of the doels and the mother and source thereof." Below was a dense paragraph in sixteenth-century script which he translated just as readily:

> *The doels were upon the earth and under the earth in a time that is gone, and shall again be upon and under the earth in a time yet to come. They are from Noth-Yidik. To them belongs a threefold life in which their destiny is fulfilled. Noth-Yidik also was upon the waters in a time that is gone and shall be upon them in a time to come. Her destiny is but one, and She abides from age to age. Kadath in the cold waste has not known Her, nor has She any dealings with the Great Old Ones, save only one. For She awaits a certain hour already spoken of. When that hour comes She shall pass into the world of men, and terrible shall be the sight thereof. And She shall thence depart into the sea, and there shall She accomplish Her work, and Her young shall enter upon the threefold life which begins in the sea and ends in black caverns far beneath the earth we know.*

Owen glanced up from the paper. "Do you have any idea what it's talking about?"

"A little." Angell poured more tea for them both. "You'll recall the reference in the Eltdown Shards that claims Noth-Yidik will play some role in Great Cthulhu's awakening. All through this text there are hints that would make sense if those refer to the same thing."

"Okay," said Owen, nodding slowly. "And does anyone know where Noth-Yidik is?"

"A very interesting question," Angell said. "The *Pnakotic Manuscript* uses a verb for her that implies that she's dead. *The Book of Hidden Things* speaks of her birth in some far future time. Then there's a very odd legend Dornly gives in his *Magyar Folklore*, the story of the Egg of Nathidech—the name's close enough that it might be the same being." With a shrug: "Or not. There is so much we simply don't know."

Owen kept his feelings off his face. Another blind alley, he thought.

Angell sat back in his chair. "I know," he said, as though he'd heard Owen's unspoken thoughts. "We live, as a writer I once knew put it, on a placid island of ignorance in the midst of black seas of infinity, and it was not meant that we should venture far." With a precise smile: "It's simply that no island can ever afford to ignore the sea for long."

He was still smiling when a knock sounded on the door.

CHAPTER 6

THE GOLDEN TREES

A ngell got up with an apologetic look, went to the entry. Owen pulled over the photostat of the *Liber Rerum Celandum*, looked up as Angell's voice went low. Another voice joined his, low and urgent, tinged with a Texas accent. Owen slid his chair back from the table, moved his right hand down to the pocket where his revolver waited.

Then the door closed, opened, and closed again. A few moments later Angell came back into the library, followed by a lean black-haired man Owen almost recognized.

"Owen," said Angell, "I'm sorry to have to cut short our conversation. This is another friend of Charles, and he's come with a message of rather some importance."

"Mr. Merrill?" said the newcomer. "Justin Geoffrey."

That was when he remembered where he'd seen the man's face before: an old black and white photograph on the dust jacket of a favorite book. "The poet?" Owen said, shaking his hand. As he'd expected, it had the same cold coarse texture as Angell's.

Geoffrey grinned. "Yeah, that's me." Abruptly serious: "An old fellow you left in a ghost town by the seashore sent me. He needs you to come with me, right now, to a place about a mile from here. There's really bad trouble."

"Okay," Owen said. An instant later, his surprise ebbed far enough for more serious concerns to surface. "My daughter Asenath," he said. "Do you know if she's—"

"The old man didn't say anything about that," said Geoffrey. "Just that we have to hurry."

"I've known Justin for quite a long time," Angell said, "and Magister Ambrosius almost as long. You may trust them both with your life—I have, more than once."

A few words of farewell, and the clatter of two locks and a door chain, and Owen and the poet were hurrying down the stair to Wayland Lane. Around them, empty windows stared blindly at one another, and a few derelict cars huddled against the curbs. Geoffrey motioned with his head and then set off southward with the loose swinging stride of the born walker. Owen matched his pace, and after a little while Geoffrey glanced at him and said, "You're heeled?"

Owen happened to know enough early twentieth century slang to make sense of that. "Yeah. I carry my .38 pretty much everywhere these days."

The poet laughed. "In Deaf Smith County where I grew up, they said a thirty-eight's a runty little excuse for a gun, but I carried one all over Europe and it saved my ass more'n once." Then: "The old man said we shouldn't run into any trouble, not if we hurry."

They hurried. "How did you meet Charles Dexter Ward?" Owen asked then.

"Oh, we ran into each other in Transylvania, and then we ended up on the same liner home in the summer of 1925. He told me that I should lie low in Providence, and he was right, but I was dumb as a box of rocks in those days. So I went to Chicago, and the other side caught me and stuck me in an asylum and shot me full of rat poison or something, and thank the Great Old Ones Charles heard about it in time to get my body shipped here. And here I am."

"Still writing poetry, I hope."

That got him a different smile, and a glimpse beneath the man's brash exterior. "You bet. I put a fair bit into the small magazines under the name John Tyler. I hope somebody gets a press going again sometime—I've got way more than enough for another book of poems."

They turned south. Owen recognized the street at once: Olney Court. "We're going to Joseph Curwen's house, aren't we?" he asked.

"Yeah. We've been using it as a base for nine years now."

"We?" Owen asked. Geoffrey grinned again, said nothing.

The last few blocks slipped past. The house Owen remembered so well still stood at 128 Olney Court, its clapboard sides badly in need of paint, its windows screened from within by cheap curtains, its front door still framed by the antique elegance of rayed fanlight and Doric pilasters. As he expected, Geoffrey led him through the gap between houses to the kitchen door in back, and in moments they were inside, passing through a kitchen freighted with memories.

"Mr. Ambrose?" the poet called out. "Here he is."

Why the memory should have surfaced at that moment, Owen could not have said then or thereafter. Maybe it was returning to the house where he'd learned alchemy from Lydia Ward, maybe it was the way that Professor Angell had said the words "Magister Ambrosius," but all at once, as he neared the parlor, he recalled something Lydia had told him in the tunnels beneath Joseph Curwen's long-abandoned farm: a detail from one of H.P. Lovecraft's stories, a note written in Latin in the script of sub-Roman Britain, a figure out of legend whose corpse Charles Dexter Ward had brought from Wales for his own purposes—

He stopped in the door to the parlor, seeing the old man sitting comfortably on a rundown sofa, wearing those modern clothes that most closely approximated the knee-length tunics and hooded cloaks that had been fashionable in Britain in the sixth century, blazing with voor like no other sorcerer Owen had ever known, glancing up at him with eyes the color of polished steel. In that moment Owen guessed a little of what those eyes had seen.

"Merlin," he said aloud. "You're Merlin, aren't you?"

The old man smiled. "*Certo*," he answered in Latin: of course.

* * *

The old man gestured him to a seat, and Owen, stunned, sat down. The poet grinned and left the room; the kitchen door opened and closed a moment later. "My grandfather's people named me Marcus Ambrosius Sylvestris," said Merlin, "but my grandmother's people called me Moridunos, or as folk were beginning to pronounce it then, Myrddin."

"And Charles Dexter Ward revived you."

"As I intended." He smiled again, seeing Owen's look of surprise. "There is more to Charles' story than you know yet. Perhaps you will hear it someday."

Owen drew in a breath to ask about Asenath. Before he could speak, Merlin raised a hand, forestalling him. "You are concerned about your daughter," he said. "Not without reason. She still lives and has the book, but she has not reached Arkham. Unless she is very fortunate she will be here soon. When she departs again you will go with her."

Footfalls sounded on the floor above, came drumming down the stair, stirring Owen's memories. A moment later a girl Asenath's age, a pale blonde with a slight boyish look, came pelting into the parlor. "Mr. Ambrose," she panted, "the sign—the one you said to watch for."

"Ah." Merlin got to his feet, motioned for Owen to do the same. To the girl, in English: "Thank you, Vanessa. Go next door and warn Justin, and then do as he tells you."

She nodded and bolted from the room. Owen watched her go, then turned to the old man.

"Your daughter is on her way here," said Merlin. "So is another, and the other must not arrive first." A gesture told Owen to move back and he did, guessing what was about to happen.

He was not mistaken. Merlin knotted his fingers together in a curious pattern, then pulled them suddenly apart and spoke four short words. Voor surged around the old man, flaring outward. All the windows Owen could see went dark at once.

"That should serve." Merlin turned to Owen. "I will need the chalk you have with you."

Owen blinked in surprise, then reminded himself who the old man was. "Of course."

A few moments later Merlin had drawn a familiar pattern of angled lines and curves in a corner of the parlor. He regarded the pattern for a moment, nodded, then crossed to another corner and drew a different pattern there, one Owen didn't recognize at all.

"Sufficient," said Merlin. He turned to Owen. "You will face grave perils soon."

"I'm okay with that."

"I know. The doctors Muñoz and Angell—" It took Owen a moment to parse *doctores Muniosus Angelusque*. "—both spoke of your courage." He turned and crossed to the first diagram he'd drawn. "Be ready."

Violet light flared in the corner at the heart of the diagram, spread, drew suddenly into a human shape. Then Asenath, with Rachel on her shoulder, stumbled out of the diagram. She looked haggard and somehow older, more so than the days since he'd seen her would explain. Behind her, the violet light flared again and spread into a shape that was far from human—

And Merlin wiped his hand across the chalk lines, disrupting the spell.

The violet light guttered instantly. By then Owen had already lunged across the room and was helping his daughter to her feet. "Dad!" she gasped. Then, ruefully: "I haven't been able to get the book to Aunt Jenny. I can't get through."

"You will need to take another path," Merlin said in English. "Quickly!" He pointed at the second diagram, the one Owen didn't recognize, and murmured something under his breath. The chalk lines flared with cold green light in response. "Go!"

Asenath took hold of her father's arm and pulled him toward the second diagram. Around them, the house had begun to tremble, as though under the tread of more than elephantine feet. Owen gathered his strength and darted forward with her.

All at once he was hurtling through an abyss full of vast prismatic shapes whose angles made no sense to him, while a shrieking, roaring confusion of sound broke over him. Ahead of him, a mass of tumbling iridescent bubbles and a polyhedron with constantly changing colors and angles seemed to pull him on. Dazzled and confused, he let himself be drawn toward a mass of prismatic shapes that rose up like a barrier before them. A sudden twist got them past the barrier, and then they plunged toward the oddly regular meeting of two great sufaces just ahead.

Just as quickly as the nightmare journey had begun, it ended, and Owen fell forward. He landed face first in what looked and felt like moss, except it was the color of bronze. As he scrambled to his feet, he spotted Asenath and Rachel close by. A ring of gray standing stones surrounded them. Just outside the stones, what looked like trees gathered close, except that they were pale gold in color and seemed to be covered with feathers. Owen clenched his eyes shut and opened them again, but the impossible trees were still there. Their branches spread over the stone circle, hiding most of the sky behind leaves the color of hammered gold.

Then Owen noticed the color of the sky.

* * *

He heard Asenath's breath catch a moment later. She'd gotten to her feet as well, and was staring past the golden leaves. Beyond, a sky the color of spring grass bent over them.

"This isn't the dreamlands," Asenath said. "I—I don't know where we are."

"Neither do I," said Owen.

Another voice spoke, one he recognized instantly. "Fortunately I can help with that—but you two need to get out of the circle right away."

He turned, motioned to Asenath and went through the nearest gap between the stones. Asenath hurried after him. As soon as they were outside the circle, voor surged and shifted behind them, flared, and then faded out.

"That was close," said Lydia Ward. "Owen, it's so good to see you again! Come on—you'll both be much safer once we get to Lilulelomaramal." Rachel chirred at her, and she laughed. "Okay, all three of you. Is that better?"

If she'd aged at all since the night in Providence when he'd seen her last, she showed no sign of it. Black hair in a torrent of braids spilled over the shoulders of a green gown that set off the dark brown of her face and hands. "This way," she said, motioning toward a trail through the wood. As they started, she glanced over her shoulder at Asenath. "You're Owen's daughter, aren't you? He told me a little about you when we worked together."

"Yes," Asenath said. "Phauz told me a little about you, too."

"I thought you had her mark on you." With a glance further back at Owen. "Both of you."

Just then a creature came darting through the air. It looked like a ruby-colored snake with bat's wings. Owen and Asenath watched it in astonishment, while Lydia walked on as though it was the most ordinary thing in the world. "Where are we?" Owen asked then.

"This world is called Melirul," said Lydia. "Just one world ulthward from our Earth."

Anth and ulth—those, Owen knew, were the directions human beings couldn't normally perceive, at right angles to all earthly directions. Until that moment they'd been abstract concepts to him. He shook his head in amazement, followed Lydia through the golden trees.

Some minutes passed before they left the wood behind. In the distance ahead, mountains rose against the verdant sky, but Owen had little attention to spare for them. Close by, a city of spires the color of mother-of-pearl rose above tawny meadows and golden orchards. Something wasn't quite right about the way the city stood in the landscape, Owen thought; a long moment passed before he realized that the city hovered above the ground at just over treetop height.

"Lilulelomaramal," said Lydia then. "It doesn't look much like Providence, does it?" She laughed, gestured. "Come on. Charles will be delighted to see you both."

It took them maybe another half an hour to cross the meadow to the city's edge. Winged serpents fluttered past from time to time, and furred many-legged shapes scuttled away when they came near. When they were halfway there, something far from human came trotting over to see them: a little like a centaur, if centaurs had been modeled on goats or small deer rather than horses. It wore no clothing; its head came to Asenath's shoulders; pale golden fur covered its body; its hooves and the short horns on its head were a deeper gold, and so were its eyes. It regarded them, and then said something in a quick lilting tongue Owen couldn't follow at all.

Lydia answered in the same language. The creature's pointed ears angled back suddenly, and it turned and bounded away toward the city. Other creatures of the same kind came trotting over to watch them, murmured to one another in the same intricate lilting language.

A little further, and they stood just outside the edge of the hovering city. Lydia called out in a different language. In answer, a ramp pivoted slowly down from above, stopped a foot above the moss. Lydia stepped onto it and motioned for the others to follow.

At the top of the ramp, the city of Lilulelomaramal spread out before them. Clustered spires, cupolas, arched bridges, broad plazas shimmered beneath the emerald sky, and all about were the people of Lilulelomaramal. They looked a little like centaurs, too, but modeled on elk or reindeer rather than horses. Russet-furred and caparisoned in curious draperies, they greeted Lydia with grave nods or a few words in their language, and she responded in kind as she led the others through the streets of the city. It didn't take long to reach what Owen guessed was one home among others, a cubic mass of pearl-colored stone with a single arched doorway at street level and a row of arched windows at the topmost floor.

They had scarcely passed through into a broad high-ceilinged room when Charles Dexter Ward—slight, pale, light-haired and blue-eyed—came hurrying down a ramp to greet them. "Owen!" he said, taking his hand. "And your daughter? A pleasure to meet you. I'm glad Merlin sent you to us. Please come with me—a meal, I imagine, and then a place to rest, for a little while." Something like dread showed briefly in the blue eyes. "We don't have much time."

* * *

"Merlin," Charles said, with a reminiscent smile. "Now there's a strange tale." He reached for the bottle of wine, filled all four glasses. "Did you know he's an ancestor of mine? He worked the same spell Joseph did." A twist got the wine bottle settled in a bucket of ice. "He had a daughter by a priestess of Minerva named Claudia Nemevia—the Nimue of the legends—and her great-granddaughter was Llunwy of Wales, who's in my family tree."

They sat in a cubical room with translucent walls, finishing the last of a meal at a circular table that looked as though it had grown in place. The food had been pleasant but strange—a pale purple something-or-other with the consistency of pudding and a flavor between bananas and pork, thin slices of something turquoise blue that didn't quite smell of violets. Asenath tasted her wine, gave her father a glazed look; Owen nodded fractionally and sipped from his own. Whatever Melirulean fruit it was made from had a noticeable mustard flavor.

"But Merlin knew exactly when he wanted to be brought back to life," Charles went on. "When I was in Britain in 1923, I made friends with a man named Paul Tregardis, a student of the old lore who had connections with secret cults in Wales. In the fall we went to Glastonbury to meet some of his friends— and a little later, at the end of October, to Caermaen in Wales, and up into the hills back behind the town, where I met serpent folk for the first time." He shook his head, laughed. "Then I went back to London and thought that was the end of it.

"A few weeks later, though, I got a package in the mail from Caermaen. It was half of a piece of black stone with an inscription on it in bad early medieval Latin, and a note asking me to keep it safe. I did, and about two months after I resurrected Joseph, I happened to mention it to him. He stared at me, laughed, and took me into his laboratory, and there was the other piece with the rest of the inscription. I wrote to Paul to tell him I knew the location of Merlin's grave and was supposed to try to recover his body." He laughed. "And Paul wrote back that his Welsh friends knew perfectly well what the whole business had been about. So we got Merlin's remains and went to work extracting the essential salts. I didn't live to see that work finished, but the last letter poor Joseph sent to Lydia mentioned that he'd brought Merlin back to life."

"And that was all either of us knew until a little over a year ago," said Lydia. "The alalume—those are the people you saw here in Lilulelomaramal, the little ones of the grasslands are the alilume—they keep a very close watch on the border between Melirul and our Earth. One day we got sent for by the Rumelelil. You'd probably call them the town council, but they get the job because they dream true dreams, and they wanted to know what it meant that they were dreaming night after night of a city rising from under the sea."

"We drew the obvious conclusion," said Charles, as Owen and Asenath both looked startled. "We told them what we knew, and then Merlin arrived. He showed up the same place you did, maybe eight months ago by Earth's calendar. Lydia and I do certain rituals there. One morning there he was. His English was atrocious but we remembered enough Latin to make up for it." Charles leaned forward. "He told us that he came with good and bad news. The good news is that the stars will be right soon and Great Cthulhu is waking at last. The bad news—"

"The Nhhngr," said Owen.

Lydia shook her head. "That's part of it. The rest is that somebody in the Radiance used the book you've got—" She nodded at Asenath. "—to call one of the beings of the outer voids."

"You know about the book," Asenath said, suddenly tense.

"Child," said Lydia, "of course I do. Even if Merlin hadn't told us you'd have it, I'd have sensed the *Ghorl Nigral* from miles off."

"What Merlin said," Charles said, "is that the thing from the outer voids has been trying to get through to Earth for ages, and the Great Old Ones can't fight it while they're bound. I don't want to think about how many worlds will be wrecked before they finally defeat it."

* * *

Not long afterward Lydia took them both to rooms on an upper floor. "You should get some rest while you can," she said. "It'll be about twenty-nine *ulemeru*—about eleven hours—before the barriers weaken again and you'll need to go."

Owen didn't argue. Though he was fairly sure it had been much less than a normal day since he'd woken up in the Mazzinis' house in Providence, weariness ached in his bones. It took him only a short time to fall asleep.

When he woke he blinked and rubbed his eyes and only then remembered where he was, and guessed that the pallid light that came through the translucent walls of the room belonged to Melirul's moon. Someone had set out a basin of cold water and the necessary cloths on a stand near the bed; he got up, washed and dressed, braced himself for the day.

The long ramp that passed for stairs brought him to a room where Charles Dexter Ward sat at a desk, reading from a scroll by candlelight. He glanced up, greeted Owen with a diffident smile. "Good morning. I think I have everything ready for the incantations we'll need."

"I'm going to guess," said Owen, "that those are right over my head."

"They're very nearly over mine." He motioned toward a chair, and Owen came over and sat. "Lydia had most of a century to study and practice while I was—"

"Indisposed," Owen suggested.

That earned him a laugh. "Good," Charles said. "Yes, we can call it that." Then: "But we need to get you and your daughter to Arkham, to the sorceress who can use the *Ghorl Nigral*—yes, Merlin told us about her—and keep the thing from the outer voids from catching you on the way. That's not going to be easy, but I think it can be done."

He considered the scroll in front of him with a wistful look. "I hope it all works out," he said then. "Melirul's beautiful and the alalume have been very kind to us, but I'd like to see blue skies again, and Providence." He glanced up, hearing footfalls on the ramp, and put on a smile.

The footfalls were Asenath's, and it didn't take her long to pull a chair up to the table. Before long the two of them were talking about the Xu language, Jeelo, and the Scarlet Circles, while Rachel dozed on Asenath's shoulder and Owen tried to follow. They were busy discussing the Five Sigils of Yaddith when Lydia came in, listened for a while, and then came over to the table. "I get the impression," she said, "that witches in New England learn a little more than they did when I was a girl."

Asenath blushed. "Thank you. My teachers in Arkham and Chorazin are really good, and Keziah Mason taught me a lot of things too."

Owen gave her a startled glance, but before he could speak, Lydia went on: "That's good to hear. If everything works out and Charles and I can make it back to the lesser Earth, I might be able to show you a few things you'd like to see." Asenath's face lit up, but before she could say anything Lydia turned to Charles and Owen. "I've been to talk to the Rumelelil. They're concerned. There have been omens." A quick gesture dismissed those for the moment. "The short version is that we should get some food and then head for Irulemelul as soon as we can."

Half an hour later, maybe, the four of them left the Wards' house. Three of the alalume waited for them on the street, and nearly a dozen more came cantering up as they started for the city's edge. Melirul's moon hovered just over the western horizon and a faint violet glow to the east spoke of the approaching day, but Lilulelomaramal still slept. Once the ramp dipped to let them down to the meadows, Owen found the alilume sleeping too: circles of adults, hindquarters inward, each head pillowed on a neighboring flank, while the young lay in clusters in the middle. Those they passed looked up, suddenly alert, and then settled back down to sleep once they knew it was only a group of alalume with four strange bipeds in the midst of them.

Meadow gave way to woodland as the glow in the east changed from violet to crimson. As they walked, Lydia turned to Asenath and said, "You don't have to draw the angles, I hope."

"Of course. It's easier with them, but with Rachel's help I don't need them."

"Is there a safe place you can go if things go wrong?"

Asenath nodded enthusiastically. "Keziah took me to a couple of them."

"Good. There might be trouble. We'll see."

The woodland gave way to the circle of stones not long after. Something seemed to trouble the air above the circle's center, a wavering like heat rising from pavement in August. The alalume conferred, and then one of them said something to Charles and Lydia.

At that instant the wavering in the center of the circle lunged toward Asenath. The air turned wintry, and something Owen could scarcely perceive, something vast and cold, drew close. "Go!" Lydia shouted at Asenath, and then turned toward the presence in the circle, raising her hands in a gesture of power. Charles and the alalume began to do the same—

And the world dissolved around Owen as Asenath seized his arm. The shrieking, roaring confusion of sound he'd heard on his first journey between the worlds broke over him again like a wave, and he plunged through an abyss of strange prismatic shapes, following a mass of iridescent bubbles and a shifting polyhedron of many colors and angles.

A vast cold presence was there as well. For an instant it loomed up, spreading to engulf them, but the shape of bubbles that was Asenath veered suddenly, and other shapes Owen could sense but not see rose up to block the cold thing's lunge. An instant later the thing was behind them, and an instant after that Owen saw two planes come together ahead at an angle that almost made sense, and plunged through it after Asenath and Rachel.

A moment of delirium came and went, and then he stumbled and caught his balance. Great oaks rose above him, reaching skeletal branches to a cold blue sky; fallen leaves lay thick on the ground. Further off, gray hills rose silent—and he heard footfalls in the leaves, too close. He started to turn, caught a glimpse of gray and white fatigues. At that same moment Asenath cried out, gripped his arm, and pulled him back into the seething chaos they'd just left.

They plunged through it at what seemed to be a different angle, past shapes that didn't quite match the ones Owen remembered from the two earlier journeys. The prismatic shapes blurred and twisted. After a time other shapes, globular and writhing, came from somewhere else and tumbled after the three of them, now drawing close, now falling back.

It occurred to Owen, as he watched the writhing shapes, that they might be pursuers.

Then Rachel and Asenath twisted toward a place where planes seemed to come together. Owen followed them, passed through a moment of delirium, and sprawled forward onto grass.

He scrambled to his feet an instant later as he caught sight of gray and white urban-camo fatigues around him. A second glance showed him that the ones who wore it were no threat to Asenath or to him, would never be a threat to anyone ever again: contorted bodies and blank staring eyes reminded him all too well of corpses he'd seen on battlefields in Iraq.

He drew in a breath, caught a faint acrid scent. An instant later fire shot through his limbs, and the world began to go dark around him.

* * *

A sudden pain in his shoulder jerked him back to consciousness. The burning in his muscles faded, and his eyesight cleared a little later. He'd fallen to his knees, he realized, and slowly got back to his feet. Asenath was picking herself up, blinking, and Rachel clambered on top of her head and addressed a plaintive chirr to someone behind Owen.

"*Incolumis paulisper eritis*," a voice said from the same direction. Only when Owen's head cleared further did he recognize the Latin phrase: you will be safe for a little while.

It was not Merlin's voice, and the figure Owen saw when he turned was not Merlin, either. Lean, long-bearded, and so wrinkled he made Merlin look young by comparison, he wore a plain robe of mud-colored cloth, and his head and feet were bare. Owen stumbled through words of thanks, and the old man motioned for them to follow him. Something about him seemed familiar, but with his mind still dazed, Owen couldn't think of what it was.

Not far off, the narrow mouth of a cave gaped open in the hillside. Inside, a few simple furnishings perched on the dry stone floor: a wooden table, a few backless chairs, a bedstead further in. The old man waved them to the chairs, and they sat. Owen was still trying to put his thoughts together when Asenath said in more than passable Latin, "Thank you, Master Belasius."

The old man nodded. "Your teacher was good enough to inform me what to expect, and it was an easy thing to prepare a fitting welcome for unwanted guests."

By then Owen's mind had finished clearing. He considered their host, and then glanced out the cave mouth, saw the slope tumble down and hide itself beneath a blanket of forest, such a forest as few countries on Earth could boast in Owen's time: green and unbroken, sweeping over rumpled hills into the distance, where a line of light spoke of the sea. "Where are we?" he asked.

"The kingdom of Rheged," said Belasius. He seemed to sense Owen's confusion, and went on. "The old woman Keziah calls it part of a land called England." Then, holding up a hand to forestall further questions: "We have little time. The others will try again, and they may well bring weapons that can strike from far off."

"I wish I knew how they got here before us," said Asenath.

"Did they follow you back through time?" Belasius asked, and when she nodded: "They simply went further than you. They arrived—" He glanced out the cave mouth, and Owen guessed he was gauging the angle of the sun. "Less than an hour before you, surely."

Owen took that in, flexed his shoulder; it felt as though he'd had an injection there. Asenath said, "If they can follow me through time, that's bad."

Belasius nodded. "Your situation is dire. There will be more bands of them waiting, and they can harry you until you must stop to rest."

"I wonder," Asenath said then. "If—" She stopped, stared at the tabletop for a while. Owen, who'd seen the same expression on her face many times, glanced at Belasius, who met his glance, smiled, and said nothing.

"If they do the same thing," Asenath said after a moment, "and go further back so they can be waiting for us, and we go to the beginning of time …."

"The Hounds of Tindalos?" Owen asked, and Asenath nodded.

"The risk will not be small," the old man said to her. "If you misjudge, you give yourself over to the same fate, but I know of no better hope for you. I will—"

He stood suddenly. "They are coming," he said. "You must leave at once."

Asenath scrambled to her feet, but Owen was quicker still. "Let's go," he said to her. Belasius indicated a portion of the cave wall, where a familiar pattern of curves and angles had been laboriously scratched into the stone. They darted over to it. Asenath took hold of his arm; violet light surged, and they plunged into the seething roaring twilight.

At first Owen thought they'd slipped their pursuers, but after an interval of something he was sure wasn't time, he glimpsed writhing shapes moving toward him and the two who led him. He tried to think of some way to warn Asenath.

An instant later, though, the mass of spheroids that guided him veered, and something shimmered and spread outward: a spell, he guessed, and hoped it would work.

For a while it seemed to hold the pursuing shapes back, but only for a while. Thereafter strange shapes followed them, and no matter what evasive moves Rachel and Asenath tried they couldn't shake them off. Finally they gave up the attempt and plunged straight ahead, or as straight as the not-space and the prismatic shapes permitted. The others leapt forward in pursuit.

The massed shapes Owen saw around him grew fewer and less intricate, the moving things less frequent. Off beyond, the not-space opened outward into vastness, and the roaring around him took on a new and more threatening note. It reminded him a little of great waterfalls he'd heard, and a little of the throaty growls of predators about to spring.

All at once the polyhedron and the mass of oblate spheroids veered, pulling him toward a place where a few remaining prism-clusters slid together at an angle. The other shapes hurtled past them and vanished. Then Owen was through, and an instant after that, he knew that they had gone too far.

CHAPTER 7

THE HOUNDS OF TINDALOS

He stood on a pale gray shore, on the edge of a sea of nothingness. An awful light that was not light moved in blurred and shimmering veils, merged into the gray abyss. All around him a tremendous silence shrieked, and there were words in the shrieking, but they were not words that Owen or any other human would ever know.

Asenath was beside him, staring out at the not-light with round eyes. As he watched, she gave him a bleak miserable glance, then crumpled and knelt on the pallid shore. Rachel made a low doleful chirring noise, and then was silent.

From far off, if distance had any meaning in that place beyond existence, a faint ripple stirred the veils. As it flowed past the shore where Owen stood, he sensed something familiar in it. Only when it was gone did he realize that it tasted of the screams of men dying in terror.

Slowly, careful to make no sudden moves, he knelt on the shore beside Asenath. It was just possible, he knew, that the Hounds of Tindalos might not scent them. The arrival of the Radiant force deeper within the realm of angular time might be enough of a distraction to keep the Hounds' attention elsewhere. If they stayed very still for a time …

Off beyond the shimmering veils, something moved.

Owen tried to focus on it, failed. The luminous gray void baffled his senses. Another movement sent ripples moving through the void, closer than the first, and another, closer still. He glanced at Asenath, saw her huddle down, lips moving in a silent desperate prayer.

Then something unfolded itself out of the shimmering not-light and stood facing them.

To call it *mager und durstig* as von Junzt had done, "lean and athirst" as his translator had rendered it, was to miss the essence of the thing utterly, but Owen knew at a glance why they had chosen those words. He could sense the terrible hunger that surged through the shape as it folded and unfolded through impossible angles, raising something that was not a head to contemplate him with things that were not eyes. It wasn't doglike in any imaginable sense, for that matter, but Owen understood just as clearly why the ancient tomes had called it a hound.

Another unfolded itself next to it. A moment later, a third appeared in the same way.

"Dad," said Asenath in an ashen voice, "I'm sorry."

He got to his feet then, stepped forward. All three Hounds turned their not-heads to consider the movement, and Owen felt their cold fetid breath upon his face.

"Dad!" Asenath cried out, appalled, but he gestured suddenly toward her, demanding silence. Memories swirled around him: a summer night in Arkham, familiar faces gathered in a not-yet-familiar living room, and a typed manuscript in Miriam Akeley's hand—

"*Iqhui dlosh odhqlonqh,*" he said aloud.

The Hounds had nothing that corresponded even remotely to expressions, and yet they seemed taken aback. One of them folded itself, and unfolded into manifestation again further off.

Owen drew in an unsteady breath, and said the same words again, louder.

The one that had retreated folded again and was gone. The others paused, then folded themselves and disappeared.

He turned. Asenath was staring at him with a dumbfounded look on her face.

"The sorcerer Eibon put a binding on the Hounds," Owen said then, "so he could go into angular time. Some Lomarian scribe stuck the words in the *Pnakotic Manuscript*, but that got lost everywhere but for the Dreamlands, where Miriam copied it." He shrugged. "I never thought I'd have to face the Hounds, but I memorized that passage, because you just never know."

She found her voice. "But the words—"

"I know." A slow smile spread across his face. "'Be on your way' in the language of Cykranosh. I've wondered for years why Eibon put that story in his book." With a shrug: "Maybe he meant it as a hint."

She stared at him a moment longer, and then got to her feet, flung her arms around him, buried her face in his shoulder, and clung to him, shaking.

He patted her on the back, finally, and looked around at the gray shrieking silences reaching away into indefinite not-light. "We're not safe yet," he said. "Not by a long shot."

She glanced up at him, red-eyed. "Not at all. Belasius thought there were more teams, and I think he's right—I sensed more than just the ones we saw."

"That's standard for them," said Owen. "The others will be further back."

Asenath managed a smile. "Or forward."

"Yeah. And if they can detect you when you jump …"

"I know. They'll be on us the moment we try to go back toward our own time." She pondered, then said, "There might be another way."

He gestured to her to go on. She glanced at the kyrrmi on her shoulder, and some silent communication passed between them.

"To Rachel," Asenath said slowly, "time isn't a straight line. It's a broken circle. There's a narrow gap between what we call the beginning and the end, a gap that can be jumped. I don't think the Radiance knows that. I don't think they can follow if we go that way."

"And you can jump the gap," Owen said.

In response, the kyrrmi chirred. "I think so," said Asenath.

He took that in, said nothing. "I know," she said. "You're thinking I nearly got us killed. But I don't know of any other way to get past the Radiance—and Rachel's sure she can do it."

After a moment, he nodded. "Okay. We can try."

Asenath took his arm, and the world dissolved around him.

As before, he plunged through the seething twilight, and the half-familiar roaring sounded in his ears. He glimpsed, just for a moment, the congeries of iridescent bubbles and the dancing polyhedron that were Asenath and Rachel, but then the angles surrounding him opened outward all at once, to the dim sounds of high shrill flutes and thudding drums. Beyond the angles there was no shape, no sound, no space, no time, no Asenath, no Rachel—

No Owen.

* * *

Finally, after an interval that might have been measured in moments or millennia, the nothingness trickled away. As it vanished, a dim sense of movement found a rhythm, turned gradually into a heartbeat. Other sensations became pressure, texture, temperature, and these coalesced into bare stone pressing against one side of a body, a hot dry wind offering little sustenance to straining lungs. A reflexive act of will became movement, hands clutching at empty air, eyes blinking open. Thought and memory returned last of all.

Owen sat up. He was lying on a flat sheet of rock scored by windblown sand. Around him spread a desolate landscape of dull browns and ochres. Here and there, something that looked like blackish-green moss huddled against the keening wind. The sky was the deep blue of a summer ocean at evening, streaked with high thin clouds and dotted with stars, and something behind him splashed red light across the scene and cast his shadow far across the waste.

He turned, blinked, rubbed his eyes and looked again.

A bloated sun the color of blood, a dozen times larger than the sun he knew, hovered just above the horizon. It was dim enough that he could look at it directly without squinting, but heat poured from it as from the mouth of an open furnace. He stared at it, dazed, and only after a moment noticed the two shapes sprawled on the stone nearby.

He tried to stand, found that his legs would not support him, crawled over to the familiar shapes. As he came close, Rachel sat up, shook herself, and then nuzzled Asenath. Asenath blinked and shifted, saw her father, and then beamed and took his nearest hand in both of hers.

Owen tried to say something, but the thin hot air caught in his throat, and he started coughing. Asenath pointed off to one side, across the stone. Owen could see nothing where she pointed, but he started crawling that way at once, and the others followed him.

He was almost on top of the seam in the stone before he saw it. Before he could go further, Asenath caught his arm, drew him back, then gestured for him to wait while she went ahead of him. He watched as she knelt on the stone before the seam, traced a complex pattern over it with both hands, then glanced back at him with a grin.

In perfect silence, the stone beyond the seam pivoted slowly upwards, revealing an open space beneath. A second glance showed a steep and oddly proportioned stair slanting down into darkness. Asenath clambered onto the stair at once, motioned for Owen to follow. Rachel bounded after them and took her usual place on Asenath's shoulder.

Inside the stairwell, the air wasn't quite so thin, and Owen felt strength returning to his limbs. He got to his feet, picked his way down the stair. Above, the stone pivoted noiselessly back down and shut out the glare of the dying sun. After a moment, Owen's eyes adjusted, and revealed a faint bluish glow trickling out of the stone walls of the stairwell. A low faint hiss announced the coming of yet more breathable air, and Asenath turned to face him, beaming.

"Where are we?" he asked her.

"Not far from the south pole," she said. "I'm pretty sure this used to be Massachusetts, but of course all the continents are in different places now. It's around two billion years after our time. That's what the Tchhcht't think, at least." Owen gave her a blank look, and Asenath said, "The species that lives now. You'll like them—well, once you get used to the way they look."

That got a laugh from Owen. "Fair enough," he said. "I gather they're friends of yours."

Asenath nodded. "Keziah brought me here and showed me how to talk with them."

"Keziah Mason?" When she nodded again: "Did she also teach you Latin?"

"Well, kind of. There's a spell."

He gestured wordlessly down the stair. Rachel chirred at him, and the three of them clambered down steps that clearly had not been designed with human beings in mind.

Maybe five hundred feet below the surface, the stair ended in a many-faceted chamber lit by the indistinct blue glow. To Owen's eyes, none of the facets looked different from the others, but Asenath hurried over to one flat surface, placed both forearms flat on it, and bowed her head.

In answer, two of the facets in another part of the chamber swung slowly open, and a black many-legged creature as tall as a man came through the gap. It looked a little like a spider, a little like a crab, and more than a little like a nightmare, but

Asenath beamed, made a clicking chittering noise at it, and pressed her hands against the creature's mouthparts. It clicked and clattered at her in response, then turned toward Owen, who copied the gesture. The mouthparts, dry and chitinous, pressed against his hands and withdrew.

"Dad, this is Thhc'h," said Asenath. "Her family's guarded the portals of Chhtc'h for a really long time—I think it's been around a quarter of a million years." She chittered at the creature, who responded in what sounded like the same language.

Asenath's eyes went round, and the two of them spoke for another few minutes as Owen looked on and wondered what they were saying. "She's here," she said finally. "Keziah."

The spider-thing clicked at Asenath then, and she looked contrite, made clicking noises in response, turned toward the gap in the walls and gestured to Owen to follow. Together, they went through the gap and into the low twisting tunnel beyond.

* * *

"Thank ye kindly," said the old woman to the spider-thing, and leaned on one of its mandibles as she settled onto the soft floor. "There," she said. "Now we can talk like decent folk." Her harsh laughter whispered back from the baroque angles of the ceiling.

Even if her back had been straight, Keziah Mason would have been a head shorter than Asenath, and age had bent her so far forward that her ears were level with her shoulders. Her face was withered as an old apple, her nose long and hooked, and her hair so thin Owen could see light gleaming off her scalp, but her eyes glinted cold and bright. Her garments, brown and shapeless, reminded him of colonial days, and near her on the floor perched a kyrrmi with a male's thick beard gone mostly gray, regarding all of them with a look that would have been amusement on a human face. Owen recalled his name after a moment: Brown Jenkin.

"I know a fair few things about ye, Goodman Merrill," she said. "This witch-child of yours went gadding about with me for a twelvemonth, and told me a story or two betimes."

"Did you know we'd be here?" Asenath asked her.

"Nay, child," said the old witch. "I knew a long time afore now that ye'd have cause sometime to flee to this lattermost age of the world, wherefore I brought ye here." She glanced at Asenath. "And ye quaked like new-made pudding to see those ye greet now as dear friends."

"I was scared," Asenath admitted.

"So ye were. 'Tis a waste of breath teaching the lore to any who can't bear a little fright." Brown Jenkin let out a chirr that sounded uncomfortably like a chuckle. "But when our paths might bring us both here thereafter," the witch went on, "nay, that I couldn't know beforehand."

She laughed her harsh laugh again, and turned to Owen. "Well, then, Goodman Merrill! Ye have more courage than most, to sit so calm before such a witch as half the folk of His Majesty's colony of Massachusetts-Bay were used to fear."

Owen gave her an amused look and said, "I've had the company of quite a few witches, Goody Mason, and haven't been hurt by it yet."

The old woman's eyes gleamed at him. "Aye, there's good cause for that. The young goddess set her mark upon ye, that's plain, and the old goddess traced the Voorish Sign over ye. The mark of the young goddess would keep any witch from harming ye, and the Voorish Sign—why, some see it and some smell it, but none will harm man or maid that bears it."

She turned to Asenath. "So ye tried to reach Arkham the way I told ye?"

"I couldn't do it," Asenath admitted. "Every time I tried the way was blocked—and they hunted us all the way to the beginning of time."

"I was afeared o' that. 'Twas wise of ye to leap to time's end. If ye go quick to the time ye hope to reach, why, ye may yet be able to do the thing."

"And if that doesn't work?" Asenath asked.

"Then hope's at an end for ye." The old witch shrugged. "That's a thing plenty o' folk have to bear withal."

In the silence that followed, Brown Jenkin padded over to Asenath's side, and chirred something at Rachel; Rachel bounded down from Asenath's shoulder, and the two of them crouched nearly nose to nose, talking in low chuffing sounds. Owen considered the old witch, and said, "I wonder if you have any advice for us, Goody Mason."

She blinked as though her thoughts had been elsewhere. "Eh? Why, yes, I do. Make the first leap ye take the longest, so far as Tsan-Chan if ye may, and then another to the right time but some other place close by. Ye can leap from there, or it may be ye can walk." The witch laughed. "I'd go along with ye, but 'tis not for me to see New-England 'til my time comes to die."

She met Owen's startled look with a little smile. "Aye, I know what manner of end I'll get. I'll have my neck wrung by a young man I was fool enough to think could learn of me, and that'll happen though I know it already. Does that surprise ye? There's a price for every power, and when ye step out o' time ye lose some deal of power to change what happens in it. That, and ye know what ye can't change." She laughed again. "That's hard betimes."

Later, after the witch had given them more good advice, she whistled Brown Jenkin back from some hidden corner of the room, accepted a hug and tearful thanks from Asenath and went hobbling elsewhere. Thhc'h brought them water in strange seven-sided troughs—"humans can't eat anything the Tchhcht't eat," Asenath explained, "so this will have to do." A little later Rachel came out of what Owen guessed was the same hidden corner looking ruffled and damp. Owen considered the kyrrmi and then sent a questioning look to his daughter, who blushed.

"She and Brown Jenkin got really friendly while Keziah and I were traveling together," Asenath said, "and she's old enough to breed so I let her go ahead. I'm pretty sure she's going to have a pup by him." With a little shrug: "I'll outlive Rachel, of course, but this way even if things go really badly I'll have a kyrrmi when she's gone."

Owen considered his daughter for a time, remembering one of the things Keziah Mason had said, and then asked, "Do you know how you'll die?"

"Of course," Asenath said. "I knew that as soon as Keziah took me through time." Then, looking at nothing Owen could see: "I'll be very old, and I'll see my fourth great-grandchild for the first time, and that night I'll go to sleep and not wake up."

"That's actually rather comforting," Owen said.

"Oh, I know." She didn't look comforted, though. "The only thing is that I can't tell where I'll be—not even in which lesser Earth." In a low voice: "It may not be ours."

He thought about that later, as they lay down in their clothes on the floor to get what sleep they could. Though he'd been through time, when he turned his mind toward his death he could sense nothing but uncertain shapes in darkness. As sleep took him, he realized what it meant: his death was not yet settled. The one thing he could tell was that it might be very close.

* * *

They woke after a few hours. A conversation with Thhc'h revealed that Keziah Mason had already gone her way. "She's like that," Asenath said in a voice that reminded Owen briefly of the little girl she'd been. "She knows we won't see each other again, and she hates goodbyes."

A little more water had to serve for breakfast. Asenath said her farewells to Thhc'h and pressed arms to mandibles, and nothing remained then but the journey. "Ready?" Asenath said, once she'd drawn a diagram in chalk on the wall of the cavern.

Owen gave her a wry glance and said, "No, but that hasn't stopped me yet."

She laughed, took his arm, and pulled him into the fourth dimension.

Once again the strange geometries and writhing things hurtled past, and the shrieking, roaring confusion of sound broke over Owen. The half-familiar shapes he knew to be Asenath and Rachel leapt ahead, drawing him along through what seemed like an immense distance. This time, though, the terrible presence did not appear and no tumbling masses came leaping after them. Finally two incomprehensibly colored planes came together at a sharp angle and he tumbled through a moment of delirium into a recognizable scene.

He was kneeling on a terrace of stone the color of onyx, with a railing of the same substance close by, carved in the form of a procession of ornate wingless dragons. He blinked and rubbed his eyes, and slowly stood up. Beyond the railing, vast pyramidal buildings of the same onyx hue rose up all around, catching the golden light of the westering sun on their upper slopes. Terraces surrounded them at intervals, and countless windows glowed. For a moment, gazing at the black pyramids, Owen thought he knew where they were, and cold dread seized him. A glance upwards, though, showed blue sky darkening toward evening, marked here and there with high mares'-tails of cloud, not the blind white sky and black stars of dim Carcosa.

"Oh, good," Asenath said behind him. He turned, saw her sitting on the black pavement, reaching out an arm for Rachel to climb. "I hoped we'd be able to get here in a single jump."

"Where are we?" Owen asked. "Or when?"

That got him a sudden grin. "Both. This is New York City about three thousand years after our time. It's called Yueh-Shi now, and it's the capital of the empire of Tsan-Chan."

Owen looked around again, took what reassurance he could from the life all around him: proof that whether the Nhhngr came down or not, someone would survive and rebuild. "Keziah took you here," he said to Asenath.

"Of course. I've got friends here, too."

Owen went to the railing. Far below, canals wove in complex patterns about the feet of the pyramids, and the scent of salt water rose on a sultry breeze. He was still pondering the cityscape when a voice he didn't recognize spoke words he didn't recognize either. He turned, to see an elderly man in robes of dark maroon standing at a nearby door, smiling at them both.

Asenath answered haltingly in the same language, and the man laughed. "Very good," he said in English, with that slight stiffness that marks a language learned from books. "You have a good memory. Perhaps you will introduce me to—"

"My father," said Asenath. "Owen Merrill of Arkham. Dad, this is Yiang-li of An-Fang. He's a philosopher."

"Merely a humble student of certain obscure branches of ancient lore," said Yiang-li. He motioned the two of them to follow him.

The room inside the door was the same onyx black as the pavement and the pyramids outside. Carpets worked in strange arabesques of gold and red covered the floor, and vermilion scrolls written in a flowing unfamiliar script hung on the walls. Yiang-li waved them to a low table in the middle of the room, busied himself at a niche in the wall from which the sounds of hissing steam and pouring water made themselves heard. Owen and Asenath sat on the floor, and Rachel glanced around uneasily and let out a low uncertain chirr.

"So," said Yiang-li as he returned with a teapot and little round cups without handles. "Your teacher told me," he said to Asenath, "that when I next saw you, you would be in some danger, and in need of counsel. Perhaps—" A motion of his head deftly included Owen. "—you will allow me to be of assistance." He poured tea, handed cups around.

"Please," said Asenath. "We're trying to get back to our own time, and there's a being of the outer voids who keeps trying to catch me when I try to get there, because of something I'm carrying. And—and there are others who've been hunting us."

Yiang-li nodded, as though none of this came as any surprise. "Let us begin with the Ma oracle." He rose smoothly, went to a cabinet, returned with a lidded iron bowl and a thick book with a handsewn binding. Owen watched, fascinated, as the philosopher took small stone disks out of the bowl, one after another, and laid them out in a pattern Owen had seen before.

"The seventh *fu*, the fourth game, the eighteenth variation," Yiang-li said then. He paged through the book and read: "'The straight path is closed but an indirect path is not. It is wise to persevere.'" He turned a page. "And the commentary: 'When this variation appears, opposition cannot be overcome directly. Another route must be taken. Help will be found in high places. It is wise to follow advice already given. It is wise to persevere even in the face of danger.'" He glanced up from the book. "That is promising, at least. I trust you have received advice."

"Yes," said Owen, remembering Keziah Mason's words. "And some of it had to do with an indirect route." He considered the stones on the table.

"You are familiar with the oracle?" Yiang-li asked.

Owen glanced up at him. "I think so. It wasn't quite the same in my time."

That earned him an unexpected smile. "Indeed? Perhaps you will satisfy my curiosity. Our traditions have it that in ancient times those who used the Ma oracle learned chants or songs instead of—" His gesture indicated the book.

"They called it the Mao games," said Owen. "Yes, I heard some of the chants."

"Often enough to recall them? No? A pity. I will hope for more travelers from your time." Then, with an odd look: "Or perhaps I will see how it is done in the Green Islands, where your people went when mine came from Chung-Kuo—I think those were called the Green Land in your time. I went there once. Twice, rather, but I only recall the once." He paused. "I was in search of old tales the people there told about Yeh-ni the greatest of sorceresses, Ah-wan the prophet, and their great and good friends. It did not occur to me to ask about the Ma oracle."

Owen processed that. "Yeh-ni the greatest of sorceresses" made a sudden dizzying sense, but not the other, despite the similarity of names. I'm no prophet, he thought, and the next thought came at once: fortunately.

Yiang-li glanced up apologetically. "But I ramble. Perhaps you will tell me more about the being of the outer voids, and the ones who hunt you."

* * *

When they finished telling him their story, Yiang-li nodded and said, "You will need to leave soon. Your teacher's advice is wise, and I will add this: seek a place you know well. Thus you may enter your own time more easily. If you have a chance, that is where it is found."

"I can do that," said Asenath. Rachel chirred in agreement.

"How soon should we go?" Owen asked the philosopher.

"Soon. This is a night of festivity, and certain ceremonies will be performed once night falls. Those will make it difficult for anyone to perceive your departure. I—"

A dim rolling like distant thunder came through the open door. Owen glanced that way, wondering if a storm had blown in, but the last red glow of the setting sun still gleamed on the summits of pyramids high up, and the first pale stars were visible beyond them. As he listened, the rolling broke apart into a complex rhythmic beat, and a high sharp rhythm joined them.

A smile creased Yiang-li's face. "Ah," he said. "The drummers are eager, and will not wait for darkness. I cannot blame them."

The dull note of a muted horn sounded above the drum-beats, undulating up and down in fluid arcs. A second horn joined it, and a third. Yiang-li got to his feet, motioned with his head toward the door. Owen and Asenath followed him out onto the terrace. High above, sunset guttered out on the peaks of the highest pyramids. On other terraces, people had begun to gather.

"What's the occasion?' Owen asked their host.

Yiang-li smiled. "Long ago, so our legends say, certain arch-sorcerers set out to bind the gods with their spells. Of course things went amiss during the little while the gods were bound, and finally certain people in the land of Chung-Kuo fled into deep caverns to save their lives. When they left the caverns and found the arch-sorcerers gone and the world fit to live in, they rejoiced. On the nineteenth day of the tenth moon, their descendants still rejoice." He gestured expansively. "A thousand years have passed since Tsan-Chan won its freedom from the motherland, and now our airship navies rule the skies and Chung-Kuo and a hundred other lands dwell under our protection, but we still remember."

Owen took that in. "Do you happen to know how long the people stayed in the caverns?"

"Scholars dispute that," said Yiang-li. "Some say they dwelt in the caverns for hundreds of years. Others say it was but a few days or weeks." He shrugged. "It was a troubled time, and little is known for certain about it."

Owen nodded in response. More musicians joined in, putting further conversation out of reach. The last sunlight vanished and the stars in the eastern sky gleamed more brightly. Owen sensed voor in motion, sweeping out in complex wave-patterns from inside one of the nearby pyramids. Yiang-li apparently sensed it too, for he smiled and bowed to the two of them. Asenath beamed and bowed to him, and Owen repeated the gesture. Then, as the philosopher went to the railing to watch the festivities and young people in orange robes began to dance on nearby terraces, Asenath led her father to a flat space of wall where Owen could just make out the faint traces of chalk marks on the stone. A few moments were enough to draw the angles again.

Asenath beckoned for him to bring his ear within range, and when he did so, she cupped her hands around her mouth and said into his ear, "The oracle said go to a high place. I'm going to take us to the highest place I know near Arkham." Owen nodded, then let her take him by the arm again and pull him at right angles to all earthly dimensions.

* * *

He was almost used to it by then: the unearthly shrieking and roaring, the tumbling prismatic shapes. Once again, the nameless presence and the negation teams were nowhere to be sensed—and then, just before the journey ended, he felt the presence again, at a distance, as though watching. The angle between planes loomed up before him, and he dove through it, braced himself in the moment of delirium that followed.

This time he landed on his feet and looked around as soon as his head cleared. The sun shone down from a blue sky, and the still air tasted of salt. Off beyond the pines, the land swept down into rumpled hills he knew, and steeples rose over distant roofs. It took only a moment for him to recognize where he was: well up on the shoreward side of Kingsport Head, where he'd come with Asenath and Barnabas in summers past. Arkham was only ten miles away.

Another moment passed before the harsh sounds further down the slope registered. Reflexes took over. He dropped into a crouch, drew his revolver and clicked off the safety in a single motion. Asenath gave him a startled look, then heard the sounds as well, blanched, and huddled down, twisting her fingers together in some witch's spell. A brief silence, and then the same sounds came echoing up from under the pines. It had been decades since Owen's tour of duty in Iraq, but the rattle of three-round bursts from assault rifles echoed in his bones.

"Mr. Merrill!" A half-familiar voice sounded off to one side. He risked a glance that way, spotted Justin Geoffrey's face above tangled brush, the gesture waving him over. A quick motion of his own sent Asenath running that way, low and fast. He waited, gun at the ready, until she was behind the bushes, and then turned and ran for it.

Past the brush the ground slumped into a sheltered hollow. Three people crouched there, and Owen recognized them all: Michael Dyson, Justin Geoffrey, and the girl he'd seen in Joseph Curwen's house. He skidded to a halt near them, said, "What are you doing here?"

"Waiting for you," Geoffrey said. "Merlin brought us."

"How did he know we were coming here?"

The poet gave him a wry glance. "You ever find out, you be sure and tell me."

Owen nodded, conceding. "Where is he?"

"Somewhere uphill," said Dyson. "We're in a hell of a mess." He motioned down the hill. "We got here around an hour ago. Not long after that a bunch of choppers landed past the pond about two miles north of us."

"Hooper's Pond," Owen said.

"Yeah. If they were following standard procedure they landed five squads. They just about had enough time to secure the LZ when that started." He motioned with his head downslope. "When I was in Afghanistan I'd have said both sides were taking a beating."

The rolling boom of an explosion broke over them then. Owen risked a glance past the brush, saw black smoke surging upward from somewhere a mile or so down the slope.

"Who's on the other side?" he asked once the roar of the blast faded.

"Merlin says it's the Yellow Sign," the girl said. "They want the book just as bad as the Radiance, so whoever wins, we lose.

Merlin's gone to find a way out." She turned to Asenath. "He said you can't go to Arkham through the hidden angles of space—and he told us why."

Owen didn't have to ask. The land sloped off to the north, marked with the traces of three centuries, whispering to him of a far vaster history he knew only in part. Somewhere that way, too close for comfort, a vast cold presence loomed up unseen against the autumn sky, facing them and watching.

CHAPTER 8

THE BLACK GOAT
OF THE WOODS

He took that in, then moved to a place where he could keep an eye on Asenath and still watch the slope below them. That also put the other three in sight. Justin Geoffrey and the girl—Merlin had called her Vanessa, he thought he remembered—hadn't changed noticeably since he'd seen them in Providence. That made the change in Dyson all the more striking. The man looked haggard and drawn, but there was more to the change than that, more than a long journey over strange roads. Owen wondered where Merlin had taken him and what he'd seen.

Another burst of gunfire sounded down the slope. Then, off beneath the pines, brief furtive glimpses of movement showed themselves. "Here we go," Dyson said. Asenath bit her lip, and then wove her fingers together and murmured something under her breath.

The movements under the pines grew closer. Owen muttered a spell of his own, closed his eyes to let vision give way to the voor-sense, and felt six centers of the life force thread their way uphill past the great surging fountains of voor he recognized as trees. It took more effort to see in both worlds at once, but he managed it, saw the voor-traces merge with the glimpses of movement. That would give him an edge if it came to shooting, he knew—but enough of an edge to make his revolver the equal of assault rifles? He hoped he didn't have to find out.

Then the mist began to gather. A quick glance showed it flowing in from the mouth of the Miskatonic off to their right. A second glance showed Asenath, bent over her knotted fingers, all her concentration focused on the spell. Vague and undefined, the mist rounded edges and blurred anything close to the ground, left the pines and the figures who moved beneath them silhouetted against shapeless whiteness. Owen braced his gun hand with the other, threw his awareness into the voor-sense as the first of the figures came close enough to be seen clearly.

"Wait," said Dyson, his voice less than a whisper. "I know him. Let me talk to him."

"Merlin warned you," said Vanessa, just as quietly.

"I'm going to risk it." He moved off to one side—drawing fire away from them, Owen knew—and then called out, "Greg! Greg Kowalsky. It's Mike Dyson."

The man beneath the pines turned toward him, fast, a pistol rising. "Prove it."

"Last December," said Dyson. "Two bottles of cheap gin and that cute little number from the Directorate of Personnel who cleaned our clocks playing Texas hold'em."

A moment's silence, then: "What the hell are you doing here?"

"You know goddamn well what I'm doing here. You got anywhere to go when the Nhhngr brings the boom down? Of course you don't."

Kowalsky said nothing. Behind him, the other five figures approached warily.

"I didn't want to do this. You know that. But if there's going to be an Earth left a few weeks from now, it's the only choice we've got. You know what happened to Project 638."

"Yeah," Kowalsky admitted.

"So it's the other side, or we all go gray and crazy before we die. Greg—" His voice cracked. "Listen to me. We were wrong.

Not just a little bit wrong. Wrong about everything that matters. All that crap about aliens? The Great Old Ones aren't aliens. They really are gods."

"They're controlling your mind," Kowalski snapped.

"No," Dyson said. "The bugs are controlling yours."

An instant later, the pistol in Kowalsky's hand barked out an answer.

Owen had been covering the other members of the negation team. Before he could draw a bead on Kowalsky, two guns roared next to Owen, a fraction of a second apart. Kowalsky staggered back and dropped. Owen braced himself for the firefight he expected, but the rest of the negation team didn't open fire. They seemed to be staring at Kowalsky's corpse.

That was as much as Owen needed. He scrambled over to Dyson, found Asenath there before him. The two of them turned him over, found the bullet hole in the middle of his forehead. Owen stifled a profanity, stared. Even an expert marksman, he knew, couldn't make such a shot through mist and the cover of the brush. Blind chance? It seemed too much to credit.

"Point those guns somewhere else," Justin Geoffrey said then. He'd risen to his feet, a long-barreled revolver smoking in each hand. "You can't kill me, but I can goddamn well kill every one of you. Try me."

The figures in camouflage fatigues didn't lower their muzzles, but they didn't open fire. Ignoring them, the poet went through a gap in the brush and crossed to where Kowalsky lay sprawled. "Well, lookee here," he said. "Guess what was giving you your orders." He thrust one of his revolvers through his belt, stooped, took hold of Kowalsky's face, and pulled.

The face came away in his hand.

Owen barely registered his daughter's sudden shocked inhalation. All his attention was on the shape in Geoffrey's hand: on one side, the perfect image of a human face; on the other, wires and levers of metal, touched here and there with a green fluid that was nothing like human blood.

"You want to find out what happened to Greg Kowalsky," Geoffrey said then, "you can ask the goddamn fungi from Yuggoth. I bet they didn't leave much." He threw the mask aside, drew the revolver. "Now get the hell out of here."

Owen didn't expect them to go, but they glanced at each other, backed away, and then turned and ran for it, heading off to the left, toward the old one-lane road that led to Kingsport. Geoffrey watched them go, and then hurried back to the hollow. "Mike?" he asked. Owen shook his head, and the poet replied, "Shit." Then, as though he'd just noticed Asenath: "Sorry, Miss."

"I thought you carried a .38," Owen said.

"Just when I was in Europe. It's a runty little excuse for a gun." He patted the two long-barrelled .45s thrust through his belt. "These, now, that's what I grew up shooting."

Another flurry of gunshots echoed up from further down the slope. "If they knew the right words, Mr. Geoffrey," said Asenath, "you'd be a pile of dust."

Geoffrey grinned. "Oh, sure, but they didn't know that." He turned. "Where's Vanessa?"

She was further up the slope, walking alongside a short, oddly dressed figure Owen recognized at once. Their conversation stopped as they reached the hollow.

"I did not think he would heed my warning," said Merlin. Then, to Owen and Asenath: "There is still hope for you. Your path leads upward." He gestured toward Kingsport Head.

"Is there any way we can keep his body safe?' Vanessa asked then, motioning toward Dyson. "If things work out and my brother comes back, I'd like to revive him."

"Your brother?" Owen asked, startled.

She grinned. "The best kid brother any girl ever had. I was eleven and Charles was six when I died of meningitis. He told me that's why he decided to followed Joseph's instructions, and I was the second person he revived, right after Joseph.

Yeah, I don't show my age." With a little laugh: "Another thirty years and I'll look old enough to buy a drink."

"You must go," Merlin said then. "Follow the ridge, and stay close to the cliff that falls down to the river. Seek the heights always. One awaits you there."

"You'll be okay?" Owen asked him.

"Once the *Ghorl Nigral* is elsewhere? Of course."

"Git," Geoffrey said, and slapped Owen on the shoulder. Owen nodded and turned, and he and Asenath hurried up the slope as yet another flurry of shots sounded downslope, closer.

* * *

The trees thinned as they scrambled uphill, gave way finally to scrub blueberry bushes and sparse grass. To either side, the ridge narrowed, so that it took only a moment to glance from the steep tumbling slope that fell to Neptune's Head and then down cliff upon cliff to ruined Kingsport, to the sheer precipice that plunged down to the waters of the Miskatonic River far below. Up ahead, the peak of an ancient cottage rose up against the white emptiness of the sky. That stirred something in Owen's memory, but too much of his attention had to go to his footing to leave him the leisure to chase it down. He followed Asenath as she hurried on.

She stopped suddenly, and he came up alongside her. Before them a chasm maybe ten feet deep barred the way. A few quick words, and then he took her hands, lay flat, braced her as she lowered herself as far as she could and then dropped. He turned, lowered himself, and fell, landing on the slanting floor. By then Asenath was crawling up a narrow defile in the far wall. He followed, trying not to notice the vast emptiness to either side.

He came out of the chasm and stopped. Before them stood a cottage with walls of gray mortared stone and a high-peaked slate roof. No door opened on the landward side of the cottage, just two lattice windows with bull's-eye panes set in antique leading. To either side a narrow ledge of stone separated the walls of the house from mist-filled space.

Asenath gave him an uneasy look. "This is—"

"I know." He knew the legends about a strange high house in the mist atop Kingsport Head. "But I don't think there's anywhere else we can go."

As though in answer, the click of an opening latch sounded from one of the windows, and it swung open. From within, a great black-bearded face peered out at them. "No, there is not," the man said, in a voice surprisingly soft. "Come in. I have awaited you a very long time."

Owen glanced at Asenath, then approached the window. A brown hand reached out, at once inviting and commanding, and Owen took it and let himself be helped over the sill.

The room inside looked as though it had stood unchanged since the first settlers from Europe landed in Kingsport harbor. Black oak wainscoting rose to waist height, with plaster above it that bulged and sagged; blackened beams framed the ceiling and scarred oaken planks covered the floor. Furnishings that might have been new when Queen Bess sat on England's throne stood against the walls, and a fire of driftwood burned on the hearth, the salt in the wood staining the flames blue and yellow by turns.

The black-bearded man helped Asenath in, then closed and locked the window. "You will be safe here," he said in the same quiet voice. "Yes, I know what hunts you, and why."

Owen considered the man, wondered what he was. Human? It didn't seem likely, not with the voor that pooled and eddied around him like currents in the deep ocean.

As though he'd heard Owen's thought, the man asked, "Do you not know who I am?" When Owen and Asenath both shook their heads, he laughed a low quiet laugh. "Your species has a short memory," he said. "Once every sailor on every sea knew of me, and in time to come every sailor will know of me again. Still, I have dwelt here in seclusion some little while."

"You said you've been waiting for us," Owen said then.

"I did indeed. I know you have little time, but it would be well for us to talk."

"I read of a man named Thomas Olney," said Owen. "He came to this cottage a long time ago, and only an empty shell of him left it."

"He asked that of me," said the man. "That an image of him would carry all the burdens he had taken up, while he himself dwelt with me. I granted him that."

"Where is he now?" Asenath asked.

"With my father in the Great Deep," the man told her.

That was what unlocked the chambers of Owen's memory. Ludwig Prinn's *Mysteries of the Worm* spoke of hoary Nodens, Lord of the Great Deep, and something in von Junzt hinted that the Lord of the Great Deep and the Black Goat of the Woods had mated in dim prehuman times, giving rise to a Great Old One that was neither quite of the greater Earth nor quite of the spaces beyond it. "Basatan," he said aloud, recalling the name.

"Not so short a memory," said Basatan. "It is well. There are two things you must know. Do not judge the first until you have heard the second." When Owen nodded: "The first is that the King has ordained that any who find a certain book must bring it to him or face his wrath."

Owen froze, but kept his reaction off his face.

"The second," said Basatan, "is that I will not be obeying the King's command." The Great Old One's voice remained soft, but something stirred in it, cold and unyielding as the great gray crag beneath them. "You know of the old quarrel. I am far from the only one among us who wills that it should end, and the thing you carry has the power to end it."

He leaned forward. "I am my father's child, and that gives me the power to send you to a place you know, where the veil between the worlds is thin. It is close to a holy place. You must go to that place quickly, for if there is safety for you anywhere, it is there. Do you understand?"

They both nodded. "Good," said Basatan. "Then it is time for you to go." One brown hand gestured and the world tore open.

It was not like those other journeys. The confusion of sound, the impossible shapes: those had no part in it. The world simply gaped, twisted incomprehensibly, and closed.

* * *

Owen found himself in near-darkness. He groped for solidity, found it: a flat hard surface beneath him, cold and rough to his hands, vaguely familiar.

"Dad?"

Asenath was close, then. "Right here," he said, and turned toward the sound. Off in the middle distance, dim light filtered through gaps. As his eyes adjusted, he made out a flat gray ceiling crossed by cracked and crumbling beams, a flat gray floor crossed by fading yellow lines, dark shapes that he suddenly realized were the rusting hulks of abandoned cars, and another shape, picking itself up from the floor, that was Asenath, with Rachel on her shoulder.

"I don't know where we are," she said. "Rachel's trying to figure out."

"A parking garage." He sat up, wondered why the voor around him seemed so familiar. Then, all at once, memories came crashing into his thoughts: images of gunfire, ancient sorcery, and a gate torn in the fabric of reality. That was when he knew where Basatan had sent them.

"We're in the old West Campus Parking Garage," he said then, hauling himself to his feet. "In Arkham. Come on. I know where we're supposed to go."

"Where?"

"The white stone."

He could hear her breath catch. "Okay," she said.

A few moments later they were out from under the cracked concrete mass of the garage, running up the wooded lower slopes of Meadow Hill. Stark leafless trees rose above them, clawed at low gray clouds. His heavy footfalls and her lighter ones rustled in the fallen leaves. Owen's breath burst from his lips in white clouds, and the air burnt with cold. All at once it was hard for him to be sure that he wasn't about to meet his own youthful self, sprinting toward the same destination. He kept running, and Asenath ran alongside him, lithe and quick as a deer.

They headed up the whaleback slopes of Meadow Hill. Old reflexes made him run low and fast, brought every movement crashing into his mind: smoke rising from Arkham chimneys, a lone seagull wheeling above the campus buildings behind him. Somewhere close by—he could feel it with brutal clarity—the presence that hunted them turned suddenly, noticing them.

Then the crest was past, and all at once they seemed to pass into another world, far from Arkham. Ahead, a grassy slope dotted with boulders left by some Ice Age glacier sloped down toward the gash of the ravine, edged with brush. Asenath sprinted ahead, and he picked up his pace. Despite the spreading ache in his muscles and the pounding of his heart, he managed to keep up with her. The presence that hunted them drew close, he was sure of it.

They veered to one side to round a mass of rock and brush, pelted recklessly down the side of the ravine. Ahead was the white stone, a vaguely cubical mass of hard pale rock rising up from the grass. They reached it moments later, slowed.

"And here you are," said a voice in the middle distance to one side, bland and genial.

Owen turned suddenly. It had been twenty years since he'd last heard that voice but he knew it instantly. The figure at the far end of the ravine was just as familiar, and twenty years had turned the hair gray but had done nothing to fill the vacancies behind the smooth facade.

"Clark Noyes," he said. He kept his surprise off his face. How could the vast shadow that had hunted them have been that of a single Radiant adept?

"Of course. Good afternoon, Mr. Merrill." The newcomer made a strangled sound in his throat. It sounded as though Noyes had forgotten what laughter was, and made only a token effort to remember. "You've given us a great deal of trouble over the last twenty years."

"Thank you," said Owen grimly. "That's quite a compliment."

He felt rather than saw Asenath's fingers twine in a spell. Noyes made a casual gesture, as though bored, and a ring of pallid flames traced itself suddenly on the ground around him, rose waist-high. "Please," he said in a dismissive tone. "Your witchcraft has no power over me."

"Big words," said Owen.

"Do you think I can't match them with actions?" Noyes said. "Think again." He gestured again and the flames vanished. "I know all the Seven Lost Signs of Terror and all the Words of Fear. The weak gods of Earth have no power against those, and neither do you."

Owen knew the meaning of those words, but kept his face from showing it. "So much for the supremacy of reason."

"Reason uses the tools it must," said Noyes in the same bland voice. Something moved behind the emptiness of his face, though, and it had nothing human in it. "While you dabbled in tomes that time has turned to nonsense, I mastered the lore of the *Ghorl Nigral* and called up one of the great powers of the nether realms. With its help I summoned Avalzant, the Warden of the Fiery Change, to carry me across the abysses of space. I walked beneath the rays of Yamil Zacra and the black flame of Yuzh. I climbed the mountain named Psollantha, terrace by terrace, overcoming powers you can't even dream of, and at the summit I faced the guardian Vermazbor and vanquished him. Now? The Earth and all its creatures are mine."

"You aren't Clark Noyes any more," Owen said then.

The bland expressionless face turned toward him. Behind the blank gaze he glimpsed the thing he'd seen a moment before, a cold ravening hunger that had nothing human in it, a will that filled Noyes' hollow shell the way a hand fills a glove: the thing that had chased them. "I am beyond anything you can imagine," Noyes' voice said. "You knelt before those feeble powers you call the Great Old Ones. Now you will kneel to me."

* * *

A silence followed, and then a voice broke it. It wasn't Owen's or Asenath's. It came from behind the two of them, and with it came an animal scent, rank and goatish.

"No, Thasaidon." It was a woman's voice, redolent with the subtle harmonies of age. "Do you think we weren't aware of this plan of yours? Think again."

"It hardly matters," Clark Noyes' voice said. "You have no power over me, not now, not while you remain bound by the spells of mere humans. All I needed was a way to this world and a living vessel to inhabit, and this creature provided me with both. A tempting opportunity, you must admit." A ghastly croaking sound tried to imitate a laugh, and failed. "A hollow husk of a human being, stripped of everything that might interfere with my will. I stepped into the empty space prepared for me. This lesser Earth is mine now."

Shub-Ne'hurrath's laugh, low and melodious, made the sound Noyes' throat had made all the more hideous by comparison.

"You dare to mock me?" said the thing that inhabited Noyes. Then, horribly, the shrill tones of another's greed burst through the blandness of Noyes' voice. "The book is here. I sense it. Give it to me or face my wrath. Give it to me now."

Asenath stiffened suddenly as a compulsion seized her, and she pulled the Book of Night from her purse. Owen tried to move, but his body would not obey him. Before Asenath could hold the book out to Noyes, though, the Black Goat took it from her hands and held it up.

Noyes lunged for the book, or tried to. His feet did not move. Startled, Owen saw that they were feet no longer. In their place, gnarled roots covered with coarse bark sank through the grass, plunged deep into the soil. Noyes glanced down as well, and then flung his hands skyward and opened his mouth to utter an incantation.

He never spoke it. Surging up from the ground, a sudden writhing change seized him. His body twisted and stiffened, his hands splayed in agony, and the bland emptiness of his face shattered at last, gave way to stark white-eyed terror.

"No, Thasaidon," Shub-Ne'hurrath said again, and an inhuman calm moved in her voice. "I know your weakness as well as you do. You have no power in this world, except through a living creature that permits you to possess it, and what that creature cannot do, you cannot do."

Noyes' face writhed in slow motion. His mouth gaped, but what came out of it was not a spell. It was his tongue, at least at first, until it thickened and lengthened, and brown cracked bark covered it. As it grew, it forced Noyes' mouth open to an impossible angle, and then his jaw and face began to flow into the growing trunk.

The Black Goat stood taller than before, and horns curled back from her brow. "You know the Seven Lost Signs of Terror and the Words of Fear, but this creature of yours shall never again have hands to make the Signs or a voice to speak the Words. Everything that lives in this world belongs to me, and what I gave to Clark Noyes, I take back. As for you, Thasaidon, stay or go, it matters not. You will not have what you wish, not now, not for long ages to come."

Something changed in the air, impalpable but definite—or was it something in Noyes? An instant passed before Owen was sure of the latter, and knew what had happened: the being that inhabited Noyes had gone.

The Black Goat of the Woods laughed again: a soft quiet laughter, the most terrible sound Owen had ever heard. "Hear me, Clark Noyes." Her voice set the air trembling like summer thunder. "The thing you called into yourself has departed. You thought you could master it. It mastered you, and it has discarded you now that you no longer serve its purpose. It will be back, but ages will pass before then, and on that day you will not even be a memory."

Owen glanced at her, then at Noyes, whose clothing had begun to split as his body thickened, whose arms had begun to split too as each finger became the end of a branch. From the branches, something green emerged; a moment passed before Owen recognized pine needles.

"Hear me, Clark Noyes." Though it shook the air, Shub-Ne'hurrath's voice stayed soft, meditative. "There was a time when no human would have dreamed of defying one of the Great Old Ones to her face. It has been too long since we last taught humanity an object lesson, and I thank you, Clark Noyes, for offering yourself.

"This is your doom. As I have remade you, so you shall remain. If the Nhhngr descends, you will die slowly with the rest of this world. If you are spared, you will stand here for years to come. Summers and winters will pass, while you sense only what a tree senses and act only as a tree acts, until finally the salt waters rise to touch your roots and release you into the hands of death. And all the while, you will remember what you were, and what you are, and why."

The last traces of human skin on Noyes turned into bark as Owen watched, and a small pine stood before him, draped in torn rags, its trunk shaped like a man writhing in torment.

Then the Black Goat of the Woods turned toward the two humans who remained.

"Grandmother," said Asenath. What communion passed between them Owen could not tell, but after a moment the head nodded once. A huge clawed hand reached downward, holding out something to Asenath. Only when she took it did Owen realize that it was the *Ghorl Nigral*.

"Give it to Tsathoggua's daughter," said the Black Goat.

"I will, Grandmother," said Asenath. "Thank you."

The immense dark shape spread outward to embrace the cosmos. "They are waiting for you," said a voice that seemed to come from everywhere and nowhere. "Go."

Then she was gone. Owen turned away from the terrible frozen writhing of the tree that had been Clark Noyes. "We'd better hurry," he said to his daughter.

"I can do better than that," said Asenath. She reached for Owen's arm, pulled him suddenly. An instant of whirling confusion passed, and they stood in front of their home on Powder Mill Street, with the familiar gambrel roofs of old Arkham rising around them. As Owen reached for the knob, he heard a curious rhythm like muffled drums, a high keening sound like shrill flutes. He tensed, then recognized the sounds: the clapping and chanting the Innsmouth folk had used for music when they were too poor to afford instruments. He pulled open the door, and he and Asenath came pelting into the entry, breathless.

* * *

The chant faltered and stopped as they came in. "Laura?" Owen called. "We're back." Familiar faces turned toward him, astonished and delighted, and a dozen voices answered, but he had ears for only one. He crossed to Laura, bent to kiss her, drew in the familiar salt scent and tried to believe that things would work out after all.

"I think that's our practice for today," Sybil Romero said, smiling. "Owen, Sennie, welcome home." Owen thanked her, and she turned to Laura. "Next week?"

"Next week," said Laura. Something troubling showed itself in her voice, and Owen suddenly guessed what it meant.

The next few minutes were a confusion of voices and movements as Laura's students said their goodbyes and left. "We got it," Asenath said, beaming at her mother, once they were gone "We got the *Ghorl Nigral*."

"You—*what?*"

"That's right," Owen told her, grinning. "Do you know where Jenny is? The sooner we can get this to—" He saw the shift in her expression, stopped. "What is it?"

"Nobody knows where Jenny is," said Laura. "The papers you sent came four days ago, and Belinda says Jenny took them up to her study that night. The next morning she was gone, and—and the only message she left was the most terrible news I can imagine."

The guess changed to cold certainty. "The Nhhngr?"

She sagged a little. "Yes. I was dreading having to tell you. How did you find out?"

He began to laugh as the absurdity of it all struck him. "Laura," he said, "I honestly don't expect you to believe this, but I heard it from a renegade negation team officer in the ruins of Sarkomand in the Dreamlands, and the person who got us there was Merlin. Yeah, that Merlin."

Laura, staring, opened her mouth to speak, closed it instead. "Mom, he's not making any of that up," Asenath said. "We've been to some really strange places."

Her mother swallowed visibly, and in a slightly dazed voice said, "So I gather." Then: "Maybe the two of you can tell me what happened—"

The front door rattled open and closed again, and Barnabas came through the entry carrying an armful of old books, a familiar distracted look on his face. He was most of the way to the stair when he glanced up, blinking, and said, "Oh, hi, Dad. Hi, Sennie."

"Busy?" Owen asked him. When Barnabas nodded, Owen went on: "We can talk later."

"Sure thing, Dad." A moment later his footfalls clumped up the stairs.

By the time the attic door opened and shut, Laura had recovered some of her composure. "We've got two hours before we should go to the East Church. There's going to be a community meeting to decide what to do—I called it as soon as I got messages on their way to our friends in Dunwich and Chorazin. Before we go, though, I want to hear what happened to the two of you."

"Do you mind hearing it over lunch?" Owen asked. "We haven't eaten since—" He stopped, realizing there was no way to measure the time that had passed since they'd shared a meal with Lydia and Charles Dexter Ward.

"For a really long time," Asenath said, finishing the sentence for him. "Come on. We can talk while we fix something."

It took most of the two hours for her and Owen to tell their story, in the intervals of making and eating fish soup and chicken salad sandwiches. Then, a little later, Owen told the story again, standing in the social hall of the East Church, a bleak Victorian brick structure four blocks north of his home, and the space around him was as crowded as Owen had ever seen it.

Nearly the whole space was filled with folding chairs. One corner lacked them; it was full instead of iridescent black blobs with one human among them, the church organist, who spoke the shoggoth language more fluently than anyone else and translated in a low whistle for those of the shapeless creatures who hadn't learned English. The rest of the room was a sea of faces turned up toward Owen: people from Dunwich and Chorazin, Kingsport and Innsmouth, along with Tcho-Tchos and people who'd lived in Arkham all along and found their way to the Great Old Ones in one way or another. Among them were friends Owen had known for years: Miriam Akeley, Larry and Patty Shray, John and Sybil Romero, Justin and Belinda Martense.

As Owen finished his story, a brief silence settled into place in the social hall, and then Tom Gilman stood up: a burly man Owen's age who happened to have tentacles instead of arms. "I've got one question," he said. "Do we know for a fact that the book's the *Ghorl Nigral*?"

Billie Whateley, who was the senior initiate in the Arkham Starry Wisdom church, looked up from the front row of seats, where she'd been huddled with Asenath over a shape Owen didn't have to see. "It's the *Book of Night*," the old woman said. "Nothing else it could be—and I've only seen two other things that have so much voor flowing through them."

Tom nodded, taking that in. "Once Jenny Chaudronnier comes back," said Owen, "we'll have all three of the treasures of Poseidonis in one place, and someone who can use them. I'm pretty sure she can do something about what we're facing."

"And if she doesn't come back?" Tom asked.

Owen had been trying not to think about that possibility, but it couldn't be evaded. Skilled as Jenny was, there were powers in the cosmos she couldn't master, and he knew too well that she might have taken one risk too many. "Then we'll all be dead soon," he admitted. With a shrug: "Until I find out otherwise, I'm going to assume that the papers she got showed her someplace she needed to go, and she'll be back as soon as she can."

The crowd took that in. "Owen," said Susannah Eliot, a priestess in the Esoteric Order of Dagon and a close friend of Laura's. "I know something about the Nhhngr, but I bet you know more. If it comes down all over the world, what's going to happen?"

His face tensed. "Without the Yr to balance it, it gradually turns our kind of matter into something closer to itself, and our kind of life can't survive that change. Everything living that gets too close to it gets transformed, and finally dies. Human beings—" More than twenty years ago, he'd read the field reports from central Massachusetts on which Lovecraft based his story "The Colour Out Of Space," and images from them surged up from memory. "We turn gray, go crazy, start to crumble, and die. That last part may take a while. After a while—a few decades, maybe a century—it'll return to space, but that'll be too late for any of us."

The silence that followed was broken only by the low whistle of the church organist, translating for the shoggoths.

CHAPTER 9

THE STONE CHILDREN

Miriam Akeley's office seemed almost unnervingly ordinary to Owen after the strange journeys of the days just past. Through the windows, he could see afternoon sunlight gleaming on leafless cherry trees; above them, clouds billowed in a pale blue sky. The thought that a color found in no earthly spectrum would spread across that sky sometime soon haunted him.

In the Van Kauran Reading Room upstairs, where Abelard Whipple watched over Miskatonic's collection of books of eldritch lore, the *Ghorl Nigral* had been tucked into a big fire-proof wall safe. Jenny had worked incantations to protect the safe, the restricted-collection room, and the old campus, but how well those would stand up to whatever powers the Radiance could bring to bear on them, Owen didn't want to find out. If Jenny didn't return in time ...

He pushed the thought away. "I've got one scrap of good news," he said. "The shoggoths have figured out a way some of them might survive. They say there's a fissure in the rock down in the tunnels below East Street they can get through. It's small enough that we can seal the top with concrete, and it goes down more than a mile. If they're right that there aren't any other fissures that lead into it, some of them can slip down it and go into something like hibernation, until Nyogtha tells them it's safe to force their way out again."

"That's good to hear," said Miriam. With a wan smile: "I wish the rest of the tunnels here went deep enough. Martha Price tells me the voormis in Dhu-Shai are pretty sure they'll survive, and they've made room for some humans, so there's a little more that can be saved." She glanced up at the clock, and blinked. "I'm sorry, Owen—I should have left five minutes ago."

"Faculty senate?" Owen asked.

"No, I'm meeting someone." She paused, then: "Martin."

He nodded. "I certainly won't keep you, then." He'd known for years that Miriam had something going on with Jenny's uncle Martin Chaudronnier, though exactly what that amounted to, neither of them had ever so much as hinted. Their business, Owen thought. He said the usual things and they left the office together.

Miriam headed for the doors onto College Street. Owen would be going the same way soon, but another errand called him first. He went the other way, turned down a short corridor that ended in a door onto the quad. Outside, Lovecraft and Great Cthulhu faced each other as before, the Great Old One arising in his might, the writer who'd reintroduced him to popular culture looking on in bewilderment. The grass around Lovecraft's statue was splashed with sunlight, and half a dozen cats lay there soaking up what warmth they could.

Owen turned to the image of Great Cthulhu, approached the altar in front of it, bowed, and repeated the ancient words of reverence: "*Ph'nglui mglw'nafh Cthulhu R'lyeh wagh'nagl fhtagn.*" From his jacket pocket, he brought out offerings: two plaited chaplets of seaweed, four silver coins, and four perfect seashells. Those went on the altar. Whether those would help wake the Dreaming Lord a moment sooner than otherwise, Owen knew better than to try to guess.

He bowed again, turned away from the statue, and saw a familiar figure among the cats. A frozen moment, and then he crossed the quad to her. "Great Lady."

"Owen Merrill," said Phauz. "Half your work is done now. Are you ready for the rest?"

Owen made himself nod. "I'll manage." The bleak mood that was on him forced its way through, and he went on after a moment: "If there's any point to it now."

The tawny eyes with their vertical slits regarded him. "Lovecraft made that mistake," she said. "He thought that since the world makes no sense humans can understand, it makes no sense at all." She reached out a hand, and the lean black and white tom came trotting over to rub his face against her fingers. "He is beginning to learn, but it is not an easy lesson."

Owen's eyebrows drew together, and then in a sudden vertiginous moment he knew what her words had to mean. It occurred to him then that the cat nuzzling her hand, with its long lanky build, its thin face and square jaw, and its general air of bewildered formality, really did look a great deal like the long-dead fantasy writer H.P. Lovecraft.

"He had no talent for being human," she said then. "I knew that when he gave me the gift I named earlier, and once the enemies of the Great Old Ones poisoned him, it was easy enough to gather up what remained of him and give him a form that suited him better. It amused me, and he was always kind to my children." Her gaze turned to the black and white tom. "Now he dwells with me. In a distant age, when my children rule this lesser Earth, he will be a teller of tales again, and for ten thousand years his tales will be remembered."

"The Nhhngr," Owen forced out. "What about that?"

Phauz looked up at him. All at once he was staring blankly into her eyes, sensing the inhuman vastness of the mind and will behind them. The will moved, and he found himself gazing out of unfamiliar eyes at a nocturnal scene he could somehow see clearly despite the darkness: a place surrounded by a tall chainlink fence dotted with rust, a gate in the fence, and by the gate, a woman with long hair, crouching in the shadows, waiting.

Something moved within the gate, low to the ground: a weasel, Owen saw after a moment. It bounded over to the woman, gripping something in its mouth that glinted as the glare of the distant streetlights caught it. The woman reached out a hand; a moment later, the glinting thing turned in the lock, and the woman slipped through the gate, left it open behind her.

The eyes through which Owen watched busied themselves with other things for a time: gauging a series of leaps from roof to porch to lawn, darting across an all but abandoned street, following the woman through the open gate and then climbing up into the trees on the gate's far side, where the harsh scents of predators set his nerves on edge. It took him some minutes to recognize the paved footpaths and half-hidden barriers of a zoo. There were still a few of those open, Owen had heard, and this one looked as though it was barely clinging to existence.

He watched the woman dart into a rundown building, return with more glinting shapes, and set to work opening lock after lock. Behind her, red pandas and squirrel monkeys scrambled out of fenced habitats and clambered into the trees. A pair of hyenas trotted toward the open gate, and an elderly lion shook itself, remembered its fierce dignity, and followed them.

The elephants were waiting for her a little further on, three of them, standing side by side just within the fence that bound them. She greeted them in their own language, and they bowed their heads in reverence. The woman knotted her fingers into the chainlink fence; something half-seen flared outward from her hands; the iron of the fence sighed and dissolved into sparkling dust, and three great gray shapes did her homage and followed her through the night. The cat through whose eyes Owen watched sprang from tree to tree.

Then a frantic human figure came stumbling out of a building where a few lights still glared, babbling words Owen could not parse. The woman walked up to him, and all at once he gazed at her, slack-jawed and silent. She placed a hand on his forehead. Owen could feel the change surge through him. Then something that was no longer human crumpled before her in adoration, rose unsteadily on hooved feet, and led the elephants to a gate sized for trucks.

As the gate swung open and a faun and three elephants made their way out into the night, Owen felt his awareness drawn back to the sunlit quad. *Do you understand?* Phauz asked him.

That was your sister, Owen responded. *Yhoundeh.*

Yes, Phauz said. *She sets her fosterlings free. Your people brought them to many places where they would not otherwise have gone, and she is grateful for that.*

How can elephants survive here? The climate hasn't gotten that warm yet.

The elephants will change—not quite so quickly as the man you saw, and not quite so far, but enough. By the time the sun rises, they will have grown coats of coarse brown hair.

"Mammoths," Owen said aloud, staring at her.

Mastodons, she said. *It is not cold enough for mammoths, nor will be for a million years as you count time. Other beasts of the warm lands will change in other ways. Even when we were bound, we kept the power to bend life to our will—and now the bindings fail.*

*But—*He made himself go on. *What good will any of it do once the Nhhngr falls?*

By way of answer she met his gaze squarely. This time he didn't plunge through the tawny eyes to a distant place. Instead, he glimpsed a little more of the being that stood before him, the immense consciousness and the implacable will. An instant later she had vanished, but the instant was enough to tell him the thing he most needed to know.

The cats gathered around the statue of Lovecraft stirred and stretched, and all but one of them made off. The one left behind, the lean black and white tom, looked up at him and mewed.

"Yeah," Owen said. "She's like that, isn't she?" He bent, scratched the cat behind the ears, and then straightened and set out for home. Laura needed to know at once, he decided, that Phauz believed there was still a chance to turn the Nhhngr aside.

* * *

"You're sure," said Laura, but the words were purely a formality. He could see in her face that she'd already accepted the news.

"As sure as I can be. I just wish I knew—" His voice trickled to a halt.

"What we can do?" She smiled, and one of her tentacles slid out to coil around his hand and wrist, comforting. "I know. Father Dagon, I know."

Everything had changed, he knew, but nothing had. Jenny still hadn't returned—he'd asked as soon as he'd gotten home, guessed what the answer would be before Laura spoke, refused to consider the possibility that Jenny was gone in some more final sense—and the efforts of the initiates to sense how long they had left before the Nhhngr descended had not yet borne fruit. If the Radiance meant to avenge Clark Noyes' fate or do anything else before the Nhhngr came, for that matter, spies, spells, and Justin's cards had turned up no sign of it.

A sudden low thump from upstairs broke into his thoughts. He glanced up. "Barney?"

"He and Sylvia have been up there for hours." With a shrug: "They've been doing that most days since Jenny warned us about the Nhhngr."

One of his eyebrows went up. "Aren't they both still a little young for that?"

Laura stifled a laugh behind one hand. "None of the noises have been rhythmic," she told him, "neither of them have looked the least rumpled, and—well, let's just say I've made sure to get their hands near my nose whenever I could come up with an excuse. No, it's not that." Then, in a more serious tone: "Though I think they might become a couple once they're a little older. I've never seen Barney look so comfortable talking with anyone else."

Just then another loud muffled *whump* came from above; it sounded uncomfortably like an explosion. "All the same, I'd better go check on them," Owen said. Laura nodded agreeably, and he extracted himself from the couch and headed for the stair.

It wasn't the first time Owen had been up to Barnabas' attic laboratory, of course. He'd followed his son up the stairs countless times to see the outcome of an experiment, to talk through something, or to administer discipline on those rare occasions when it had been necessary—it was easier for Barnabas to handle that when it was in the shelter of a familiar space. Even so, remembering his own childhood and the shared bedrooms and constant turmoil of foster homes, he tried to minimize his intrusions into Barnabas' private world. That didn't keep him from pushing open the unlocked door and stepping through.

Beyond the door, dim light filtered in through an attic window, revealed a few pieces of old furniture, tall bookshelves weighed down with a wild assortment of books, a sturdy wooden table against the far wall half covered with laboratory glassware. Out of sight around an ell, low sounds and a familiar tuneless whistle told Owen where Barnabas was.

He scarcely noticed, though. His gaze caught on a figure in a chair near him. At first he thought it was Sylvia d'Ursuras, and he opened his mouth to say something to her, but realized that it wasn't just the dim light that made the figure's hair and face looked gray.

Owen went closer. It looked like a statue of Sylvia in fine gray stone, rendered with more than photographic exactness, down to the last stray hair—but no one in Arkham had anything close to the necessary skill, and Barnabas had shown no talent for art and no great interest in it. A blank moment passed before it sank in that the statue was dressed in a homespun blouse and skirt Owen had seen Sylvia wearing more than once, and he realized what sat in the chair.

He turned toward the ell just as Barnabas came out of it, carrying a small object Owen didn't recognize at first. Staring at him, Owen forced out one word: "Why?"

Barnabas motioned for him to wait, then crossed to the silent stone figure. As the light from the window spilled across the boy, Owen realized that the object in his son's hand was an old-fashioned perfume atomizer half full of pale golden fluid. Owen followed, saw the nozzle of the atomizer press against the statue's nostrils, heard the quick little hisses as Barnabas squeezed the bulb twice in one nostril and then twice in the other—

He knew what to expect then. He'd seen the same thing eighteen years earlier in a small town tourist trap, but it was still a shock to watch stone turned back to flesh, the change spread across Sylvia's face. As it reached her hairline, Owen turned to face his son.

"Dad," said Barnabas then. "The Nhhngr affects everything organic. Stone isn't organic. If people get turned to stone for a century or so, the Nhhngr can't touch them."

Owen realized his mouth was open. He closed it, tried to find words.

Sylvia spoke first. "Oh, hi, Mr. Merrill." She was blinking, as though she'd suddenly woken from a nap. To Barnabas: "How did it work? I don't remember a thing."

"The dose was exactly right."

"Wonderful. Then we're ready to go."

Owen looked from one of them to the other and back. He wanted to shout at them for attempting anything so risky, but common sense stopped the words before he'd even finished thinking them. When every living thing on Earth was going to turn gray and crazy and slowly die once the Nhhngr descended, how could he criticize anyone for taking risks?

"That's brilliant," he said finally. "I mean that." Sylvia blushed, and Barnabas looked away and grinned. "Come on downstairs," Owen went on. "You need to talk to the elders."

Sylvia got to her feet, shook herself. "I'm good with that. Barney?"

He nodded after a moment. "Yes."

* * *

"So that's what we did," said Sylvia. "And it worked."

She'd done most of the talking. Barnabas sat beside her on the sofa, his gaze fixed on the floor. Around them, as many of the elders of the Starry Wisdom Church and the Esoteric Order of Dagon as could be gathered in half an hour sat in something close to stunned silence.

Billie Whateley spoke first. "I'd like to know what the risks are."

"We don't know," Sylvia admitted. "The books in Aunt Jenny's library don't say—but I think it's less risky than the Nhhngr."

Billie's face tensed, but she nodded. Owen, standing next to the couch, glanced at Sylvia and said, "Rose and Arthur Wheeler spent most of a century under that spell, and came out of it just fine. So I think it's worth trying."

For a moment no one spoke. "Barney," Laura said then, and he glanced up. "How many people can you do that to?"

"Four thousand, nine hundred thirty-two pounds," Barnabas said at once.

"The dose is by body weight," Sylvia explained. "That's how many pounds of human body the chemicals we've got will petrify. That would be around thirty adults or a hundred children. If we can get more chemicals, of course, we can do more than that."

"Get me a list," said Noah Bishop, who was standing in back.

Sylvia extracted a pen and a notepad from her purse, wrote for a few moments, and showed the list to Barnabas. When he nodded, she handed it to Noah. He looked it over, nodded once, turned and left the parlor. The front door opened and closed a moment later.

"A hundred children," said Susannah Eliot, in a quiet wistful voice. "That would mean a good deal, to save that many."

"Mostly young children," Barnabas said suddenly. "They're lighter and we can save more of them. Enough older children and teenagers to take care of them. Two grownups who know how to do things. I can show you the figures if you want."

"What I want to know," Billie said then, "is who's going to undo the spell."

"Michaelmas," Sylvia replied. "He's made of brass, so the Nhhngr won't affect him."

That got a sudden murmur of surprise from most of the elders. "You didn't know that?" Sylvia went on. "He was made in 1362 by the second best sorcerer the family's ever had, Luc le Chaudronnier. He can keep the antidote safe until the Nhhngr's gone, the stars are right, and plants and animals can come back to this lesser Earth from the others."

Owen turned, regarded them for a moment. "You worked out all the details, didn't you?"

"We had to," Sylvia said. Her gaze, cold and measured in a way no fifteen-year-old's should have to be, met his. "We've got to save something."

The assembled elders glanced at each other, and Owen knew that they would agree.

"I have one question," said Susannah. "What about the kyrrmis?"

"We've worked that out too," Sylvia said. "It's especially important to save the young witches and their familiars, and it takes only a tiny dose to petrify a kyrrmi, so we can do all of them without having to leave more than two children behind."

"You've tested it?" Susannah asked.

Sylvia considered her for a moment, then said, "Yes." She reached into her purse again, brought out a small gray shape, and set it on the coffee table in front of her. Owen glanced at it, then stared. Curled up as though asleep, Wilbur lay there, a shape of gray stone.

"Sylvia," said Billie Whateley in an ashen voice. "How *could* you?"

"He's okay." For the first time since she'd begun explaining the experiment to the elders, a quaver ran through Sylvia's voice. "He's safe. Even if the Nhhngr came down right now, it wouldn't hurt him at all." She swallowed visibly. "And if I'm one of the ones who's chosen to be turned to stone, I'm going to hold him in my lap, so the two of us can wake up together."

Billie bowed her head, conceding. "I'm sorry. I shouldn't have said that."

"It's okay." Sylvia picked up the silent shape, kissed it, and put it back in her purse.

Another silence slipped by. There were words Owen wanted to say, but the customs of the Starry Wisdom forbade him to utter them. Fortunately Tom Gilman spoke them instead. "Barney, you said some teenagers should be saved. I think you two have earned it."

"I'm not the best choice," Barnabas replied.

Owen glanced at his son. "That's not your choice to make, Barney."

He met Owen's gaze briefly and then looked away. "I know, Dad."

An instant later the front door slammed open. "We've got trouble," Noah Bishop called from the entry. "Helicopters, lots of them, headed this way. The alarm's being sounded." The bell of the East Church rang in the middle distance just then, high and harsh.

"Why didn't our watchers see them?" Billie Whateley asked, appalled.

"Damn if I know," Bishop said. "I don't know how we're going to evacuate in time."

"We're not," said Owen. As a seventh-degree initiate, he had the right to take charge of the local Starry Wisdom community in an emergency if no one challenged him. He could see with brutal clarity what would happen if they tried to flee Arkham now, in the midst of an attack by the Radiance, and that left only one alternative. "We've got almost a thousand here who can fight, and that's not counting shoggoths. We can take them. It's the only chance we've got."

A moment's stunned silence, and then Noah Bishop nodded. "I'm good with that." That was all it took, and the others agreed, some tentatively, others with sudden fierce grins. "You know what to do," Owen told them. "Do it."

He turned to Barnabas and Sylvia. "Get the chemicals and head for the deep tunnels, now. Ask the shoggoths for help if you need it. We'll get as many children down after you as we can. Use the potion on them. Don't drink it yourselves until you know we've lost. Okay?"

Barney lunged to his feet and darted up the stair. Sylvia went after him. Off in the distance, Owen caught the low threatening rhythm of helicopter rotors in flight. He bent to give Laura a kiss, went for his pistol, then headed for the door.

* * *

Outside all was seeming confusion. Young men carrying weapons came spilling out of doors all along Powder Hill

Road, sprinted to the assembly points they'd been assigned. Older men and women hurried at a slightly less punishing pace toward the places where they'd be working sorceries or directing the struggle.

He forced his mind clear and headed for the university, his assigned place in a crisis. Across Walnut Street and Parsonage Street, and then onto College Street: the way to the old campus was all but hardwired into Owen's bones and blood. Others would be converging there too, but for the moment it looked as though he was first. He reached out with his voor-sense, perceived running figures moving that way, then caught the very different trace of something sliding the same direction below the streets and grinned in relief.

He got to the main doors of Hutchinson Hall, ducked inside. As he started through the entry, something moved up the stair from the basement. The movement coalesced into a woman he knew: Brecken Kendall, the organist for the Starry Wisdom church, who taught music at the parochial school and lived close by. Long black hair tied loosely back gave her a disheveled look; her face was lined with worry.

"Hi, Brecken," he said.

She gave him a startled glance and then visibly relaxed. "Oh, hi, Owen. We came as fast as we could. Do you know what's happening?"

He explained about the helicopters. By then the "we" had begun to put in an appearance: shoggoths, sliding one after another up the stairs, seven of them in all. They greeted him with piping voices, and he whistled in response. A flurry of movement, and four of them slid into Hutchinson Hall's central corridor and flowed toward the doors, moving faster than a man could run. The other three stayed close to the organist for the moment.

Just then a dim whisper of sound came down the stairwell from above. It resolved into footfalls, steady and patient. Owen turned, saw the lean form of Abelard Whipple descending the stair, noticed a faint acrid scent that he couldn't place.

"All's well," said the librarian, with his usual air of genial distraction. "It won't be safe for any living thing to go up to the Van Kauran Reading Room for at least six hours, though. Perhaps one of our shapeless friends here can bar the stairway."

It took only a few moments of whistling to get that settled. One of the shoggoths repeated the message to give to humans—"the air upstairs will kill you"—and settled onto the lowest steps of the stair, with another hidden in the shadows of the basement stair for backup. That left Owen, Abelard, Brecken, and one shoggoth. "I believe our place is in the faculty lounge," said Abelard. "Shall we?"

The faculty lounge was a few doors past Miriam's office, a pleasant room with armchairs, sofas, a little wood stove in one corner for heat and hot water, and heavy windowless walls, a crucial reason for its role in emergencies. Miriam was already there. So was Will Bishop, who'd been a student of Owen's in Dunwich, then one of Miriam's graduate assistants, and now taught mathematics at Miskatonic, and so was Michael Peaslee, technically a professor emeritus but still constantly on campus. They looked up sharply from cups of tea as Owen and the others came in, and like him, grinned in relief once they saw the shoggoth. "The cavalry has arrived," said Will.

"Thank you," the shoggoth said in English, in a voice that sounded uncannily like Brecken's; Owen gathered that it knew the idiom. Brecken smiled at it and whistled a response, and the two of them settled on a sofa.

"I've seen to the collection," Abelard said to Miriam. "I don't imagine anyone will get past our friends here, but if they get to the fourth floor they won't get further." Owen glanced at him, then at Miriam, but knew better than to ask; he'd long guessed that the restricted collection of books on sorcery had secret defenses, and it was comforting to have that confirmed, especially with the *Ghorl Nigral* residing there.

Michael Peaslee poured Owen a cup of tea, motioned with the pot to the others, nodded when they declined. For a time no one said anything. Then a shoggoth-voice sounded in the corridor outside, warning that a group of humans was approaching the main doors.

Owen got to his feet and went to the door, waiting to see if his gun would be needed. Another few minutes passed, and then a second whistle came: the humans were friendly, it said, and brought good news.

Not long thereafter Larry Shray came down the corridor, looking rather like a bandit with a shotgun slung over one shoulder and a bandolier of shells running across his chest. He followed Owen into the lounge, greeted everyone cheerily and said, "We're good so far. The main Radiance force is across the river in the old campus—something upward of a hundred of them. They tried to get a couple of teams in here from the south, but something caught them just outside of town and ate them." To Brecken and the shoggoth: "There were bones left, so it wasn't any of your friends."

"What's the plan now?" Owen asked him.

"A message's on its way to the Deep Ones," said Larry. "Most of our people are heading north to the river. If the Radiant force attacks, we stop them. If not—" He shrugged. "I don't think anyone's willing to evacuate at this point, so we're probably going to have to take them."

"Okay," said Owen. "Where's our side's command post?"

"Your church." Larry gave him a questioning look. "What are you thinking?"

"I'm not sure yet," Owen lied. "But I think there might be another way."

* * *

By the time he stepped out onto College Street an eerie silence gripped Arkham. He could feel eyes watching him as he headed north, knew which broken windows in the empty buildings across the street concealed old men and women from Dunwich with hunting rifles that could hit a squirrel a quarter mile away, but nothing moved down the street but the wind.

There was another way, he told himself, something besides the brutal mathematics of the kind of firefight he'd faced in Iraq, the long lists of dead and wounded people he knew. All those years ago in Chorazin, he'd convinced one negation team to back down from a fight they couldn't win; later, in the tunnels under Brooklyn's Red Hook neighborhood, he'd tried the same thing, and would have succeeded if a Mi-Go hadn't countermanded it. Could he do it again? There was only one way to find out, and a memory of Michael Dyson's face just before he'd died convinced Owen that he had to try.

He got to the East Church without incident, looked up so the men who crouched in the bell tower with deer rifles could see his face clearly through their scopes, went in the back door. "Owen!" Tom Gilman called out. "We got the news from your end of town, and we've just heard from the Deep Ones. Once they get here we're going across the river."

"I want to try something first," Owen said, and sketched out his plan. By the time he was finished he was at the center of a little knot of silent men and women.

"That's either a really smart idea," said Tom then, "or a really dumb one."

"I know," Owen said. "I think it's worth a shot, though."

No one argued, and moments later Owen found his way to Peabody Avenue, and headed down the middle of it, staying in plain sight. Someone had found him a piece of white cloth and stapled it around one of the metal-tipped wooden poles that served to open the church's upper windows. Whether the Radiance would pay any attention to a flag of truce was anyone's guess, but Owen held the thing up and hoped that he wasn't throwing his life away.

Rust lay heavy on the Peabody Avenue bridge and a few pieces of the pavement had already gone tumbling down into the rushing Miskatonic below, but Owen's footfalls rang firmly on the concrete and steel. From there the avenue ran straight toward the abandoned campus. The Radiant force had their defensive perimeter somewhere near the old quad, he was sure of it. The only question in his mind was whether they'd start shooting the moment they saw him.

He passed tumbled remnants of gambrel-roofed houses, vacant lots where brown weeds grown tall over the last eight years rattled and shook in the cold wind. Derby Street came sooner than he'd expected. Beyond it stood the cracked concrete pedestal where the statue of Cthulhu had been, and the ruins of the old gray building that had been the Arkham Sanitarium and then the Lovecraft Museum. Orne Library's Gothic spires rose straight ahead, the windows below them covered with plywood sheets long since gone gray with sun and rain. He veered left to pass between the library and the graffiti-stained brick walls of the Armitage Student Union.

As he came out from between the buildings, facing the square mass of Morgan Hall and the delirious angles of Wilmarth Hall across a wilderness of head-high brown weeds and bare saplings, a man's voice rang out: "Stop right there."

Owen stopped, slowly raised the makeshift white flag higher. "I've got a message for your team coordinator," he called out. He couldn't see the Radiant force, but the voice had come from somewhere in the middle of what had been the quad a decade before.

A silence passed. "Don't move," the voice said then, "and if our detectors show any trace of sorcery we're going to blow your lying ass from here to Salem."

Owen waited. A low murmur told him that someone was talking into a radio. Minutes passed, and then the same voice called out: "What's your message?"

"You're outnumbered and outgunned," Owen said. "Your machines ought to tell you that we've got shoggoths on the other side of the river, our human force has you outnumbered by nine to one, and the Deep Ones are on their way." He paused as a faint tremor troubled the ground, wondered what it meant. "The teams you sent in from the south didn't make it. You want to fight, be my guest, but you won't win."

Silence gripped the empty buildings around him.

"There's another option," said Owen. "You can get out of here. If you head north toward Ipswich, nobody's going to stop you." Another tremor came, stronger. He had to fight to keep his balance, and a crack zigzagged through the pavement in front of him. "You don't have a lot of time to find shelter before the Nhhngr comes down out of space—and you know as well as I do that your allies aren't going to protect you from that."

A faint murmur told of another conversation over the radio. Another silence followed.

"The chief says no dice." Was that weariness in the man's voice, or something more? "She says if you want us out of here, you're going to have to—"

A powerful shockwave jarred the ground, sent buildings swaying and crumbling, and the pavement buckled and broke open in front of Owen. He staggered, caught his balance, glanced up as the tremor continued, and stared in amazement.

As he watched, great masses of concrete broke off the sides of Wilmarth Hall and crashed to the ground with a roar, sending clouds of dust billowing into the shaken air. More shocks set the ground swaying. At first Owen thought the ground was shaking the building, but a closer look showed him that it was the building that was shaking, and setting the ground in motion.

The building—

Or something within it.

"You might want to reconsider," a familiar voice called out from somewhere behind Owen. "And don't pull those triggers, or you'll find out what I can do to bullet trajectories."

He risked a glance back over his shoulder, saw a short plain figure with mouse-colored hair coming from between the two buildings behind him. Relief swept through him, dizzying.

CHAPTER 10

THE MOTHER OF DOELS

Another shockwave set the ground reeling, sent more dust billowing upwards. "The Mother of Doels is awake," Jenny called out again through the rumbling noise. He gave her a look of speechless astonishment, looked at the building, at her again. "Her Young are hatching inside her," she went on. "Get in her way and you'll be on their menu."

The thing in Wilmarth Hall shook again, sending another cascade of concrete and glass down onto the pavement. Owen could see something greenish, pulsing, and translucent through gaps where the familiar rugose walls had been. Orifices opened and spat out tumbling shapes he recognized, after a moment, as broken drywall, flooring, abandoned office furniture.

"I hope your team coordinator isn't too close to that building," Owen said then.

"She was inside," the voice in the weeds admitted.

"Then Noth-Yidik's already fed her to her Young," said Jenny. "You can still run."

"You're not running," the voice said.

"I can communicate with Noth-Yidik," Jenny told him. "You can't."

Another shock set the quad trembling as the thing that had been in Wilmarth Hall shook itself like a wet dog, sending the spires on its back tumbling high into the air and down again.

One spire landed point first on the far side of the quad and buried half its length in the earth like a javelin, jolting the ground hard. Through the dust, Owen could see something where the building had been: a greenish, shapeless mass in which pale presences shifted and squirmed.

As the roar of the collapsing concrete faded, a woman's voice called out. "You—the guy who came up here first. You're Owen Merrill, aren't you?"

"Yeah," Owen called back.

"Some of us want to know if you'll accept surrender."

"Heffler!" the first voice barked, outraged.

"Shut up," said Heffler, and in a tone of disgust: "sir."

"That's cause for—"

The sharp crack of a single pistol shot rang out through the tumult, and the sound echoed back from the buildings. Something landed hard in the weeds.

"Anyone else want to argue?" Heffler said. No one did.

Owen and Jenny gave each other startled looks. "Why?" Owen called.

A lean dark-haired woman in gray and white camo came out from among the weeds. "I knew Mike Dyson," she said. "I know what he did, and I'm pretty sure I know why. You've got zero reason to do anything but waste us, but I heard about how you handled that business over near Buffalo." With a shrug: "And it's more than we're going to get from the Mi-Go."

"If you're planning on trying something stupid," Owen said, "you're better off taking your chances with the Mi-Go."

A bitter laugh blended with the fading echoes of Wilmarth Hall's collapse. "No," said Heffler. "No, there you're dead wrong."

Owen glanced at Jenny, who nodded fractionally and gestured toward the sidewalk near them. He nodded in response and called out, "Okay. Any of you who want to surrender, drop every weapon you've got and come over here with your hands high. The rest of you—"

The vast shape that stood where Wilmarth Hall had been lurched and began to move. The heaps of broken concrete that lay around it slid and tumbled out of its path. The shape slammed against the empty shell of Morgan Hall, and it collapsed with another tremendous roar.

"—had better start running," Owen called out, once he guessed he could be heard again.

For a moment no one moved. Then men and women in gray and white uniform, dozens of them, came toward Owen with raised hands. They looked dazed and uncertain, but when Owen motioned for them to gather on the sidewalk in front of the Armitage Union, they obeyed.

"We'll have to wait until she's gone into the river," Jenny said then.

The vast greenish shape lurched again and slid at an angle across the quad, snapping off saplings as it went. The gap between Orne Library and Pabodie Hall, the engineering building on the far side of Federal Avenue, was too narrow for it, but it shoved through anyway, leaving rubble where a good half of each building had been. Once it was past, Jenny motioned—the noise was too loud for speech—and Owen, using gestures, got the prisoners lined up and marched them through the gap between Armitage Union and what was left of the library.

On the far side, he stood with Jenny and the prisoners and watched in silence as the immense mass of the Mother of Doels slid through the empty college neighborhood, turning abandoned houses into matchsticks as it went. Finally it reached the riverbank and slid down into the water, sending a great surge of spray up into the air.

"Hands clasped on your heads," Owen told the prisoners once the roar of the waters had faded into silence. "Single file down the middle of Peabody Avenue. Try anything and you're going to find out why that's a really bad idea."

No one argued. They put their hands on their heads and began trudging down the street.

Owen turned and hurried down Peabody Avenue to the head of the line of prisoners. Heffler, who was first in line, gave him a flat wary look that could have meant anything. As they reached the northern end of the bridge, Owen said to her, "I can't promise anything, you know."

Heffler nodded. "I figured." Owen handed her the white flag, and she took it.

The bridge rang beneath negation team boots. Owen glanced over his shoulder, made sure that none of the prisoners had left the line and that Jenny was following. He faced forward again just as John Romero and Tom Gilman, deer rifles in hand and tentacle respectively, came out from behind a tumbledown warehouse on Water Street. They looked dumbfounded. For a moment Owen wondered if they'd watched Noth-Yidik go into the water, but they were staring at the prisoners, not at the wreckage across the river. He grinned, and hurried toward them.

* * *

"I'm not sure who first thought of putting Noth-Yidik's egg inside a building," Jenny said. She was sitting at a table in the social hall of the Starry Wisdom church, hands wrapped around a cup of coffee, while church elders and priestesses gave each other incredulous looks and Deep Ones and shoggoths looked on. "According to Chalmers, her human servants run in family lineages like the ones we had in Kingsport, and they're even more secretive. All I know is that Wilmarth Hall was designed as a brooding rack right from the start, with plenty of gaps inside the structure for the egg to hatch and Noth-Yidik's new body to take its proper shape."

"What you're saying," Miriam Akeley said then, "is that for twenty-eight years I had my office inside one of the Great Old Ones."

Jenny nodded. "Her body has plenty of channels and chambers in it for her Young. The architect put hallways and offices in those while she wasn't using them."

Miriam shook her head in amazement.

"And now she's where she needs to be. If the Nhhngr doesn't reach her, she'll grow to her full size, and the doels will spend a few centuries at sea, swim to shore, pupate, and hatch after a thousand years as flying polyps. She'll live for a hundred million years or so and then lay her egg and die, and the cycle starts again." She sipped coffee. "But there's more to it than that. The Eltdown Shards say that she plays an important part in Great Cthulhu's awakening. I didn't know what role that was—I don't think anyone did—until Owen got me Halpin Chalmers' papers."

Laura, sitting beside Owen, gave him a smile, and he smiled back.

"Noth-Yidik's a daughter of Yog-Sothoth," Jenny went on. "Her father's the gate and the guardian of the gate, and she takes after him. Now that she's in the ocean, she's become the Gate of the Lesser Deeps—and it's through that gate that Cthulhu will pass once the stars are right. So her awakening brings us a big step closer to his return. That's what Chalmers said, and the only way to confirm that was to go to R'lyeh—so I did."

Utter silence filled the social hall.

"Halpin Chalmers figured out some astonishing things," she went on. "He knew more about the barriers that separate our Earth from the greater Earth than anyone since Alhazred's time. Those barriers are wavering now. That's how I could go to R'lyeh, and come back in one piece—" She allowed a tired laugh. "Though it wasn't easy. But I needed to go, because some passages in the papers gave me the clues I needed to figure out that the Nhhngr is on its way.

"And as far as I know, there's only one way to stop it. Until the stars are right and the bindings placed on them dissolve, the Great Old Ones can't turn it aside. More precisely, there's only one being who can bring down the power to do that, and he's dreaming in R'lyeh."

"That doesn't sound like we've got much of a chance, then," Susannah Eliot said.

Jenny turned toward her. "We've got all the treasures of Poseidonis, and I've copied the runes on the Seal of the Abyss that holds Cthulhu in his tomb. This afternoon I'm going to sit down with the *Ghorl Nigral* and every other tome that might help, and work out the ritual. At least in theory, it should be possible to break the Seal of the Abyss and wake the Dreaming Lord. At least in theory, I know how to do that, and that's what I'm going to try to do."

Watching her, Owen suddenly recalled what Yiang-li of An-fang had said. Yeh-ni the greatest of sorceresses, he thought. When people listen to the stories Yiang-li was talking about, will they think of a plain middle-aged woman sitting on a wooden chair in an old church basement and explaining how she was going to try to save the lesser Earth?

"Miss Chaudronnier." The voice had a Deep One accent. Glancing toward its source, Owen thought he could see a face he recognized: Mha'alh'yi, a Deep One sorceress he'd known for twenty years. "If there is anything we of Y'ha-nthlei can do to assist, you will tell us."

"Of course," said Jenny. "As soon as I know what's going to be necessary, you'll hear about it. It won't be long." Something bleak showed in her face then. "We don't have much time before the Nhhngr comes down. Maybe a week at most."

That called up another silence, more brittle than the first. "I know it's not as important," said Billie Whateley after a moment, "especially with—with that on its way, but we've got another thing to sort out. What in the Old Ones' names are we going to do with the prisoners?"

"I didn't expect them to surrender," Owen admitted. "I thought they'd run."

"I bet," said Tom Gilman. "I don't know what to do with them either, but Father Dagon, it was something to watch the two of you marching them down Peabody Avenue."

"I think we should talk to them," Laura said then.

That got blank looks, but one of the others—Teresa Chonle, the *ngam khilao* of Arkham's Tcho-Tcho community—glanced at Laura and said, "I don't see how it could hurt."

Laura nodded as if that settled the matter, and turned her wheelchair toward the door.

* * *

The prisoners were sitting on the bare concrete floor of an old warehouse south of Water Street, each one well away from the others, under the watchful eyes of a dozen young men from Arkham and the muzzles of an assortment of guns. Weathered fiberglass skylights set into the roof let in a brown blurred light. The prisoners stared at the concrete, faces set hard, as though braced for something. Owen glanced at them, then at the motley group of priestesses, elders, and initiates who came to confront them, and tried to make himself believe what he saw.

"Is one of you in charge?" Laura asked.

A moment passed, then Heffler glanced up at her. "Our team coordinator and her staff got eaten and our unit coordinator took a bullet. I think I'm the senior squad officer here." She glanced back at the others. "Anyone gonna argue?" When none did, she turned back to Laura. "Are you in charge of your side's forces here?"

"Not exactly," Laura admitted. "I'm the head of the local lodge of the Esoteric Order of Dagon." She gestured at the others. "The elders of the Starry Wisdom church, the *ngam khilao* of the Tcho-Tchos, and others who help run things here. We don't do things the way you do."

Heffler met her gaze, said nothing.

"We're trying to figure out what to do with you," Laura said then.

"You're going to off us, of course," Heffler replied with a little shrug. "We knew that when we surrendered."

Owen stared at her, considered asking the obvious question. Before he made up his mind, Laura asked it instead. "Then why did you surrender?"

"Because the alternatives are a lot worse. Do you know about Mi-Go brain cylinders?"

"I know they exist," Laura said.

Heffler nodded. "And you know about the Nhhngr—and those are the other two options. If we'd run for it, or stayed under General Directorate command and followed orders, the Nhhngr comes down and we all turn gray and crazy and crumbling and take our merry sweet time dying. If we'd stayed and didn't follow orders, we get to be part of Earth's number one export. Compared to either of those, a quick death's pretty decent, and if that means I get fed to a shoggoth I'm gonna wish the damn thing *bon appetit*."

Jenny turned to Laura, said "May I?" When Laura nodded, the sorceress turned to Heffler. "And what will you do if the Nhhngr doesn't come down?"

Heffler paused, braced herself visibly, and said, "Then your side's going to wake up Cthulhu—and if that happens we're all worse than toast anyway."

The priestesses, elders, and initiates of Arkham gave each other baffled glances. "How do you know we're going to do that next?" Jenny asked.

"Because that's what the Weird of Hali says," Heffler replied.

"Then you know something we don't," said Jenny.

Heffler regarded her for a long silent moment, her face hard with disbelief.

"Nobody on our side left the Moon Temple of Irem alive," Jenny said. "You know that better than we do. Until six years ago we didn't even have fragments of the Weird."

The blood drained from Heffler's face. "But—" She stopped, tried again. "Every time our teams tried to stop part of it from happening, your side got there first. Everywhere—Arkham, Kingsport, Providence, New York City, that place out near Buffalo—"

"Chorazin," said Owen.

"Yeah. We tried over and over again to get control of Arkham so we could keep you from using the geonoetic currents, and every time your side brought in assets we didn't know about and stomped the crap out of us." Her voice shook. "Every—single—time."

"That's the Weird's doing," said Jenny. "Hali was a prophet, remember. He knew everything you would do before you even thought of it—and it's his Weird that's been dragging you down." Then: "What I don't know yet is what the Weird says about the Nhhngr. I need to know that because I'm going to stop it if I can."

Another moment passed, and then Heffler said, "It doesn't say anything about that." To the others: "I'm about to break PSOs. If you're going to object, do it now." No one spoke.

"PSOs?" Owen asked.

"Permanent standing orders," Heffler said. "You live and die by those if you're negation team personnel. PSO number one is that you never let out secure information that might get to your side, period—and that's what I'm about to do." She closed her eyes, drew in a breath.

Without warning, a pistol barked.

* * *

Owen turned, fast. One of the guards had fired. Close by, one of the prisoners toppled forward, and the fluid that spread around him was dark green rather than red. A strange weapon dropped from his hand. In the instant that followed, two other prisoners lunged to their feet, the guards pointed their guns, Owen reached for his revolver—

And then everything slowed and stopped. To Owen, it felt as though the air had suddenly congealed around him. Out of the corner of one eye, he saw that Jenny had raised her right hand, the fingers bent into strange curves.

"*Kalath ak Kadath astu Kamathaoth,*" she said. "I invoke the Doom of Nithon!"

Her fingers shifted, and the two prisoners who'd stood shrieked and crumpled to the floor. The air loosed its grip on Owen, but he didn't bother to finish reaching for his gun. The guards stared at Jenny, and so, as the spell shifted, did the other prisoners. She stood there with her hand raised until reddish spines stabbed through the uniforms of the fallen ones and pushed the masks that looked like faces askew, revealing alien shapes beneath.

"Mi-Go," said Jenny, lowering her hand. "They're better at masks than they used to be."

Heffler turned slowly, looked at each of the three corpses, the displaced masks and the pools of spreading green blood, then gave Jenny an unnerved look and settled back into her place. Owen nodded to the guards, and two of them hauled the corpses away one at a time.

"Okay," Heffler said then. "For what it's worth, I didn't know about that."

"I know," Jenny answered. As Heffler stared at her: "The Weird. What does it say?"

She nodded after a moment. "What I know is the English translation. Our side had that done by a guy named Thompson back in eighteen-something. You want the Latin or the original Duriac, you gotta talk to someone from Research." With a bleak laugh: "If there's anyone from Research still alive. Most of them bought it when the Binger project went pear-shaped. But here's what I know." She drew in a ragged breath, began to recite.

"You who have filled this fane with blood and fire
And broken what you cannot comprehend
Never shall have the thing that you desire.
No! All your deeds shall only speed your end.
Your doom is sure, no matter how you bend

The destinies of Earth. Across the sea,
In lands thrice harrowed by the curse you send,
Where paths of moonlight stretch across the lea,
Two children of a distant age I call to me.

"Three signs I bring. Your direst doings will
Not turn them back nor slow your destined night:
A door shall open by a stone-crowned hill
To bid the sleeper wake and rise in might;
The gem of Egypt's king, long lost to sight,
Brought back shall be to its forsaken space
Where dwells the Watcher that abhors the light;
A dead man's hand beneath the sandy place
Shall free the forces put there by an ancient race.

"Three treasures shall they have: a ring of gold
One hand alone can wear; a book of spells
Brought out of strange abysses; black and cold,
The blade of which lost Alar's legend tells.
These shall call forth from ocean's deepest wells
One who abides. Where gray tide meets gray stones,
And four join hands above the rocky fells,
Your doom then comes—I write it on your bones—
For then the gods of Earth shall rise to claim their
thrones."

A long silent moment slipped past. "You knew that," Laura
said then. "And you still thought you could win."

"Half our people," said Heffler, "thought it was the ravings
of a senile old fool. The other half thought we could beat it."
Laura considered that, and shook her head slowly.

"May I?" Owen asked her then. When she nodded, he
turned to Heffler. "I'm going to ask some things you probably
won't answer. The first is how soon to expect the next attack."

Heffler met his gaze. From behind her, a harsh-faced man said, "Might as well tell him, Judy. It doesn't make a damn bit of difference at this point."

"There won't be a next attack," Heffler said. "You're looking at what's left of the last negation force this side of the Hudson valley. When word got out about—" She stopped.

"Project 638," Owen suggested.

That earned him a moment of hard-edged silence. "Yeah," Heffler said. "So you knew about that too. As soon as the negation teams heard, most of them broke discipline and went to ground. I'd bet good money that any team coordinators that objected got fragged on the spot."

"And the Mi-Go?" Owen asked.

"What we were told," Heffler said, "is that all the bugs that are surgically adapted to live on Earth went to the shelters weeks, ago, except for a few field operatives. Their orbital base has been pulled out past the asteroids for the time being. The Nhhngr's as dangerous for them as it is for us, and their spacecraft are living creatures. If those go gray and crazy and crumbling—"

"Yeah," said Owen. Then: "How soon will the Nhhngr get here?"

"We don't know," Heffler admitted. "Too damn soon."

Owen nodded. "Thank you." He turned toward Laura, the others.

"Can I ask something?" the harsh-faced man said then. Owen turned back to face him. "If the Nhhngr comes down, could you at least do us the favor of shooting us?"

It was Billie Whateley who answered. "If that happens, a lot of us will be taking poison. I'll ask the witches who'll be brewing it to make sure there's enough for you." Then: "And I'll see if we can find something for you to eat in the meantime. I'm still not sure what to suggest we do with you, but there's no need for you to starve while we figure that out."

Heffler, the harsh-faced man, and most of the others were staring at her by the time she finished. Owen thought he could guess why, and cold anger flared in him. "This war was your idea, not ours," he said. "If you'd just gone off somewhere and done your thing, we wouldn't have cared. All we wanted was for your goon squads to leave us alone."

All at once he couldn't bear their presence any longer, and turned away. He could feel their gaze on him all the way to the door.

* * *

Outside a brisk autumn breeze came whistling through Arkham's streets, blew thin mare's-tails of cloud across a cold blue sky. Owen drew in a ragged breath. The Weird, he thought. We finally know the Weird. That wasn't what had his heart pounding, but it meant more than the knotted emotions inside him, he knew that well enough.

He was still trying to clear his mind when a voice called his name. He glanced up, to see John Romero coming toward him. "Two people just came down Old Kingsport Road. They say you can vouch for them."

By then Owen had glanced past him and spotted two familiar figures standing in the street. He was about to say something when he thought of the three disguised Mi-Go, walked to them instead and reached out a hand. Justin Geoffrey grinned and shook it, and then Vanessa Ward pressed it with hers; both hands had a coarse dry texture he knew at once. "Yeah, I can vouch for them," he said. "Hi, Vanessa. Hi, Justin. Any idea where Mr. Ambrose is?"

"I wish," the girl said. "He told us where to go and then went back into the woods—but he told us to bring you a message." When Owen motioned to her to go on: "He says to watch for the Yellow Sign. He says the King's forces are gathering, and you have to be ready. He says—he says it won't be long."

She swallowed visibly. "And he wants me to pass on another message to somebody else. I don't know who."

A silken voice from behind Owen answered before he could. "The message is for me," Phauz said, from what had been empty sidewalk an instant before. She stepped past Owen, turned to regard them all. "And I already know what it is."

Vanessa's eyes went round, and she made an old-fashioned curtsey. For just an instant, Owen glimpsed what she'd seen: the slender figure of more than human height, the golden skin, the feline head with pricked ears.

"My father's servants gather in the hills above Kingsport," Phauz said, in her human form again, as cats scampered out of nearby alleys to wreathe about her feet. "There they will stay, or perish. The servants of the Radiance thought they could come that way, and the flesh has been stripped from their bones."

"Was that your doing, Great Lady?" Owen asked her.

The tawny eyes turned toward him. "Not mine alone."

All at once the unquiet air above Arkham was full of presences on the edge of sight. Owen glimpsed forms humanlike and utterly unhuman, diadems and horns and animal heads, billowing robes of light and shadow, faces and faceless shapes turned in a direction Owen's mind couldn't quite process. Ulthward, he guessed—ulthward, toward Carcosa.

"Basatan permitted your child to bring the book here," Phauz said to Owen then, and he sensed somehow that he alone heard the silken voice. "So did my mother. So did Nodens—the Lord of the Great Deep could easily have taken it from her as you leapt from time to time. So did another." The tawny eyes considered him, amused. "Your spell would have done little if dread Tindalos had not chosen to call off his Hounds. Another, my sister of the winged elk, protected you the whole way, as I did. Another, eldest on this world, wove the pattern in which we all dance." She stretched upward, became part of the multitude gathered there. Her voice came ringing down: "We will not permit the old quarrel to wreck this world. What we can do to prevent that, we will. What we cannot do …" The rest came in a whisper: "You must do."

Then Owen blinked, tried to clear his vision and his mind. He had fallen to his knees on the sidewalk. John, Vanessa, and Justin Geoffrey were staring at him, and so were others who had come out from the warehouse: Laura, Jenny, most of the priestesses and elders. As he pulled himself to his feet and saw his reflection in the glass of a nearby window, he realized why: the mark of a cat's footprint Phauz had placed on his forehead in Providence ten years before blazed with tawny golden light. It faded as he watched.

"We have help," he managed to say.

"I know," said Jenny. "I saw them—I think we all did."

Laura wheeled over and took his hand. He gave her a grateful look, forced his mind clear. "I'm sorry I walked out," he said to the elders. "It was just—" He groped for words, found none.

"I know," Susannah Eliot said. "Trust me, I know."

"If we're done here?" Jenny asked then. When that got nods and agreeable words from the elders, she turned to Owen and Laura. "Do the two of you have time to talk? Owen, I want to hear how you got the *Ghorl Nigral* back. Then—" Her expression tautened. "There are some things you both need to know."

* * *

Jenny nodded slowly as Owen finished his story. The parlor of the big farmhouse on Benevolent Street was uncharacteristically quiet. Justin, Belinda, their children, Molly Mazzini and the d'Ursuras girls had been called away by the clanging bells—scattered books and a sink full of half-washed dishes told that story clearly enough—and had not yet returned. Three cups of tea and a teapot on the table between them completed the scene.

"That's fascinating," Jenny said. "Especially about Belasius. Some of the legends about Arthur talk of Merlin's teacher, a hermit called Bleys, who lived in the kingdom of Rheged."

"Might be the same person," said Owen.

"Did you know that Ludvig Prinn claimed to have met him?"

Owen and Laura looked startled. "That's not in *Mysteries of the Worm*," said Laura.

"No, it's not," Jenny agreed. "Prinn mentioned it in a letter to one of my ancestors, Jean-Paul d'Ursuras—it's in the library of the Université de Vyones now. He said he met *Bleis praeceptor Merlini* in the hills south of Carlisle when he was in Britain in 1437."

"Bleys, the teacher of Merlin," Owen said. "And Prinn's usually careful about history."

"He wouldn't have been human, would he?" Laura asked. "Bleys, I mean."

"Probably not," Jenny agreed. "Some humans live that long, but if you hear about someone doing that it's usually one of the elder races in disguise." She sat back in her chair. "What makes this interesting is that Arthur was caught up in the same war we're fighting. The Radiance in those days tried to sweep away every scrap of civilization in the West, so it wouldn't be able to hold out against the empires they were trying to build. They meant the Saxons to go straight across Britain and lay waste to Ireland. Arthur stopped them, with Merlin's help, and that's why Irish monks could spread learning all over Europe over the next few centuries."

Owen nodded slowly. "I hope you have the chance to meet Merlin," he said then.

"So do I." With a sudden smile: "If the legends are anything to go by, though, that'll happen when and if he wants it to." Jenny refilled three teacups, and her smile guttered. "I'm sorry to say the news I've got is less pleasant."

They gestured for her to go on, and she said, "I was delighted to hear about Tish—thank you for letting me know—and on a whim, before I tackled the rest of Chalmers' papers, I decided to find out about Barry and Kenji." To Laura: "I don't know if Owen's mentioned them—Barry Holzer was a housemate of ours when we were going to Miskatonic, and Kenji Nakamura was—well, 'friend' was what we thought. They got married right after they graduated." Laura nodded, and Jenny went on. "So I used a scrying spell, and I found them." She swallowed. "More precisely, I found their brains. They were just past the orbit of Mars."

"Oh my God," said Owen.

"I know." She stared at the table, or through it. "They weren't alone. The thing they were in was the size of an asteroid and it was chockfull of brain cylinders. I'm pretty sure there were other craft going the same way, more than a few of them."

"The squad officer mentioned that," Laura said after a moment of utter silence.

"Earth's number one export," said Jenny. "Yes. I don't know enough about astronomy to be sure where they were going, but it looked like they were headed for the outer solar system."

"Yuggoth," said Owen.

"That's my guess." She picked up her teacup, gave it a dubious look, set it down again. "There's a passage in the *Testament of Carnamagos* that suggests the Mi-Go use brains for computers. It's hard to be sure, since Carnamagos was writing two thousand years before humans first tried computer technology, but that's what it sounds like." With a bleak little laugh: "He said not to let the Mi-Go put your brain in a cylinder. 'Your brain shall be made a slave of theirs, laboring in numbers as in a mine or quarry'—that's what he wrote."

"Okay," said Owen. "So—all the empty towns I went through."

"That's part of it," said Jenny. "The economic crisis was another part."

"Do you have any idea who did that?" Owen asked. "I always figured it was the Radiance, but Mike Dyson said it wasn't and I believe him—and I know it wasn't our side."

"I think it was neither side," Jenny said. "Economies crash and civilizations fall—" She made a little helpless gesture. "The world is like that. But the Mi-Go took advantage of it, and harvested a lot of brains. You probably heard of those ads about jobs out west. I'm pretty sure they were doing it on an industrial scale: anesthetize a thousand at a time, extract the brains, incinerate the bodies, on to the next batch."

"The way we treat livestock," said Owen, wincing.

"Basically. They had other facilities in eastern Europe, India, some other places. I don't know how many people went into them, but it's probably a pretty stunning number."

No one spoke for a while. "I know it's selfish of me," Laura said then, "but I hope none of our people got taken."

"Not as far as I know," said Jenny. "It helps that so many of the people of the Great Old Ones weren't really part of the money economy when that was still going, but there's more to it than that. I met a woman in Buffalo who'd been thinking of going out west, and got warned against it by the Black Goat in a dream. I didn't know what to make of it. Of course now I do."

Another silence came and went. "So that's my news," Jenny said finally.

Owen considered her. "What now?"

"Off to campus to study the *Ghorl Nigral* and start putting the ritual together. I hope you can spare the time to help; it'll go a lot faster with two of us."

Owen glanced at Laura, read the answer in her eyes, nodded. "Of course. How soon?"

Before Jenny could answer, the front door rattled and opened, and footsteps sounded in the entry. Jenny got up, beaming. "Justin, Belinda—" Then they came into sight and she saw their faces. In a different tone: "What's wrong?"

"We've been down to see Josephine," said Belinda. "I know she's okay, but—" The sentence trickled away in a helpless gesture of tentacles. Jenny took that in, obviously baffled.

"Your younger niece," Owen told her, "and my son figured out between them how to make the same potion Mad Dan Morris used on Rose and Arthur. It's for the children, so the Nhhngr can't affect them." Turning to Justin and Belinda: "How many?"

"Barney said sixty-three," said Justin.

Jenny's expression, shifting slowly from horror to acceptance, reminded Owen intensely of the emotions he'd felt in the attic laboratory. "Yeah, I know," he said to Jenny. "We do what we have to." She met his gaze, nodded slowly.

CHAPTER 11

THE COLOR OUT OF SPACE

The stair up to the reading room echoed with footfalls as Owen and Jenny climbed it. Windows at each landing showed Arkham huddled beneath blue skies. Though the teams of initiates who kept watch gathered in chambers out of sight, and the young men who stood guard with more mundane weapons knew better than to show themselves, a tense silence gripped the town. It crouched, Owen thought, like a beast at bay.

They reached the top of the stair and Owen knocked on the old oaken door once, three times, once. A moment passed, and then a heavy lock slid open. Abelard opened the door; blue eyes glinted as he waved them in. "Yes, I thought the two of you would be here shortly," he said.

Upham Library's Van Kauran Reading Room, the place where the restricted collection was kept, couldn't have been less like the basement room beneath Orne Library if the builders who'd restored the old structure had arranged that on purpose. A square room with wooden bookcases lining the walls and long oaken tables occupying the center, it had clerestory windows and skylights with white glass overhead. Though he'd spent many hours there since his return to Arkham, Owen still felt a little jolt of surprise when the door opened onto filtered sunlight and dark varnish instead of gray steel bookshelves under fluorescent lamps.

As he came through the door, a familiar voice spoke: "*Prae-clare hoc actus.*" The words were Latin, of course: that was very well done. At a table nearby, a short man with a wispy white beard sat with a book of lore open before him. Voor blazed in him like lightning.

Merlin got to his feet. To Owen, he said in Latin, "I rejoice that you are well. It is a long road from Partridgeville." Then, to Jenny: "*Magistra.*" In his accented English: "Perhaps this tongue will be more suitable."

"My Latin's rusty," Jenny admitted. "Who are you?"

Merlin smiled. "I need not tell you that. Shall I prove myself by repeating what our father said to you when you came alive from Carcosa with the Ring of Eibon on your hand?"

She took that in. "Why are you here?"

"To assist you, of course. Our father knew long ago of the peril the world would face in this latter age, and willed that you have teachings of sorcery from before the *filii Lucis* destroyed so many of the old books. That I agreed to do—and once Charles Dexter Ward revived me, and I saw that other matters needed my attention, I took them in hand as well."

"You did that a lot for King Arthur, didn't you?" Owen asked.

Merlin glanced at him, and something stirred in the steel-gray eyes. "Arthur," he said. "Lucius Aurelius Artorius, we called him, but the hill tribes, my grandmother's people, said Arthwr the Bear. He was as tall as you—big enough to wrestle with giants, folk said." He laughed. Then, abruptly serious: "We have much to do. Abelard?"

The old librarian came over with a stack of four books. Owen recognized them at a glance: the *Ghorl Nigral*, the *Book of Eibon*, Prinn's *Mysteries of the Worm*, and the *Necronomicon*. Once they rested on the table beside Merlin, Abelard went back to his desk, returned with six manila folders stuffed with loose sheets of paper. He handed those to Jenny, who opened them. Owen, looking past her, recognized the contents at once: the papers Abelard Whipple had been working on since before Owen first visited the old restricted-collections room beneath Orne Library twenty years back.

"*Gratias ago tibi, magister*," Merlin said then, glancing up: I thank you, teacher. Then, in the same language: "When I asked you to take on this labor I knew you would not fail me." Abelard nodded, and then turned to Owen and motioned him away to the far end of the room.

"They'll be busy until sometime tomorrow," Abelard told Owen in a low voice. "She'll have to learn the principles of the greater sorcery, and then the two of them will construct the ritual that might save us all. He'll send you a message when they're done."

"Those papers were what you've been doing all these years," Owen said. He thought of Abelard's seeming ageless-ness and Merlin's words, and realized what scent he'd caught on the stairs that morning. "Abelard," he said then. "When did Merlin ask you to do that research?"

The librarian's blue eyes turned to him. "A very long time ago."

"When you were called Belasius."

A slow smile spread across the librarian's face. "Good," he said. "Very good. Not the first human name I've taken, just as Abelard Whipple will doubtless not be the last." Glancing at him: "I wonder if you've guessed what I am."

"The poison was kind of a broad hint," said Owen. "Serpent folk?"

Without warning, the old man next to him vanished. In his place stood a mighty shape fully eight feet tall. Muscles rippled beneath a skin covered with mottled green scales. Hooked claws, each sufficient to disembowel a man, tipped three-fingered hands and three-toed feet, and a muscular tail swept behind. Eyes like polished black stones regarded Owen from a viper's head; two long fangs arced down from the upper jaw.

"It hass been usseful to me," said the creature, "that sso many over the yearss have underesstimated my sstrength." A blink of an eye, and Abelard Whipple stood beside him again.

Owen took that in. "Does anyone else know?"

"Of course. Miriam knows—that was necessary, so she'd understand the defenses I've placed on the library—and I'm tolerably sure Jenny has guessed. And of course Merlin."

"You taught him," said Owen. "Merlin, I mean."

The bright blue eyes glanced at Owen again. "As I taught Jenny." With a shrug: "Merlin knew me when it wasn't quite so necessary for my people to hide themselves. Do you recall the title Pendragon? In Welsh it was once *Pen y Dynion Ddraig*, 'chief of the serpent people.' Uther and his son were not of our people but they earned our loyalty, thus the title."

"I'd like to hear that story sometime," said Owen.

"If we're still alive a week from now, I'll tell it," said Abelard. "And if all turns out well, more of my people may just come to Arkham. That wouldn't surprise me at all."

"They'll be welcome here," said Owen.

"I know. That's why they'll come." Then: "You should go. There's much still to be done before the Nhhngr descends."

* * *

Silence huddled in Arkham's streets as Owen hurried back home from the university. Once he was inside, the smell of fish chowder helped him feel a little less lost; so did the long close embrace Laura gave him. So, in its own way, did the sudden *whump* from upstairs that shook the house timbers. "Barney and Sylvia have been busy for hours now," Laura explained once he settled on the sofa. "Noah Bishop found them more of the chemicals. So they're sure they can take care of all the children and have some left over."

"That's really good to hear," said Owen. "Do you know where Sennie is?"

"I've got my suspicions," said Laura, and Owen laughed.

"After dinner," she went on a little later, "they'll be waiting for me at the lodge hall. I'd much rather spend this evening with you, but—"

"But you're the Grand Priestess and they need you." He took her hands. "The only reason I'm not heading for church this evening is that Billie's the senior initiate and I'm not."

"I'll be back as soon as I can," she promised. "Do you know what Jenny's planning?"

For once, he didn't have to force a smile "She's in the restricted stacks getting lessons in sorcery from Merlin. Abelard says the two of them are going to draft a ritual together."

Laura shook her head. "I'm still trying to fit my head around the idea of Merlin alive and here in Arkham. Do you think we can invite him over for dinner, once all this is over?"

He threw his head back and laughed, a great rolling laugh that rattled the windows. "Thank you," he said then. "I don't know, but I promise I'll ask him."

The warm confident mood the laugh brought him stayed with him as the day slid past. A little past five, Barnabas and Sylvia came down the stairs, looking tired but pleased; she said her goodbyes and hurried home, he explained that they'd finished making the potion and another two thousand, five hundred eleven pounds of human flesh could be turned to stone the next day.

"And the antidote?" Laura asked.

"We've made that already," Barnabas said. "It takes a lot less of that per pound, and the chemicals are easy to get, so we made three times more than we need. One batch goes with Michaelmas, one goes down with the children in a sealed glass bottle, and we're still figuring out where to put the third batch. One way or another it'll be there when it's needed."

"Thank you, Barney," she said then.

He looked away, but grinned. "Sure thing, Mom."

Asenath hadn't come home yet when dinner was ready, so it was just four of them, Owen, Laura, Barnabas, and Pierre, sitting around a table well stocked with chowder, salad, home-made bread, and raw fish done Innsmouth style. By unspoken agreement they didn't talk about the one thing that was on all their minds, and so the evening went pleasantly. After dinner was over and the washing up was done, Pierre made his little crouching bow and headed for his room in the basement, and Barnabas gave his parents a hug each and climbed the stairs. Laura went into their bedroom, got the nine-tasseled stole of a Grand Priestess of the Esoteric Order of Dagon, wheeled out again and gave Owen a kiss. A few minutes later she was gone, and Owen sat on the sofa and stared blankly out the windows at the gathering evening.

After a little while he got up, went to the bookshelf, and came back with an old favorite, Justin Geoffrey's *The People of the Monolith*. When he opened the book, he found no solace:

> Until those cold bright hieroglyphs on high
> Come right at last and set the Old Ones free,
> That is not dead which can eternal lie,
> And with strange eons even death may die.

He clenched his eyes shut. Before he could do anything else, a knock at the door provided a welcome distraction; he hauled himself up from the sofa, went to the door, and found Justin Martense waiting outside. He waved him inside, said, "What's up?"

"Jenny's on campus, Belinda's at the lodge hall, I was going slowly crazy staring at the walls, and I figured you probably were doing the same thing."

Owen let out a harsh laugh. "Close enough." The two of them went into the parlor; Owen waved Justin to a seat, then asked, "Beer, or—"

"Or," Justin said. "Definitely or."

Owen went into the kitchen, came back with a bottle of local whiskey and a couple of glasses, and finally processed what his friend had said. "Hold it. Belinda's at the *lodge hall*?"

Justin nodded. "She finally decided to go ahead and rejoin the Esoteric Order of Dagon. Once all this is over and everything's calmed down again, I'll probably apply for membership too." He raised the glass Owen had just filled for him. "Cheers to whoever made sure the Order's meetings don't conflict with Starry Wisdom church services."

Owen raised his glass, tapped it against Justin's. "Laura and I'd both been in a fix if we'd done anything else. Not just us, either, these days." He downed a swallow of the whiskey, let it round the edges of his fractured mood. "I'm glad to hear that about Belinda."

"She misses the services," Justin said. "She doesn't talk about it much, but especially since she got Laura's book—" A shrug punctuated the sentence. "Most of the people who made things so ugly for her after the business at Dunwich are gone now, and the rest don't want Laura to rip their ears off. Which she would, bless her."

Owen nodded and raised his glass, acknowledging the point. A companionable silence passed, and then he asked, "Any idea where Sennie is?"

Justin chuckled. "Well, yes." Owen shot him a hard glance, and he went on. "I figured it's nobody's business but theirs. You know Belinda got her stepmom's engagement ring? She gave it to Robin a week ago after a long talk. I'll let you guess why." When Owen's gaze didn't falter: "Don't you dare tell me that you and Laura waited until you were married."

Owen relented. "No," he admitted. "We didn't quite wait for me to propose."

That got him a grin in response. "Neither did we. Those two are really well suited to each other, like you and Laura." He held out his empty glass.

"And you and Belinda," Owen said, refilling it and then his own.

They talked about other things while the night deepened. "If you can do it," Justin said after a while. "If you and Jenny wake the Dreaming Lord and all the prophecies come true ..." His voice faltered for a moment. "What happens then?"

"I have no idea. I don't think anybody does." That was true, too, and it reminded him of what Judy Heffler had said in the warehouse where the prisoners still waited. Even the most daring of the old tomes, when they spoke of Great Cthulhu's awakening, drew back from guessing what he would do once he rose from drowned R'lyeh. Maybe, Owen thought, not even Great Cthulhu knows what he'll do.

"I actually sat down and read some H.P. Lovecraft the other day," said Justin then. "You know what he said about what happens when Cthulhu awakes, right? 'Then mankind would have become as the Great Old Ones; free and wild and beyond good and evil, with laws and morals thrown aside and all men shouting and killing and reveling in joy.'"

Owen snorted in derision. "Yeah." Then: "The thing is, laws and morals are just fancy names for the rules people work out so they can get along. You don't go around killing people, because people don't want to be killed and they'll shoot you if you try—that's where laws come from. You don't cheat your friends, because you don't want them to tell you to get lost—that's where morals come from. Humans followed rules like that long before the seven temples were desecrated." He sipped whiskey. "The elder races did the same thing when R'lyeh was still above water. So I don't worry about that."

"Okay," said Justin. Then, considering him: "What do you worry about?"

"Other than the obvious?" When Justin nodded: "What kind of a world we'll be in once the Great Old Ones do whatever they decide to do with it."

"I get that," said Justin.

* * *

After another hour or so, when the clock warned that the rituals at the Esoteric Order of Dagon lodge hall would be winding down soon, Justin made his unsteady way home. Maybe ten minutes later, the latch of the front door clicked, the door opened with barely a whisper and closed again, and Asenath came into the parlor. She looked dazed and rumpled, and her hair was a tangled mess, as though she'd tried to smooth it with her fingers and given up the attempt halfway through. She didn't seem to notice her father at first, and got halfway across the parlor before she glanced his way in surprise and let out a little wordless cry.

By then, Owen had seen the gleam on the third finger of her left hand. He'd thought of a dozen different things to say to her, but what came out was, "Good evening, Sennie. Nice ring."

She blinked, and then reddened. "Thank you, Dad. It's—"

"Annabelle's. I recognize it." He didn't, but it seemed wiser to avoid an explanation. "I'll let your mother know you're home once she gets back," he said, and made a shooing motion toward the stairs. She beamed at him, stopped on the first step and looked back at him. "You're the best dad anybody ever had," she said. "I mean that."

Moments later she was gone, and after a decent interval the house's elderly plumbing gurgled and hissed. Owen tried to turn his attention back to *The People of the Monolith*, and failed. Memories surged again, drew him back twenty years to his first encounters with Laura: the autumn morning in Innsmouth when he realized how much he needed her, the afternoon a few days later when they'd made love for the first time, the night journey that brought the two of them to Dunwich and the beginning of their life together. Now, if the little Earth survived, it would be Asenath's and Robin's place to set the cycle turning again. If—

He was still brooding over that when the front door opened a little less stealthily and Laura came in. He got up, greeted her with a kiss, helped her out of the wheelchair onto the sofa. She let out a long ragged sigh and, once he sat next to her, slumped against him. "The most astonishing thing happened," she said then.

"Belinda?" When she gave him a startled look: "Justin came by earlier."

She nodded, slid an arm around his waist; he bent and kissed the top of her head. "Yes," she said. "I've hoped for years that she would return to the order someday." Then, glancing up at him: "And after the ceremony she mentioned a bit of news about my stepmom's ring."

"Sennie had it on her hand when she got home this evening."

Laura nodded, closed her eyes, smiled. "Not that it's any kind of surprise, but I'm happy for them both. If things work out we can have the wedding as soon as they're ready."

"If," he said. After a moment he burst out: "I just wish that for once, we could live without something hanging over us. The Radiance, or—"

"I know," she said. "You didn't grow up with that."

Embarrassed by his own outburst, he didn't answer.

"Owen." She was looking up at him, the way she'd done all those years ago in the house north of Arkham where they'd first made love. "Do you regret it?"

He considered that. "No," he said finally. "Not at all. We've had twenty really good years together." That earned a wistful smile from her, but he went on. "And if I'd gone down the other road, the way I expected to go, I'd be facing the same thing anyway, with no idea what was happening and no way to do anything about it."

She reached for him, drew him down into a kiss.

Later, she nestled down into their bed, closed her eyes. He bent over her, kissed her cheek, slipped on pajamas, and left the room. Sleep was still far from him, and so he found his way mostly by feel across the unlit house to the stair, and up to his study. Darkness framing Asenath's door told him that she and Rachel had gone to the Dreamlands as usual, and a thin line of lamplight under Barnabas' told him that his son was awake: bent over his desk, no doubt, with some obscure volume of nineteenth-century hyperphysics open in front of him. Owen smiled, went into his study and closed the door behind him.

He thought about lighting the lamp by his own desk, but walked to the window instead, looked out over Arkham's silent roofs, black and huddled under the stars. A few dim lights gleamed in windows, that was all.

Then a different light streamed upwards from a building off in the middle distance. At first he tensed, wondering if a fire had broken out, but the light shone pale as the moon. Beams shot out through skylights, surging and fading, and then rising in a crescendo to dazzling intensity before fading out into a blackness that endured.

Voor came rippling past him in the night. That was when he realized that the building from which the rays of light had risen was Upham Library, and knew that Jenny and Merlin were still at their labors. He watched the light and the voor for a time, then picked his way back down stairs, settled down next to Laura, and sank into troubled sleep.

Only one dream remained in his memory when he woke the next morning. In the dream he wandered through dark tunnels, passing silent shapes of gray stone. Most of them were children, but here and there he passed people he'd known: Laura's parents Annabelle and Jeff Marsh, Justin's Aunt Josephine, Larry's Grandma Pakheng, Cicely Moore from Chorazin, and others. The last of them was the woman he'd glimpsed on the way north with Nyarlathotep, the one who'd brought a meal and received a blessing. She stood the way she'd been standing when Owen saw her last, hands clasped to her chest, a look of awed delight on her face.

Then he passed beyond the stone figures, into a greater darkness. Something waited, something that he knew was ancient beyond memory before the stars spawned Great Cthulhu, a half-shapeless presence that gazed down at him with heavy-lidded eyes lit from within like coals. *Hali called you,* said something that was not a voice. *I made the plan that brought you into being. The Crawling Chaos, the Black Goat, Yhoundeh, Phauz, Basa-tan, they guided you. Now comes the hour on which all depends. Are you prepared?*

There was only one answer he could make. "No," he said aloud, "but I'll do what I can."

The smoldering eyes met his gaze, but the not-voice said nothing.

Then Owen blinked awake, to find himself lying in bed next to Laura. The first cold light of the new day trickled in through the window. He drew in a long unsteady breath, sat up, bent to kiss Laura as she slept, and then got up to face what had to be done.

* * *

Afterward, looking back on the last day before the Nhhngr came, Owen recalled only bright splintered images tumbling past one another:

"I met Phauz in the Dreamlands," Asenath said, shoulders hunched, eyes fixed on the floor. They were all were sitting in the parlor after breakfast. "We talked, and she showed me how—how to do what Merlin did, and open a door to Melirul. And—and she told me I could take one other person with me—just one. Mom, Dad—"

"You're going to take Robin, of course." Laura said at once. Asenath looked up at her with wide eyes, then clenched her eyes shut and nodded.

"Sennie, dear," Laura went on, "of course you are. Your father needs to help your Aunt Jenny, your brother has to take care of the children, and I—" Her voice wavered for an instant, and Owen knew her well enough to sense the dread and grief she'd been keeping in check since the news first came. "If things don't go the way we hope, my place as a priestess is here, to do what I can to make things a little easier for the members of the order, for as long as I can."

Asenath started crying, got up and crossed the room to where her mother sat and gave her a long tearful hug. Owen got another, and Barnabas a brief awkward squeeze. Then Asenath sat, dabbed at her eyes with a handkerchief, and drew together the shreds of her self-control.

"How soon will you go?" Owen asked her.

"I don't know yet," she admitted. "I have to talk to Robin— but it's going to be today."

Again, two hours later, Owen and a dozen elders sat in the old classroom underneath the Esoteric Order of Dagon lodge hall, facing twenty or so teenagers whose red eyes and tense resolute faces said most of what needed saying. "We've got all the kids under twelve taken care of," Sylvia d'Ursuras was saying. "And we've got enough left for fourteen of us and two adults. The others decided Barney and I should take the potion, because we know how to make the antidote if more has to be made once we get revived. They drew straws to choose the other twelve, and then everyone voted on which two adults to choose."

"I'm going to risk a guess," Billie Whateley said. "Mr. and Mrs. Martense."

That got the first smiles Owen had seen on the teenagers' faces in days. "Yeah," said Sylvia. "All the kids think they're really nice. It'll mean a lot to have them there if we wake up after a couple of hundred years, and everything else has changed."

"How soon will you be going down to the tunnels?" asked Noah Bishop.

"As soon as we're done talking here," Barnabas answered.

That called down a hard-edged silence. Susannah Eliot broke it, hauling herself to her feet and saying, "Well, I hope you can spare the time to get a blessing."

Barnabas ducked his head and said, "Please." He knelt, and Susannah placed her hands on his head and murmured words in the Deep One language. Owen got up then and so did Billie Whateley, and they began giving a blessing in Aklo to the teens who came from Starry Wisdom families. Then fourteen-year-old Rebecca Waite, whose parents had been born in Innsmouth, asked Owen for his blessing; Amos Moore, a big sixteen-year-old from Chorazin, asked the same favor from Susannah; Sylvia, whose family came from drowned Poseidonis and belonged to neither tradition, knelt with a luminous smile and received both; and Teresa Chonle finished blessing the three Tcho-Tchos, beamed, and blessed each of the other teenagers as well. A barrier had fallen, Owen knew, and if any of them survived, something had been kindled that would spread and grow in the years to come.

Again, maybe an hour after that, Owen picked his way down crumbling stone stairs that were old centuries before the first white settlers came to Arkham. The flashlight in his hand did little to shift the weight of the darkness around him. The Arkham he knew was far above, wrapped in a growing silence as its inhabitants braced themselves for the Nhhngr.

"This way," said Barnabas, just in front of him, and gestured with his flashlight beam. Tunnels led in three directions from the foot of the stair; Barnabas went into the leftward tunnel, and Owen followed. Behind came thirteen teenagers and more than twice as many adults.

After a short distance, the tunnel ended in a space too regular and smooth-walled to be a cavern. There the children sat in ragged rows. Owen recalled with aching clarity the first time he'd seen Arthur and Rose Wheeler, on display in a small-town tourist trap: the same perfection of detail down to the last stray hair, the same desolate stillness. The children before him were dressed in warm clothing; some of them clutched stuffed animals, blankets, or some other keepsake; most of the older children looked frightened, most of the younger ones confused.

"Here," said Barnabas, turning to face the others. A few words of attemped comfort, a few embraces and kisses, and twelve teenagers sat. Working together, Sylvia and Barnabas measured out doses into beakers from a big bottle of brown glass, and one at a time the twelve drank. Owen knew what would happen, but it was still hard to watch the stiffening, the graying of the skin, the blankness spread across the eyes. It was harder still to watch family members try to keep their feelings in check as they backed slowly away.

Justin and Belinda sat down next. Belinda had Annabelle with her; she spoke quietly with Sylvia, extracted a baby bottle from her purse, gave it to Sylvia and got it back a few moments later with a dose of the potion. The nipple of the bottle went into Annabelle's mouth, guided a little clumsily by mouth-tentacles, and Belinda clenched her eyes shut as the change took place. Without opening her eyes, she reached out a tentacle, and Barnabas gave her a beaker. She drank it, and got her arm-tentacles curled around the baby just before the change took her as well. Justin watched the process, then got his dose, raised it in an ironic toast, and drank.

"Your turn?" Owen asked his son as Justin finished changing.

"Yeah." He went past the children to the stone wall, got a glass bottle full of golden fluid and a sealed jar, brought them back with him while Sylvia said her goodbyes to a little knot of Chaudronniers and d'Ursurases—her grandfather Martin, her parents Charlotte and Alain, and her older sister Emily. Her brother Geoffrey was already among the silent shapes.

"What's in the jar?" Owen asked.

"An atomizer and instructions," said Barnabas. "If something happens to Michaelmas, once somebody else finds us down here, they'll be able to use it."

"Smart," said Owen, and Barnabas grinned. Owen gave him a hug, let go of him.

Sylvia sat down, extracted the silent gray shape of her kyrrmi from her purse, and then smiled at Barnabas. The boy measured out the last of the potion into two beakers and sat beside her. He downed his dose without hesitating, set the beaker down, and got his hands on his thighs before the change took him. Sylvia got Wilbur settled in her lap, drank her dose more slowly, and reached over to put one of her hands on top of one of his before she stiffened and went gray.

Owen turned away, then, suppressing a shudder. The Chaudronniers met his gaze, and Martin nodded. Without a word, he joined them, and they went back up to the surface.

* * *

Again, as morning drew on toward noon and clouds rolled in over the hills west of town, another set of farewells: Asenath's and Robin's. Asenath's face was swollen with tears, Robin's pale and composed. "Here's the antidote," Owen said, hefting an old nylon backpack. In it, wrapped in blankets, was the third bottle Barnabas had prepared, and another atomizer in an airtight jar. "One way or another, once Great Cthulhu wakes and the barriers between the lesser earths unravel, you can cross back." The two of them knew that as well as Owen did, and Owen knew as much, but repeating the words helped keep his dread at bay for the moment.

Robin took the backpack, shouldered it and got it settled. While he was busy with that, Asenath went to give her mother one final hug, and started crying again.

"If things work out," Owen said to Robin, "I'll look forward to having you as a son-in-law." He made himself go on. "And if things don't work out—please take good care of her."

Robin met his gaze squarely. "I will, Mr. Merrill—and thank you." Owen clapped him on the shoulder and forced a grin. Robin went to say something to Laura, and then Asenath flung herself into her father's arms with enough force that Owen had to draw his head back to keep from getting a faceful of kyrrmi. Rachel chirred apologetically at him, and he patted Asenath on the shoulders, said the expected things, tried to give her what comfort he could.

She drew back, made herself smile up at him. "Give our best to the Wards," Owen said, and she promised she would and turned away. A complex diagram in chalk already waited. She pointed her right forefinger at it and repeated seven words Owen didn't know. Green light flared in the midst of the diagram, and the lines opened up into immeasurable spaces. Asenath gripped one of Robin's arms and stepped forward. Green light flared once more, and Laura and Owen were alone in the parlor. He turned to face her, but he could find no words to say.

Again, a little after noon, as he gathered up the dishes from lunch, a tapping came at the kitchen window. Owen looked up, startled. A big raven perched on the windowsill, peering in with one beady black eye. As Owen watched, it tapped on the window again, and eyed him.

Guessing why the bird was there, Owen opened the window, and it clambered inside and hopped to the top of the kitchen faucet, where it gave Owen another close look and let out its croaking cry. There was a word in the cry: "Now."

"Merlin sent you, I bet," Owen said to it.

The raven gave him a curt little nod, and made another cry. In it was the word "Aye."

"Okay," said Owen. "I'm on my way."

The raven nodded again, just as curtly, then hopped back out the window and flew away. Owen turned to Laura, who had watched the whole exchange from beside the kitchen table.

"I'm impressed," Laura said. "Tell Jenny she's welcome to have dinner with us—and of course that goes for Merlin too."

"I'll tell them both," promised Owen, gave her a kiss and headed for the front door.

Then, finally, he stood at the foot of the stair that led to the restricted-collections room. He wasn't the only one who waited. Miriam was there, so was Martin Chaudronnier, so was Abelard Whipple, and so was Will Bishop. Will greeted him with a grin and said, "They ought to be down any minute now. It's been something to watch."

"What's been happening?" Owen asked.

"Voor," said Will. "I'm pretty sure that space has two more dimensions than I thought."

"If we survive this," Owen said, "you should tell that to Barney one of these days."

Will grinned. "I'm going to be counting the days until Barney starts classes here. I talked to Matt Waite the other day, and he says he's got Barney doing five-dimensional Lobachevskian geometry in his math class, and lapping it up. You've got one smart—"

He fell silent, and an instant later Owen heard footsteps on the stairs. He looked up, sensed the searing intensity of Merlin's voor, and then noticed another center of voor, even more brilliant: blinding as a magnesium flare, but fading out into violet at the edges. Only when she came into sight was Owen sure that the second center of voor was Jenny.

Through his eyes, she looked no different. He tried to square that with the coruscating glory his voor-sense showed him, and finally understood: the alchemies that roused Merlin to a second sorcerous life and the longevity of the serpent folk had swept aside the machinations of the Radiance and brought Jenny all that she needed to become the sorceress she was capable of being, fit to stand beside Haon-Dor, Eibon, Malygris, and Merlin. He bowed to her as she reached the foot of the stairs, and she gave him a startled look, then said, "Don't you dare."

Merlin, for his part, sized up in a glance the ones who awaited him. He bowed to Martin as he would have bowed to a king of sixth-century Britain, and said "*Dominus.*" Next he bowed to the professors, less deeply, and said "*Magistri.*" To Owen, he gave the smile of a companion on the road and said in Latin, "I thank you for all that you have done. Are you prepared?"

"As well as I can be," Owen said in the same language, smiling too despite his fears.

"We've done everything we need to do," Jenny said then. "There's a little more than twenty-eight hours left before the Nhhngr descends."

"Can you stop it?" Miriam asked pointblank.

"Maybe," Jenny replied. "I'm going to try."

"And I," said Merlin, "will go now to prepare the way. It occurs to me that certain enchantments will be useful to keep you safe while the work proceeds." He bowed to her, and before she could respond, knotted his fingers together in a complex pattern and vanished.

As the others stared, Owen gave Jenny a sidelong glance and said, "Can you do that?"

"I know the principles." She shrugged. "Someday, maybe."

"No doubt." More immediate concerns pressed forward in his mind. "I don't know if you're free, but Laura wanted me to ask you to dinner tonight."

"Please," said Jenny. "We have some things to talk about."

"I hope you can spare a little time before then," said Martin, with a troubled smile.

"Of course I can." To Owen: "Seven, maybe?"

CHAPTER 12

THE ENDING OF THE WEIRD

A brief flurry of rain drummed on the windows as Owen got the dishes in the sink. It was just the three of them now, Owen, Laura, and Jenny, bringing together the threads they'd begun to spin eighteen years ago, twisting them into a cord that might possibly save a world.

He went back to the table as Laura poured herb tea. "The two of us weren't alone in the library," Jenny was saying. "Tsathoggua joined us. Did you know that he's the god of sorcery?"

"'As Hastur is king of the Great Old Ones and Cthulhu their high priest,'" Laura quoted, "'Tsathoggua is their sorcerer, and all who were mightiest in sorcery studied it in his school.'"

The sorceress nodded, sipped from her cup. "That's from the *Testament of Carnamagos*, isn't it? I thought so. But it's more than that. My father's been preparing for this since Cthulhu and the King first quarreled, long before our ancestors crawled out of the sea onto dry land. He foresaw it all." A gesture gathered up more than two millennia of terrible events. "The ironic thing is that I figured out the thing that mattered most before he appeared to us."

"That," Laura said, "doesn't surprise me at all."

Jenny blushed. "A lot of it was Owen's doing." She turned toward Owen. "I started from the second thing in Halpin Chalmers I showed you before you went to Partridgeville."

"Something about spirals and whorls and a treasure house," said Owen.

"'The treasure houses of them that dwell below,'" Jenny quoted. "That phrase reminded me of something I'd read a few years ago. It took me a while to chase it down, but I found it in some back issues of *Notes and Queries*. It's a curious story. Somebody named Charles Selby got a stone tablet around 1875 from a rural family near Caermaen in Wales, and wrote to *Notes and Queries* asking for help with it. He included some of the writing, and it's the same script as the tablet Léon Muñoz gave me. The discussion went on for years, and finally in 1894 an ethnologist named William Gregg published a partial translation of that one line. Then you sent Chalmers' notes back from Partridgeville, and after a long night I had the whole text deciphered.

"It was mostly a list of places and the moon paths that connect them," Jenny went on. "But it's easier to show you the thing that matters." She took a map of eastern North America from her purse, started to unfold it. Owen took one end, and they got it spread out on the table.

"Look at the pattern," Jenny said, pointing to places on the map. "Arkham, Kingsport, Innsmouth. West through Lefferts Corners to Chorazin and on into Ohio. South by Providence and New York City through New Jersey and into Virginia. North through Maine into the Maritimes. What shape does it make?"

Laura saw it first. "Father Dagon," she breathed. "The Sign of Koth."

"Exactly," said Jenny.

Owen leaned forward, considered the map. "Okay," he said. "And the moon paths were put there by the serpent folk back in the Permian. I wonder why they did that."

"Tsathoggua had them do it," said Jenny. "So it could be used in our time."

Laura glanced up. "You'd need to find the eye to do that."

"I already have," said Jenny, "and that was what showed me what all this is about. The eye of the Sign of Koth, the point from which you have to begin tracing it to awaken its power, is on top of one of the cliffs by Kingsport, the one called Neptune's Head." She leaned forward. "That's why Basatan lives on Kingsport Head. Have you ever wondered why one of the Great Old Ones lived for so long in that one little corner of this one little Earth?" Owen gestured for her to go on, and she said, "He's there to guard the eye of the Sign of Koth."

"Why?" Owen asked.

"What do you do with the Sign of Koth?" she asked in response. Before he could answer: "You use it to reverse a spell."

Then he understood, and his eyes went round.

"Exactly," she said again. "That was the secret all along— the secret of the moon paths, the secret of the Weird of Hali, the thing that sent both of us to Chorazin and Red Hook and sent you to Providence, the reason why the Radiance spent centuries trying to control this corner of the planet and the people of the Great Old Ones kept on being sent here to try to loosen their grip. If I traced the Sign of Koth in front of the Seal of the Abyss that wouldn't do enough to bother, but with the Sign already traced in the living voor of the Earth across lands and seas, and the voor flowing freely for the first time in millions of years, that's another matter. If it's done in the right way it can break the Seal and set Cthulhu free."

Owen stared at her, then at the map. "That's what Chalmers was talking about."

"Yes. 'The secret is in the earth.' It's not something buried, it's the pattern of the moon paths themselves. That's what will free the Dreaming Lord if anything can."

"Can you do it?" Laura asked her.

Owen and Jenny both turned from the map to her. "Maybe," said Jenny. "I know what has to be done, and I think I can do it, but—" She glanced at both of them. "There aren't any guarantees. If I can do what I have in mind, it's going to be the most difficult work of sorcery any human has ever done. If I can't—" She shrugged. "This isn't the kind of magic you walk away from. If it fails, I won't survive, and neither will anyone else who takes part in it."

In the silence that followed, Jenny looked at the map and Laura looked at Owen. He returned the glance, saw the answer to his question in her eyes before he could ask it, and turned to Jenny. "Let me know what you need and I'll do it."

Jenny glanced at Laura, saw the same unyielding acceptance in her face, then closed her eyes and nodded. "Thank you," she said aloud.

He nodded. "How soon do you want to start?"

"First thing tomorrow." Meeting his gaze: "Michaelmas can drive us down to Kingsport—the Cadillac's still got that many miles in it, and we've got the gas." She forced a smile. "From there, it's an easy trip up to Neptune's Head."

"I'm good with that," Owen said. He reached out to Laura, felt her hand curl around his.

* * *

That night, after Jenny went back home, he and Laura made love, slowly and deliberately, savoring their time together. Afterwards, lying in a tangle of limbs and tentacles and mingled scents, Owen recalled the passion and frantic haste of their first couplings. If it all ended in the days ahead, his life snuffed out in the ritual Jenny had in mind, hers trickling away beneath the horror of the Nhhngr, it still felt as though the circle was complete. Laura's question rose in his memory, and he choked back laughter. Regret was the last thing on his mind just then.

Morning came too soon. They shared a breakfast of chowder and raw fish, held each other for a time that was not long enough. Then she got into her wheelchair, drew in an unsteady breath, and said, "I'll send out word to the other lodges of the Order, and to as many others on our side as I can. Their prayers and spells will be with you—and so will mine."

He thanked her and kissed her, made himself smile and stand there in the entry as she wheeled out the door and headed for the lodge hall, then went back inside. His revolver went into his jacket pocket. Then he went into their bedroom, dug in one of his dresser drawers, and found a relic twenty years old: a flat packet of red cloth fastened to a loop of red cord. Abigail Price, the old witch of Pickman's Corners, had made it for him one fall morning, filling the packet with leaves the Black Goat of the Woods had blessed, and he'd kept it safe down through the years since then so that it still had power to protect him. He slipped the cord over his head, got the packet settled under his shirt, and left the room.

When he went out the front door Laura was out of sight, which was a small mercy. He turned and set out for Jenny's house. Arkham spread out around him in silence beneath a cold blue sky. He had never noticed before how much the voices of children marked the difference between a living town and a dead one. The thought that all Arkham's children sat in the tunnels far under the town, cold and silent as stones, sent a feeling like ice down his spine.

He saw the old Cadillac parked in front of Jenny's house long before he got there. By the time he'd crossed the street to the block her house was on, the door had opened and Jenny and Michaelmas came out onto the sidewalk. The house they left felt silent as a tomb, and Owen thought of two other cold still figures below.

"Good morning, Mr. Merrill," said Michaelmas, impeccable as always. Owen returned the greeting, exchanged silent nods with Jenny. Michaelmas climbed behind the wheel as Owen and Jenny settled into the back seat. No more words needed saying. The engine grumbled to life, and the Cadillac headed for Peabody Avenue and the road to Kingsport.

There had been a mall beside Old Kingsport Highway when he'd first come to Arkham, Owen recalled dimly, but no trace of it remained. Willows and pines clustered along the roadside once the highway started to climb out of the Miskatonic Valley, and if some of the roots thrust aside dark shapes, he couldn't tell if they were fragments of a broken parking lot or masses of stone from Valusian times. Further up the willows grew thicker, and the highway plunged into country not even the toughest of the old colonists had tried to settle, a land of bleak barren hills where everything human seemed worlds or ages away. Miles passed, and at length scattered farmhouses appeared in sheltered hollows. Most of them had been repainted in the past few years, but they crouched silent now behind shuttered windows and bolted doors.

Finally the Cadillac came out from under the trees and what was left of Kingsport spread below, a waning crescent of empty buildings around a harbor swollen with the rising seas. The line of hotels along Harbor Street had become a belt of crumpled ruins pounded by the surf, and not even that much remained of the old marina and the maritime district behind it. The route Owen and Laura had used all the years they'd lived in Dunwich and summered in Kingsport was half gone now, and Michaelmas turned up unfamiliar streets toward Bluff Road, which ran along the crest of the hills past Hooper's Pond and an old brick powder-house to the ridge above the Miskatonic River. There he could see Arkham across miles of river and meadow, the white Georgian steeples in the sunlight blazing like beacons against the hills north of town.

Then he glanced up, and his blood ran suddenly cold.

In the far distance, off beyond the distant hills, a faint shuddering light troubled the blue of the sky. It reminded Owen of an aurora, but the color belonged to no earthly spectrum.

"I know," Jenny said in a low voice next to him. He glanced at her, and she went on: "It came through the magnetosphere over the north pole late last night. It's spreading across the upper atmosphere right now, and once it gets to the south pole, down it comes." Despite it all, she managed a smile. "So we have more than enough time for the ritual."

He could hear in her voice the immensities they meant to challenge, the thin and fragile hope that was all they had left. Cold terror shot through him, but he would not let it touch his expression or his voice. "Good," he said. "Let's do it."

Her smile brightened. "That's the plan."

A few minutes later Michaelmas turned right onto the one-lane road that climbed up the hills to the landward side of Kingsport Head. Tall pines stretched their boughs over the road and mercifully blotted out the sky. Owen cleared his mind, braced himself for the work before him.

The car rounded another curve, slowed, and stopped. A glance through the windshield showed why: a landslide had come crashing down to block half the road.

Michaelmas got out of the car, opened the door on Jenny's side. Owen, impatient, opened his own door and climbed out onto the fractured blacktop. A glance at the other side of the car warned him that his presence was briefly unwelcome, and he walked a short distance away, breathed in salt air as it rushed through the pines.

"Miss Jenny," said Michaelmas then, "may I say it has been a pleasure to know you."

"Thank you, Michaelmas," Jenny said indistinctly. Then: "If everything goes well, I'll see you in Arkham in a few days at most."

"I'll look forward to that, Miss Jenny," said the butler. He climbed back into the driver's seat. Jenny moved away, and the Cadillac backed up, made a smart turn, and headed back down the road. Owen could hear the growl of the motor as it headed back toward Arkham.

"Okay," Jenny said then. Despite the keening of the wind, her voice seemed unexpectedly loud. "It's not much further to Neptune's Head."

* * *

They did not hurry. There was no point in hurrying, though the shuddering glow in the upper air had spread over a quarter of the sky by the time they reached the place where they needed to be. There was work to be done, and enough time to do it. When it was over, either the two of them would be dead and the lesser Earth would die soon thereafter, or—

Or the Weird of Hali would be fulfilled.

"The altar needs to be found, not made," Jenny said as the road stopped in a thicket of shore pines. Refuse dumped there over the decades rose up in low mounds: defunct mattresses, broken furniture, a dead appliance or two. "That's the one thing we need."

"How about that?" said Owen, motioning at a rust-streaked white shape near them. It proved to be a refrigerator of the sort students used in dorms, small enough to tuck under a desk.

"That'll do. Do you think you can carry it?"

He settled the question by heaving the thing up from the ground. It took some scrambling to get it through the thicket, but a few minutes later they came out from under the pines and climbed up the last ragged slope to the bare top of the cliff named Father Neptune.

Seen from the crest, ocean spread out gray-green to the far horizon, tracing an arc from east-northeast, where the high ramparts of Kingsport Head blotted out a quarter of the sky, to the dim shape of Marblehead a little west of due south. Below, ruined Kingsport huddled around its central hill. Wind hissed in the pines, and the sound of surf came up faintly from the rocks below. Above, the baleful trembling light of the Nhhngr spread over the sky.

"Here," said Jenny, indicating a flat spot toward the middle of the clear area. Owen put the dead refrigerator down, stood guard while Jenny opened her shoulderbag and got everything in place for the working. When she was done, the makeshift altar had a black cloth draped over it, and strange figures had been traced on the cloth in something that clearly wasn't fabric paint. Four amulets of curious aspect sat at the corners of the altar. At the center was a shape of brown clay a foot or so across, incised with Aklo characters, and shaped like a five-pointed star.

"Okay," she said finally. "It's ready."

"Let me know what you need me to do."

That earned him a quick bright smile. "First of all? Keep a close eye on the trail up here. Once I've cast the Greater Forbidding of Malygris, we'll be safe, but until that's far enough along—" A shrug. "We still may be in danger. Merlin said he was going to do some protective workings, but I don't know what those will accomplish."

"What if the Mi-Go try something?"

"Then we're almost certainly dead." With a little shrug: "If we're lucky, what we heard was right and they're far out in space or in underground shelters by now."

Owen considered that and nodded, then went to the side of the clearing near the pine thicket, drew his pistol, and stood there with all his senses wide open. Seventh-degree initiate of the Starry Wisdom that he was, he'd learned ways of detecting movement and intention that didn't rely on eyes and ears, but even those could be deceived. He cleared his mind, waited.

Behind him, Jenny began to chant.

He noticed little change at first. Then the spell began to take effect: a blurring of the air, a wavering of perspective. Thereafter, a little at a time, the world beyond the hilltop began to go mad. Lines and shapes twisted with sickening slowness. Trees stopped pointing at the sky and bent at incomprehensible angles. The stone crags further off folded and unfolded like the limbs of the Hounds of Tindalos. Weird forms began to lurch out of the confusion toward him or plummet into the unseen, and a low murmuring confusion of sound seemed to fill the air, as though something was shrieking and roaring somewhere far away.

Jenny's voice fell silent. After a moment, she said, "There. That's done."

Owen turned. The view toward the ocean was just as blurred and confused as the one he'd been facing. "We're safe?"

"Against anything but the Great Old Ones." She started digging in her shoulderbag. "Now I need to create the link between this thing—" She indicated the brown shape on the altar. "—and the Seal of the Abyss in R'lyeh. If the King's going to stop us, that's when he'll do it." A shrug indicated how little they could do if that happened. "If any lesser powers try to interfere, though, the Vach-Viraj incantation might slow them down enough to matter. I want you to walk counterclockwise around the altar, ten or fifteen feet out, and recite the incantation."

"Now?"

"As soon as you're ready."

He nodded once, put his pistol away, walked away from the altar, and began circling slowly, reciting the words of the spell. "*Ya na kadishtu nilgh'ri stell-bna Nyoghtha: K'yarnak phlegethor l'ebumna syha'h n'ghft:*" memories came cascading with each word. He'd chanted the Vach-Viraj incantation hundreds of times in Starry Wisdom rituals in Dunwich and Arkham, invoked its powers in the ruins of the van der Heyl house near Chorazin on a night shot through with thunder, called on it for protection in the tunnels under Red Hook. "*Ya hai kadishtu ep r'luh-eeh Nyogtha eeh, S'uhn-ngh athg li'hee orr'e syha'h:*" every word had its meaning and power, and he'd studied them all. He concentrated on those, tried not to notice as Jenny's low chanting before the altar sent tremors rippling out through the voor of the world, drew tremendous forces together and directed them in a sudden rush toward the greater world's anthern pole and the vast city that lay drowned beside it.

Despite his efforts, Owen felt the energies reach their goal and accomplish their work a moment before Jenny fell silent. In the hush that followed, his voice seemed unnaturally loud. If the King in Yellow meant to intervene, he knew, that would happen within moments. The sky would tear open at right angles to all earthly directions, a towering figure with tattered yellow robes would loom above them, the Pallid Mask would bend to contemplate them, and their utter annihilation would follow promptly thereafter.

He reached the end of the incantation, and turned inward to face Jenny, who had the *Ghorl Nigral* open before her. The Ring of Eibon shone on her hand, bright as a star. After a moment, she drew in a ragged breath, and said, "Okay, that's done. Now for the final step." A motion of her head called him to the side of the altar.

"What do I need to do?" Owen asked then.

"It's really simple." She indicated the altar. The shape of clay she'd set on it had changed its substance; it was stone now, the color of hoarfrost, and letters in a forgotten alphabet spilled out from the center along its five rays. A penetrating cold seemed to radiate from it. "The Blade of Uoht needs to go through the heart of that thing."

"That sounds easy enough."

A shake of her head dismissed that. "No. It's simple, but it's not easy. For all practical purposes, that's the Seal of the Abyss in drowned R'lyeh, put there by the King himself, and it'll fight back, with all the power he put in it, to keep from being broken. Your job is to drive the blade through the Seal; mine is to keep the counterspells from destroying you before you can do that. Neither of those will be easy."

Owen considered her, and nodded. "Now?"

With an unsteady smile: "Might as well."

She handed him the Blade of Uoht in its scabbard. He drew it, set the scabbard beside the altar. The blade, long as his forearm, cold as interstellar space, swallowed up all the light that touched it. The hilt was long enough to grip with both hands; he planted his feet well apart, raised his hands, and aimed the blade to stab straight down. Then, remembering, he murmured the spell from *The Book of Innsmouth* that would strengthen his grip on rope or oar or blade.

"Ready?" he asked.

Jenny turned the pages of the *Ghorl Nigral*, found the passage she needed, raised her right hand and traced a symbol in the air. Violet incandescence surged from the Ring of Eibon. "Ready," she told him.

He braced himself, and brought the tip of the Blade of Uoht down slowly toward the frost-colored shape on the altar.

* * *

The riposte came at once, a sudden twisting force that sought to wrench the hilt from his hands and send the Blade of Uoht spinning through the air. Owen struggled with it, barely kept control of the weapon. The force that fought him was inhumanly quick, jolting the blade one way and then another, and all he could do was cling to the hilt and keep the Seal of the Abyss from breaking his grip entirely. He struggled to master the blade and drive it down toward the Seal, but nothing he did seemed to help.

At the outer edge of his awareness, Owen could hear Jenny's voice chanting words in Aklo, protecting him from whatever sorcerous protections had been woven into the seal, but it all seemed distant, meaningless. Panic clawed at him, reminded him of the Nhhngr falling slowly from space, the ghastly fate waiting for every living thing on Earth if it finished its descent. He shoved the thought away, forced his attention back to the Blade of Uoht, strained his muscles to the utmost to drive the point downward, and failed.

Then, faintly at first, another strength seemed to join his.

For a moment he wondered if one of the Great Old Ones had intervened, but the strength that steadied him felt far too human for that, and far too familiar. It was as though other hands braced his, another will pressed down on the hilt. He thought he could guess whose they were.

Presently, others seemed to join in, adding their own force to his efforts. Faintly, at the furthest edge of his awareness, Owen sensed circles of initiates around the globe, their faces taut, their hands joined, chanting names so dreadful that few dared even to whisper them except at direst need. He flung his attention back to the blade, drove the hilt down again with all his strength, and the tip of the blade moved a fraction of an inch closer to the hoar-colored stone.

The Seal of the Abyss lashed back at him with furious strength, but Owen knew now that it could be beaten. He steadied himself, ignored everything but the blade in his hands and the cold stone beneath it. The strength that was not his own flowed into him, added itself to his utmost effort. A hair's breadth at a time, the Blade of Uoht descended.

As its point wavered just above the upper surface of the stone, Jenny set the *Ghorl Nigral* upon the makeshift altar, spread her arms wide, and began to intone words in a strange tongue Owen was sure he'd never heard before, words that rolled and thundered and brought voor rushing toward them from the furthest reaches of the universe. Her arms rose, the Ring of Eibon blazing on her hand like violet lightning, and then she brought her hands together and rested them atop the pommel of the Blade of Uoht. The pressure seemed slight, but it drove the point down into the stone.

For an instant nothing changed—and in that instant Owen could see the Seal itself in R'lyeh, vast as a mountain, surrounded by black waters, holding shut the titanic doors of the temple-tomb of the Dreaming Lord. Through that image he sensed something of what lay at the heart of the Seal of the Abyss, the terrible purpose and the terrible grief. A mask the color of bone seemed to bend toward him, its eyes blank holes, its features reduced to bare lines. Words formed in his mind: *I set this seal in its place that the greater Earth should not be destroyed,*

*and all that came from that, the sweet and the bitter, I acknowledge
as my own deed. You who would break the seal and loose what I have
bound, whoever you may be, dare you do the same?*

The thought of putting himself on a level with the king of
the Great Old Ones left Owen aghast, but he knew better than
to think he could evade the question. *Yes,* he thought at it.
*Whatever happens because of it—yes. The unbinding's my deed as
the binding was yours.*

Be it so, came the response.

All at once a vast silent explosion flung him away from the
altar. He landed hard on bare stone more than ten feet away.
With a desperate cry, he surged to his feet, flung himself back
toward the altar, the Blade, the Seal of the Abyss.

"It's okay," said Jenny in a choked voice. She'd been flung
the other way, and was lifting herself out of a muddy hollow in
the rock surface. "It's—it's done."

Only then did Owen look at the altar. The Blade of Uoht
stood upright there, stark and irrefutable, half its length sunk
in the dead refrigerator.

To either side, the Seal of the Abyss lay split into two uneven
halves.

Staring at it, he went around the altar, helped Jenny stand.
In a silence broken only by the wind's hissing and the distant
sound of surf, the two of them approached the altar.

The Seal had not quite perished. A bluish-white light, bit-
terly cold, played around the two fragments, leaping and gut-
tering like a dying flame. Something about the light seemed
familiar to Owen, and after a moment he began to nod.

"What is it?" Jenny asked.

"The Radiance," he said. "It was never more than a distant
echo of—of that."

They waited. The light flared and faltered, rose and fell,
flared one last time, and went dark forever. In the long moment
that followed, a great slow tremor passed through the voor of
the world, faded slowly to stillness.

"What happens now?" asked Owen.

"I have no idea," Jenny admitted. "I don't know that any-body does." She drew in a long ragged breath. "But I think we should watch the sea."

They turned away from the altar, and Jenny gestured and uttered a sentence in Aklo. The twisting and blurring of the Greater Forbidding of Malygris faded out, and once again they could see the ocean reaching off to the sky's edge, the great gray mass of Kingsport Head rising to their left, the headlands tumbling down to their right to the roofs of Kingsport, and the trembling light of the Nhhngr, the Color out of Space, stretch-ing across the sky from north to south.

A moment later, as if in response, the ocean began to draw back from the land.

Owen stared, and only after a moment realized what he was seeing and why. The water drew back almost to the edge of sight, baring miles of sea floor to the sunlight, and then rose up in a massive green wave and came surging back.

Jenny let out a little cry and turned away, clenching her eyes shut. Owen put a hand on her shoulder, hoping to offer her some shred of comfort, and then turned to face Kingsport. He would not let himself look away. The people of drowned Posei-donis still remembered those who had witnessed the drown-ing of Susran, Lephara, Pneor and Umb, and the town that had sheltered so many survivors of the drowned lands deserved a witness to its own last moments.

It was over more quickly than he'd expected. The great wave rolled right over Orchard Island and Hog Island, rushed into the harbor and over the town, and rose and rose until finally only the half-collapsed brick shell of the old Congregational Hospital on the central hill stood above an expanse of churning brown water. Then the wave receded, and took most of the town with it, leaving shattered ruins and bare foundations in its wake.

Moments passed. The sea drew back again and came roll-ing in a second time, completing the work of the first wave.

Very little remained when that second wave went sweeping back out into the Atlantic deeps, and Owen turned to the south, looking toward the horizon to see if a third wave was on its way.

Once again the sea rose up, but this time it didn't stop rising. For one terrible moment Owen thought he was seeing a wave vast enough to sweep right over the top of Kingsport Head, but then he realized that the great gray-green shape rising at the horizon's edge curved away to either side, and an instant later he saw other shapes, high and sharp as mountain pinnacles, break from the sea's level far behind it. The thing surged upwards, and he knew what had set the ocean moving. "Jenny," he said in a toneless voice. "Jenny, you need to look."

She looked, and her breath caught.

The mighty shapes rose higher, and became unmistakable— the crown of an immense head and the upper tips of two colossal folded wings. Another surge forward and upward, and another, and the tentacled face rose above the roiling surface of the sea; more, and green water sluiced off mighty shoulders; still more, and the massive musculature of the chest broke free of the ocean. Step by step, a mountain walked or stumbled, rising from the cold Atlantic until it stood knee-deep in the ocean, towering over Kingsport Head, a colossal sea-colored shape half-silhouetted against the shuddering auroral light. The Mother of Doels had accomplished her greatest work and opened the portal from far R'lyeh. For the first time in sixty-five million years, Great Cthulhu stood potent and titanic upon the surface of the little Earth.

* * *

The Great Old One raised his head, then, and let out a tremendous ringing cry. It was a summons, Owen knew at once, and before he'd even noticed the movement he'd begun to step forward in response, toward the cliff and the vast shape beyond it.

Jenny caught his arm just as he stopped the motion, sensing that the summons was not meant for him.

A moment later it was answered.

The air went suddenly chill. Owen glanced back over his shoulder, and then turned slowly toward the west, though he knew already which of the Great Old Ones had come. Tall as Cthulhu but gaunt as winter, clad in tattered yellow robes, his long white hair whipping about in a rising wind, Hastur stood there, facing his half-brother and ancient foe. Something about him was not as the tomes described, though it took Owen a moment to realize what it was.

The Pallid Mask was gone. For the first time in sixty-five million years, Hastur had bared his own face to the world. Dim prehuman legends spoke of those long narrow eyes and long-lobed ears, that thin nose and pointed chin—but had they mentioned the haggard angles of the face, the tremendous intensity of the dark unhuman eyes? Owen could not recall.

High above the cliff, silent and unmoving, Hastur and Cthulhu faced each other, the king and high priest of the Great Old Ones, and the fate of the greater Earth hung in the unquiet air between them. Time passed, unmeasured, and then a third stood in the south, facing them.

She was tall as they were but midnight-colored, from the coarse pelt on her haunches past the glorious abundance of belly and breasts to the great curving horns that traced mighty arcs across the sky. Shub-Ne'hurrath, the Black Goat of the Woods with a Thousand Young, stood facing them both, and reached out to them, imperious, demanding. Cthulhu responded at once, his great clawed hand grasping hers. Hastur regarded her for a still moment, and then the white six-fingered hand that had hurled planets from their orbits reached out, took hers in its grip.

As one, all three looked toward the north, and Owen and Jenny looked that way as well. Moments passed, and then something moved high up on the tallest crag of Kingsport Head, small and lithe, bounding from rock to rock. Straining to see, Owen thought at first that it was an ordinary house cat, then blinked, for it seemed to become larger at each leap. A lynx sprang across a chasm between tall stones, a puma flung itself from there to a lower crag, a great golden creature with white fangs like scimitars made the final vertiginous bound to the cliff named Neptune's Head. For a moment after it landed, Owen thought he saw a woman with unkempt hair and rumpled clothing walking toward them, but the figure stretched and blurred upwards, and her form changed. Lithe as a child but tall as the others, bare to the waist and clad in a garment of shimmering light below, her head golden and feline, Phauz had arrived.

She reached out her hands as her mother had done, smiled at Cthulhu and at Hastur. A titanic green hand took hers at once, but again the King in Yellow paused, regarded her. She met his gaze, still smiling, and after a moment he nodded and took her hand in his.

It was only then that Owen realized what he was seeing. A line from a poem whispered in his memory: *Four join their hands where gray rock meets gray tide.* He waited, wondering.

Then the four Great Old Ones opened their mouths, and the sound began. It was not music, not unless the roaring of hurricanes is musical, but there was a structure to it that reminded Owen of music. The voices rose and fell, whirled and gyred around one another, and they caught his awareness, drew it up into their dance.

Suddenly Owen realized that Jenny was speaking to him— had been speaking to him for some moments, a hand tugging on his arm to try to catch his attention. He blinked and managed to focus on her. "Owen," she said, "can you hear me?" He nodded, and she went on. "You want to get flat on the ground and cover your eyes and ears before they finish their working."

He blinked again. "Sorcery?"

"Their kind of sorcery," she said, and pulled on his arm, urging him down.

He managed the movement, lay belly to the ground with his palms over his eyes and his thumbs blocking his ears. One final glance showed Jenny taking a similar position.

Even with his ears sealed, Owen could hear the not-music pulsing through his bones, and through the bones of the planet. It seemed to be getting louder—or was the structure he'd sensed drawing taut, pressing forward to some unimaginable fulfillment of its own?

The sound reached a crescendo, and abruptly stilled, leaving a deafening silence behind it. A moment passed, another, and then the world tore open around him and its fragments tumbled into a lightless abyss.

CHAPTER 13

A STILLNESS IN ARKHAM

Endless voids of sentient blackness rushed past Owen. He could no longer feel the stone beneath him. He could no longer feel his own body. He dimly sensed great shoals of shapeless things lurking and capering around him, but could not tell how he perceived them. Then he heard the high keening of shrill flutes, the deep thudding of muffled drums, and knew a little of what was happening: Yog-Sothoth, the Gate and the Guardian of the Gate, had opened the way to the greatest of the Great Old Ones, blind Azathoth. For a moment that spanned all of eternity, the flutes and drums sounded, and then faded to silence as Azathoth withdrew.

Thereafter, atom by atom, the world reassembled itself.

Presently he could feel his body again, and the stone beneath him. He was lying belly down, fingers over his eyes, thumbs blocking his ears. The question that haunted him was what kind of world he would find when he sat up, and he knew there was only one way to find out.

Cautiously, he pulled his thumbs away from his ears, and heard nothing stranger than the hissing of the wind in the pines and the distant rush of surf on the rocks far below. After a moment, he moved his hands aside, blinked, tried to focus.

The first thing that met his gaze was a tiny brown beetle picking its way patiently across the rock, busy with its own affairs.

That it was there and alive meant more to him just then than anything else he could have named. An inordinate fondness for beetles swept through him, and he waited until the little creature had passed him by and was clambering happily into a patch of lichen before he drew his hands up under him, pushed up, twisted into a sitting position.

Around him was the familiar gray sweep of Neptune's Head reaching off southward to the cliff's edge, with the green surging sea beyond it and the horizon beyond that. Nothing seemed to have changed at all. Movement to one side caught his attention; Jenny was sitting up, dazed and blinking. He tried to say something, failed, and then looked up.

Blue sky streaked with mare's-tails of cloud met his gaze. The baleful trembling light was gone. Something halfway between a laugh and a sob passed through him as he stared upwards.

"I know," said Jenny.

He glanced at her then. "I bet."

She was the greatest sorceress of that age of the world, he'd known that for years, and he had even more reason to know it at that moment, but just then she didn't look like a sorceress. A thin, plain, middle-aged woman, her rumpled clothes stained on one side with mud, stray pine needles sticking out of her graying hair—or maybe, he thought, that was what great sorceresses looked like. All at once he started laughing, remembering what she'd been like back when they'd first met, what he'd been like in that same distant time.

"What is it?" she asked.

"Thinking about how long a road it's been since the house on Halsey Street."

She laughed too. "I won't argue." Then, serious again: "One thing, though. If you ever hear me say that I know the first thing about sorcery, will you please kick me?"

"The working the Great Old Ones did?"

Her nod confirmed it. "I could sense a little of it. Just a little—but it was like Rembrandt next to a child with a crayon."

A familiar voice spoke from behind them. "I think you judge yourself a little too harshly."

They glanced over their shoulders, saw the tall figure standing there, robed in garments the color of crimson flame. "Nyarlathotep," Jenny said, breaking into a smile.

They began to stand, but the Crawling Chaos gestured, quelling the motion, and then walked between them to the seaward side of the clifftop and turned. "The Great Old Ones did what you could not," he said, and sat on the bare stone facing them. "But you—both of you—did what we could not. A fair exchange, all things considered."

"And—it's done?" Owen asked.

"It's finished," said the Old One. "The long war's over at last."

Owen opened his mouth and then stopped, trying to bring together the vast uncertainties around him into a few simple questions. Nyarlathotep allowed a wry smile, and said, "You want to know what's happened to the Nhhngr, the Radiance, the Mi-Go, your people in Arkham—and the Great Old Ones. I've come to tell you a little about each of those, for my masters wish you to know: you, the other humans, and the elder races on this world.

"Yog-Sothoth came in answer to the invocation you witnessed. With Azathoth's consent and the power Great Cthulhu called down from realms beyond the greater Earth, he dissolved the bindings the Radiance placed on the Great Old Ones, and opened certain doors. You've both seen very slight displays of his power, but this—this was not slight. The Nhhngr is gone; it's been sent back to its proper place in the cosmos, where it's in balance with the Yr. It never should have been brought by itself into this region of space, and we've seen to it that no future species can do what the Mi-Go did.

"As for the Radiance, it's gone as well: thrust through a portal to another place. Those who surrendered or fled earlier we left alone—they're of no concern to us—but the ones who held firm, the adepts and initiates and the few members of negation teams who stayed with them to the last, were another matter. They won't trouble this or any other world again."

"I'd like to know where they went," said Jenny.

The black unhuman eyes glanced her way. "There are places in the greater Earth that it's not well for humans even to know about. Yog-Sothoth sent them to one of those. The one mercy we granted them was that death wasn't unduly delayed."

Jenny took that in, and nodded.

"The Mi-Go who were on this planet also won't be seen again. On Yuggoth—" He gestured. "A remarkable species, the fungi from Yuggoth, with immense potential. From now on, they'll be pursuing that potential in their proper realm, outward from Yuggoth into the Ghooric zone. If they ever again venture inside the orbit of Cykranosh, Yuggoth will have an unfortunate encounter with one of its own moons."

"You can do that," Owen said, wondering.

"We could once and we can again. The King is on Yuggoth now, explaining matters to the Mi-Go. He's already burnt the Yellow Sign onto the face of Yuggoth's closest moon as a gentle reminder. We don't anticipate any further trouble from them."

"Can anything be done about the brain cylinders?" Jenny asked.

"Nodens has already seen to it. Each of the ships went through a different gate, into realms the Mi-Go cannot endure. The brains will have strange destinies, but that's true of every living being now that the Weird is accomplished."

Owen and Jenny both nodded, said nothing.

"The people in Arkham already know what's happened," the Crawling Chaos went on. "From the way voor is moving, certain statues are turning back into living beings." He glanced at Owen. "That was clever. The Mi-Go aren't the only species that has remarkable potential."

Owen managed to mumble words of thanks, and the Old One went on. "As for the Great Old Ones, my presence here should tell you most of what you need to know. Certain quarrels have been settled once and for all. Certain of my masters who were not present sixty-five million years ago have made their will known, and the choices that opened the way for the Mi-Go and gave the Radiance its foothold won't be repeated."

"I'm really glad to hear that," said Jenny. "I'm a little surprised, though, that the world doesn't seem to have changed at all."

The Crawling Chaos gave her an amused look. "The world is as the Great Old Ones shaped it," he said. "The Radiance and the Mi-Go could spoil it in places, but they never had the power to change its nature. Why should my masters make it different now?"

Jenny took that in, and nodded slowly.

* * *

For a time nothing spoke but the wind in the pines and the distant surf. "I'm glad that Phauz was part of it," Owen said then, "there at the last. She did so much to make this happen."

Nyarlathotep glanced at him. "The King has a worthy heir." The two humans gave him startled looks, and he nodded. "Far in the future, when both Hastur and Cthulhu have withdrawn into contemplation, she will rule the greater Earth. That had been prophesied, but there were some who doubted it. Now those doubts are settled." He considered Jenny and said, "A certain Great Old One you know well will be gratified."

"The prophecy was Tsathoggua's," Jenny said in a quiet voice. "I know."

The Crawling Chaos rose to his feet. "But all these are matters for another time. Just now it's important for the two of you to return to Arkham."

Jenny gave him a tired look. "I know—but it's a long walk."

"Trust me to arrange matters better than that," said Nyarlathotep. "My car's on the road."

Owen hauled himself to his feet, turned, and blinked. Where the little broken refrigerator that served them for an altar had been, a cube of black stone rose out of the bare rock, with the Blade of Uoht rising out of the center of it. Something about the way the blade seemed to fuse with the stone suggested that it would not move again.

"The Blade of Uoht has accomplished its work," Nyarlathotep said then. "It seemed fitting to my masters to leave it here as a memorial."

"And the *Ghorl Nigral*?" Jenny asked him.

"Has returned to its proper place in lightless N'kai. It was needed here for a time, but no longer." With a hint of amusement: "There are many other tomes to keep you occupied."

Jenny laughed, and the three of them headed down the slope to the trail through the pines.

Nyarlathotep's car was a long black shadow at the end of the road. "Its time is almost over," Nyarlathotep said. "A pity. More than one age will pass before I'll have the chance to drive anything quite so fast again." He gestured with his head. "You'll want to sit in back. We'll be picking up someone else."

Owen opened the door for Jenny, closed it, and then went around the car and climbed in. The engine rumbled to life, and the car shot down the road at a speed no human driver could risk, dodging past the landslide on two wheels and plunging beyond.

The pines rushing past sent Owen's mind spinning twenty years back, to another journey in the back seat of Nyarlathotep's car, Laura nestled close to him, as a night of shadows and deaths barely evaded gave way to the gray light of dawn.

It was different now. Sunlight of a winter afternoon streamed cold and angular through the trees, the woman sitting beside him was friend and comrade rather than lover and bride-to-be, and the age-old war he'd joined on that earlier night had just ended forever. He drew in a long slow breath, released it as slowly, let himself begin to believe that the long nightmare was over at last.

All at once, as the road sped past, he knew when and how he would die. He sensed the old man's body he'd have then, worn out by a long life, sinking gratefully into stillness as friends and family gathered around. Other glimpses came surging into his mind an instant later: each pine the car rushed past stretched into an arc from fallen seed to fallen log, and the gray stone beneath them traced out its vaster arc from sediment on the floor of a long-vanished Paleozoic sea, through a thousand geological changes, to sediment on the floor of a sea that would not be born for a hundred million years to come. He blinked, tried to clear his thoughts, found everything around him unfolding into time, the way he'd seen all things on that terrible night twenty years back, and glimpsed in brief intervals since then.

Jenny glanced at him and smiled. Did she perceive what had happened to him? An instant later he was sure of it, and in that same instant he could see the arc of her life, her bitter childhood and youth, the dazzling awakening of power that had come to her twenty years back, the long struggle since then, and then beyond, reaching toward an unimaginable destiny in the far future. He forced his attention back to the moment. The sense that had opened up in him remained, a promise and a challenge.

The road led on. Most of the way to Kingsport, the car took a sharp right onto a slightly less dilapidated two-lane highway, whipped around one curve after another, and began to climb into the hills. "It really is gone, isn't it?" Jenny asked then. "Kingsport, I mean."

"Its time was over," said Nyarlathotep. "It would have drowned soon anyway."

"I know—and this way, at least I'll always remember it the way it was." She closed her eyes, and Owen knew how little comfort that thought offered her just then.

Another few miles, and the car turned onto Old Kingsport Road. The hills rose up, uncompromising in the winter light, and the willows clawed at the sea wind. Unfamiliar shapes moved half-seen beneath the willows. Owen wondered whether Yhoundeh's fosterlings had reached those hills yet, or if older and stranger things had come out of hiding now that the world had changed. The new sense in him stirred, told him that both were true.

Halfway to Arkham, the car slowed and rolled to a halt. Owen looked up, saw someone standing on the side of the road: a man on the far end of middle age. Lean harsh angles of the face, black hair streaked with gray, curious garments— white shirt, knee-length trousers, leather boots with toes turned up to points—whispered of something Owen couldn't quite remember.

The passenger side window rolled down as the car came to a halt, though Nyarlathotep didn't press any buttons. "Excuse me," said the man on the roadside in a mellow Bostonian accent. "Can you—" Then he looked in through the window and laughed. "Nyarlathotep," he said. "Well. I admit I'm surprised."

"Are you? Perhaps you'd welcome a ride to Arkham."

That got a sudden grin. "Yes, and thank you. We're in the hills above Kingsport, aren't we? I thought I recognized the shape of the land."

Nyarlathotep motioned for him to get in, and the door opened and closed. The man glanced back, saw Owen and Jenny. "Good afternoon," he said. "I wonder if we have friends in common. I'm Randolph Carter."

"I thought so," said Jenny, and introduced herself and Owen as Nyarlathotep started the car moving again. "We're both friends and former students of Miriam Akeley."

Carter nodded. "I thought as much. She's mentioned you both, of course—and a certain young lady I've seen tolerably often in the Dreamlands rather resembles you, Mr. Merrill."

* * *

Through the winding miles of the hill country, and then down the long uneven slope to the Miskatonic River: the last part of the journey was achingly familiar to Owen. He scarcely noticed that the car passed other people in curious clothing, as it wound down through the stillness of the afternoon toward Arkham and home. The sense that had opened up in him murmured of the long bitter history of that corner of the world, but that, too, made only the faintest impression on him just then.

Then the outlying buildings of the old town slipped past, Old Kingsport Road turned into Peabody Avenue, and Nyarlathotep slowed the car as people came streaming out of the buildings to welcome them. A left turn onto College Street and two blocks through a gathering crowd brought the car to the old campus, and there Nyarlathotep stopped and gestured Owen, Jenny, and Carter toward the doors.

Outside the car all was cheering and shouting, faces familiar and unfamiliar, human and unhuman. Owen had scarcely closed the car door when Asenath came pelting over to him and flung her arms around him. She had tears streaming down a face alight with joy and relief.

"Back so soon," he said, scooped her up in his arms, gave her his cheek to kiss.

"Robin and Mr. and Mrs. Ward are here too. Dad—the barriers are gone."

He tried to process that, failed.

"They're gone. The little Earth is part of the greater Earth again."

He squeezed her, set her down, tried to fit his mind around the words she'd said.

"Mom's over this way," she went on, and all but dragged him through the crowd toward one of the doors of Hutchinson Hall. People shouted his name and cheered, but he barely noticed them. A glimpse of Miriam's white hair gave him his bearings, and a moment later—

Laura.

She surged from her wheelchair as he reached her and flung her arms around him, then nearly toppled as her tentacles gave under her. He held her up, buried his face in her shoulder, repeating her name over and over again. She was laughing and crying at the same time, and he held her for a long while before helping her back into the wheelchair.

The crowd suddenly hushed, then, and Owen turned. Nyarlathotep was standing atop his car, hands on hips, considering them all: humans, Deep Ones, shoggoths, and stranger beings.

"You already know the news that matters most," the Crawling Chaos said then, his deep voice echoing from the buildings to either side. "The Weird of Hali has been fulfilled, Great Cthulhu is awake, and the Radiance is extinguished forever. The world is very different now.

"My masters wish me to say two things to the humans among you. First, that they trust you won't be foolish enough hereafter to think that the world belongs to you, as the Radiance taught, and as humans have been rather too prone to believe from time to time. Your numbers are greatly lessened, the elder races are free from the constraints the Radiance placed on them, and a Great Old One many of you could name is seeing to it that the wild places are full of wild things again. Not all of them are material as you know matter, and some of them consider you their rightful prey. You'll be wise to step more carefully on the land than you've done before now.

"Second, the world is different, but it's still as you shaped it. The wastes you dumped in the waters and the sky, the sprawling things you flung over the land, none of that is any concern of my masters or of mine; from our perspective, those things will be gone soon enough not to matter. You may decide to do something about those—but if you do, it's your concern, not ours."

In the silence that followed, Owen found his voice. "What you're saying, Old One, is that we made a mess, we get to clean it up."

"Exactly," said Nyarlathotep.

"Fair enough," Owen replied.

A female voice with a Deep One accent spoke then, from somewhere in the middle of the crowd; looking that way, Owen thought he saw Mha'alh'yi's face. "Old One," she said, "if we of the elder races choose to help the humans in that work, will that be permitted?"

"You and the humans may decide that as you wish," said the Crawling Chaos. "It's not of concern to my masters, or to me."

Martin Chaudronnier spoke then, from somewhere on the far side of the car. "Old One," he said, "I trust that you and your masters aren't going anywhere."

"Not at all." A smile creased Nyarlathotep's dark face. "Those who remained with this little Earth during its time of torment will not abandon it in its time of healing. If anything, you may expect to see my masters and their emissaries more often than before."

"I'm glad to hear that," said Martin. "For now, though, do you have any counsel for us?"

"For now?" said Nyarlathotep. "Rejoice."

He flung up his arms, and his form stretched and blurred. Vast black wings beat the air, and for just an instant Owen saw a three-lobed burning eye gazing down upon them. Then the world reeled, the sky opened and closed at right angles to all earthly directions, and Nyarlathotep and his car were gone. In their wake, a tremendous stillness hung over Arkham, rose up past the high thin clouds to the untainted sky beyond.

* * *

"Rejoice," Miriam said then. Hers was one of the first voices to break the hush after the Great Old One's disappearance. She was standing a little beyond Laura, up against one of the Doric pilasters of Hutchinson Hall's entrance. "That strikes me as very good—"

Her voice trickled away. Owen gave her a startled look, realized that she was staring past him, across the crowded street, toward a lean figure in odd clothing.

"Oh my God. Excuse me for a moment," Miriam said then, and pushed her way through the crowd. Over the sounds that began to fill the street, Owen heard her voice: "Randolph!"

Asenath had been standing next to her mother, but she heard Miriam just as clearly, and stared after her. After a frozen moment, she mumbled something, moved a short distance away. Owen watched her bow her head and twist fingers together in some witch's spell. All at once she let out a wordless cry and darted away into the crowd.

Owen gave Laura a baffled look, but she shrugged. "Where's Barney?" he asked then.

"Down in the tunnels. Miriam said he didn't want to leave until he was sure that all the children were fine."

"Sounds like him."

"Doesn't it?" With a sudden smile: "But everything went the way it should."

"That's good to hear," said Owen. "I—" He stopped, seeing a pair of familiar faces in the crowd. "Lydia!" he called out. "Charles!"

They turned, hurried over. "Owen," said Lydia Ward, beaming. "And you must be Laura. It's so good to finally have the chance to meet you—"

A dark shape interrupted her, flinging itself toward her. Tentacles wrapped around her knees, and four eyes in an alien face turned upwards, imploring. Whatever passed between them was closed off from everyone else, but Lydia looked up with a luminous smile. "And thank you for taking such good care of Pierre for me."

As the two women began to talk, Owen turned to Charles Dexter Ward. "Your sister should be here in Arkham. She and Justin Geoffrey got here two days ago."

Charles nodded, smiling. "I know. I met them just now. And Merlin?" When Owen gestured his ignorance: "He'll be in the woods, then—that's where he likes to live. We'll see him just as soon as he decides to appear." Owen laughed, conceding the point.

A moment later the door behind them clattered open, and Barnabas came through it, with half a dozen teens behind him. "Hi, Dad," he said, as calmly as though nothing worth mentioning had happened since their last parting. "It worked."

"That's what I hear," said Owen, grinning. He scooped up his son in his arms, hugged him, then set him down again.

"Hi, Mr. Merrill," said Sylvia, who'd come through the door a moment later, her kyrrmi perched on her shoulder. "Did Aunt Jenny come back with you?"

"Hi, Sylvia. Yes, she's out there in the crowd somewhere."

"Nope," said Barnabas.

Owen glanced at him, then followed his gaze and saw Jenny extracting herself from a knot of well-wishers a few feet away. "Hi, Sylvia. Hi, Barney," she said. "Laura—thank you. I sensed the voor your people were sending our way the whole time."

"I'm glad," said Laura.

The door clattered open again, and Justin came through it. Belinda came a moment later, with Annabelle cradled in two of her arm-tentacles and Josephine clinging to a third. "Owen!" Justin cried, and threw his arms around him. "God, I'm glad to see you."

"Likewise," said Owen, grinning. "You're both okay?"

Justin let go of him, ducked back into the shade of Hutchinson Hall. Belinda handed Annabelle to Josephine with a broad smile, gave Owen a tight tentacular hug. "Oh, we're fine," she said. "I honestly don't remember much—I just felt stiff, and then I blinked awake."

Meanwhile Justin turned to Jenny. A pause, some bit of wordless communication Owen couldn't read, and then he put his arms around her, gently, as though a sudden movement might crush her. Belinda gave Owen a final squeeze and let go of him, and a moment later her arm-tentacles wrapped around them both. Owen glanced at Laura, and she beamed.

Another flurry of movement in a crowd no longer hushed, and Asenath came pelting back, three others following her at a more sedate pace. One of them Owen recognized at once; the other two were middle-aged women in ornate many-layered gowns of curious cut, one blonde, the other brown-haired. "Mom, Dad," Asenath said breathlessly, "these are friends of mine and Miriam's from the Dreamlands, Randolph, Serin, and Aysh, and I'm so glad you finally get to meet them." She turned to the two women and started talking in a quick many-voweled language Owen was sure he'd never heard before.

Randolph Carter, laughing, shook Owen's hand, then took Laura's and murmured something in French. Introductions followed, with Asenath translating. In the midst of it, Owen turned to Carter and said, "I admit I'm wondering how you got here from the Dreamlands."

"So am I," said Carter. "It was rather sudden—one moment I was walking on the road from Nir to Hlanith, and the next I was in the middle of a willow thicket in hills I thought

I recognized. I found my way to the nearest road, and you know the rest."

"That seems—" Owen stopped, tried to find a word. "Merciful, almost."

"I'm quite sure mercy had nothing to do with it," said Carter. "Great Cthulhu wants us here for some reason of his own. Still—" A sudden grin creased his face. "I won't object."

"I bet," Owen said. "Did Miriam find you just now?"

Carter nodded. "And introduced me to her fiancé." Owen gave him a startled look, and he grinned again and said, "There should be an announcement—ah, here it is."

* * *

"Excuse me." Miriam's voice came through the sounds of the crowd. She was standing on the porch of one of the buildings across the street, with Amber perched on her shoulder and people clustered around her. Owen recognized Martin, some of his family, and Will Bishop close by. "I have a few announcements to make. They're nothing like so important as the news that Nyarlathotep brought, but I think some of you will want to hear them."

The crowd went gradually silent, turned toward her.

"First, I know we've all had our lives upended by the events of the last few weeks, but I'm pleased to say that Miskatonic University will be open on Monday as usual. Next semester we'll have at least one more guest lecturer than we'd been expecting, and I think quite a few of you will be interested in hearing what he has to say."

Owen glanced at Carter, who met the glance and nodded.

"Second, it's been a very great honor to serve as president of the university during the years just past, and I'm more grateful than I can say for all the help I've received from all of you—students, faculty members, staff, and the Arkham community. We've kept Miskatonic alive and thriving through changes

I don't think any of us could have possibly imagined a few years ago. At this point, though, it's time I handed over the job to someone else. The faculty senate has accepted my resignation, and unanimously elected Will Bishop as Miskatonic University's next president. I hope you'll give him all the support you've given me."

That got cheers and applause, as Will climbed up onto the porch and shook Miriam's hand. As the crowd quieted again, someone raised a voice in a question Owen couldn't make out. "Yes," Miriam said, "I'll still be teaching my scheduled classes next semester, and no doubt I'll make a pest of myself around campus for the foreseeable future." As the laugh finished, she went on. "Which brings me to my last, rather personal announcement.

"I think most of you know Martin Chaudronnier. Some time ago, he asked me to marry him, and when this last crisis began, I agreed that if we both survived, I'd say yes. And here we are." More cheers and applause echoed off the buildings. "Under the circumstances, we don't see any point in delay. The ceremony will be at noon tomorrow, in the quad if weather permits. Grand Priestess Laura Merrill will officiate, and I hope all of you will come. Thank you, and—" She broke into a smile. "Nyarlathotep had some advice for us all, and I suggest we take it."

In the cheering and shouting that followed, it was Aysh who seemed to understand best. She asked Asenath a question in her own language, said a few words to Serin, and then went a short distance away, to a bare spot of sidewalk up against the flank of Hutchinson Hall, where she sat. A little drum shaped like an hourglass made its appearance from under her outermost gown; she gave the head a sharp tap with her fingers, then began to beat a lively rhythm.

Heads turned. Emily d'Ursuras's was among them, and she turned and ran. She was back a few minutes later with a case containing a flute, and hurried over to where Aysh sat.

Aysh smiled up at her, and kept drumming; Emily put the instrument together, raised it to her lips, and began to play a high, skirling melody over the top of the drumbeats.

Others reacted similarly. Owen watched John Romero duck into one of the college buildings and come out with a deep-bodied drum in his hands. He sat next to Aysh, gave her a grin, and then picked up the rhythm. She smiled at him, and began playing faster patterns around his beat. A little while later Brecken Kendall walked over to where Emily was playing, gave her a luminous smile, raised her own flute, and started playing an intricate counterpoint to Emily's melody. Out in the street, where Nylarlathotep's car had been, people began to dance.

Sybil Romero came out of the crowd then, hurrying over to Laura. "Mrs. Merrill!" she said, raising her voice to be heard over the drums. "Can we?"

Laura gave Owen a questioning glance and he grinned, kissed her, and then stepped aside. Sybil sat on the sidewalk next to the wheelchair, and the two of them began to clap, matching the rhythm of the drums. A moment later the keening of the Innsmouth chant rose up to twine around the melody from the two flutes. One by one, Laura's other students appeared and joined in, and the drummers sent their own rhythms leaping around the beat of clapping hands.

By then most of the street was full of people dancing. Owen saw Miriam and Martin out in the middle of the crowd, Will Bishop and his husband closer by, and then suddenly Asenath and Robin spun past, weaving among the older and slower dancers. Lydia and Charles Dexter Ward went by; Randolph Carter and Serin began a complicated Sydathrian dance, and beyond them, in a shady place near the drummers, Justin and Belinda held each other close.

Then Justin Geoffrey came strolling past, grinned at Owen, and walked to the end of the street. Judy Heffler stood there among a knot of former negation team members, all of them in ordinary clothes that didn't quite fit, all of them with bewilderment written on their faces. The poet walked over and said something to Heffler, who looked even more startled. They spoke for a few moments, and then Heffler nodded and the two of them joined the dancing crowd. Not long thereafter Vanessa Ward spun past, dancing with Amos Moore, the two of them grinning as though they shared some unspoken secret.

Not far away, Barnabas and Sylvia sat against a brick wall, one of his hands resting in one of hers, and Owen suddenly saw their marriage, their children, the proud lineage of loremasters that would rise from them. The sense of time that had opened up in him on the road down from Neptune's Head unfolded again, and he saw—

He saw the future of the lesser Earth, stretching out across two billion years to the time of the Tchhcht't beneath their bloated dying sun. He saw the intelligent species that would rise and fall after the end of humanity's era, and the others who would be born while humanity still lived, and would think of them as a cryptic elder race guarding archaic mysteries. He saw the whole arc of the human future, from the long years of confusion ahead through the rise of the mighty empire of Tsan-Chan and beyond, age upon age, to a continent not yet risen from the sea that would harbor the last humans.

He saw the whole arc of time, as he'd done twenty years back in the old East Campus Parking Garage, staring into the eyes and mind of Yog-Sothoth. In place of the dazed confusion of that earlier vision, though, this one settled quietly into place in the back of his mind, a frame against which other thoughts could move, other actions be seen. The long harsh history of the land surrounding him whispered to him again, and he glimpsed all at once some of the directions it had been headed all along, some of the things that could be done to bring it to its fulfillment.

Had the Radiance failed in Alexander's day, a not-voice said, *you would have sensed this as soon as you beheld Yog-Sothoth.*

Phauz spoke to him, he was sure of that. *Despite the curse they laid on this world, the glimpses you received guided you again and again. Now that their deeds are dust in a rising wind, it is no wonder that you have received the gift that Hali had all those years ago—and it is well for you and your people that you have it.*

That was when he understood what had happened to him. Ah-wan the prophet, he thought, and knew in the same moment that Yiang-li had spoken nothing but the truth.

He blinked, brought his attention back again to the present. Just then a movement caught his eye. A cat he recognized, a lean black and white tom, sprang up onto a window ledge on the first floor of Hutchinson Hall. From that vantage the cat pondered the scene with a baffled look. Don't worry about it, Owen thought at the cat, glimpsing its strange trajectory across the ages. You'll understand eventually.

He glanced at Jenny, who stood there watching the cat with a quiet smile on her face. The music was loud enough by then to drown out anything less than a shout, and so he didn't bother; he simply gestured toward her and smiled. She gave him a startled look, then after a moment smiled and took his hand, and the two of them joined the dance.

ACKNOWLEDGMENTS

Like the earlier novels in this series, this fantasia on a theme by H.P. Lovecraft depends even more than most fiction on the labors of earlier writers. Lovecraft himself, of course, provided most of the raw material for my tale. Inevitably, perhaps, for the final movement of a work based on his imaginative vision, I drew on nearly every one of his famous stories and quite a few of his less well known tales for raw material. Lovecraft's good friends Robert E. Howard, Henry Kuttner, Frank Belknap Long, and Clark Ashton Smith also provided a great many details for my story; so did Arthur Machen, whose work Lovecraft admired; and so did C.S. Lewis, whose planetary trilogy was an important influence in various ways, some more roundabout than others.

The references to Merlin and the Arthurian legend generally are based on many years of reading about the history behind the old tales of Camelot. *The Quest for Merlin* by Nicholas Tolstoy and *The Age of Arthur* by John Morris were particularly influential in shaping the vision of the Arthurian era that appears in brief glimpses in this story.

The divination cards used by Justin Martense, as noted in two previous books in this series, are a variant of the Gypsy Witch cards, a traditional American cartomancy deck.

As I look back over this project, two other debts come forcefully to mind. The first is to the writers and readers of *Weird Tales* magazine—"The Unique Magazine," as it called itself—and more generally to the authors and audiences of the weird tale in its golden age in the early twentieth century, when H.P. Lovecraft was one of the most glittering stars in a firmament ablaze with raw imaginative force. The seven volumes of *The Weird of Hali* are in a real sense a homage to the *Weird Tales* era, and especially to the soaring creative vision of its greatest writers, of whom Lovecraft was unquestionably one. If I have replaced some of the social and moral attitudes of that era with others I find more congenial, and woven in a philosophy that differs from Lovecraft's mostly in that I rejoice in some of the things he dreaded most, that's every author's prerogative, and it shows no lack of delight in the work of the authors whose extraordinary creations have influenced me so profoundly.

A second debt is owed to my readers. I sketched out the plot of *The Weird of Hali: Arkham* and wrote a first draft of Chapter Twelve when the first book had not yet seen print; I finished the initial draft when the first two novels were available and the third was about to appear, and did the final revisions when the sixth book was a few weeks from publication. The enthusiasm of the readers of the first two volumes made it easy to finish writing, revising, and preparing the manuscript of this final installment of the series.

I also owe, as before, debts to Sara Greer, who read and critiqued the manuscript. I hope it is unnecessary to remind the reader that none of the above are responsible in any way for the use I have made of their work.

Printed in the USA
CPSIA information can be obtained
at www.ICGtesting.com
JSHW032133021023
49524JS00006B/6

9 781912 573974